Barbara Speake w
cut and obtained a first degree in Psychology and a
Master's degree, before moving to England in 1972 following her marriage. She was a research psychologist for
a number of years, before obtaining a Master's Degree
in Clinical Psychology. For over twenty years she has
practised as a clinical psychologist, as well as holding
various management positions both in the UK and in
New Zealand. She and Terry have two grown-up children.

Primed by the Past is her second crime novel.

By the same author

Secrets Only Sleep

PRIMED BY THE PAST

Barbara Fagan Speake

Published by
Country Books
Courtyard Cottage
Little Longstone
Bakewell
Derbyshire
UK
DE45 1NN

www.countrybooks.biz

ISBN 978-1-906789-52-7

Acknowledgements

I would like to thank the people who read and commented on various drafts of my book including: Sandra Smith on this side of the Atlantic and Teresa Covill and Marcia McInerney on the other side. My brother-in-law, Tom Covill, an attorney and avid crime reader helped with the various legal aspects. But it is to a fellow writer, Trevor Williams that I am most grateful. His editorial suggestions were invaluable. Thanks also to Dick Richardson for his publishing support.

I would also like to thank George and Evelyn Manson and their friend, Susan Riddell for helping me to create my main character and lending me their hometown of Huntly in Scotland for her birthplace. Each year they provide a home from home while my husband fishes and I write. George and Susan both have police backgrounds and they helped me invent a past for Annie Macpherson. As I interviewed them and they talked about their experiences, my new character came alive for me. I hope they like her.

A love of reading and of writing was instilled in me at a very young age and for that lifelong gift, I will always be indebted to my late parents, Teresa and Joe Fagan.

To my late parents, Teresa and Joe Fagan

Prologue: fifteen years earlier

It was always at this time of day that she felt sad. There were never any tears – that wasn't tolerated. But she was sad nonetheless. Sad to see her best friend run off, knowing that she couldn't invite her in to play, that she couldn't be like other ten year olds. She never knew what she was going to find behind that door.

As she put her key in the lock, on that glorious spring day, her hand shook slightly. Velvety silk red curls fell around her face, disguising the taut expression, the biting of the lip.

With all her senses heightened, the silent counting began.

One ... the key turned in the lock. Good sign. *Mommy can't be too depressed today, or she wouldn't even bother locking it.*

Two ... no radio blaring. That was definitely positive. That meant there was no frenetic activity. *Maybe I can get the supper on without being disturbed.*

She had an official classification, the one that the 'too weary to care any more' social worker had given her: 'Young Caregiver'. But it didn't make her life any easier having a label. It didn't take away the constant worry. *Only one person can help me.*

Three ... *something isn't right.*

'Mommy!'

The little girl felt her stomach go funny, the way it always did when she was scared, really scared. The usual spot in the den, the one facing the TV, was empty. The indentation was there, on the right hand side of the couch, but not her mom, nor her cigarettes or ashtray. Panic set in. Her eyes widened like a cat on the prowl.

Perhaps the kitchen, but no, that too was empty. Actually, it was worse than that, it was clean. Everything was in its place. The ashtray was empty and there wasn't even the smell of stale smoke. But there was a smell of something else, a lemony smell. Was it disinfectant or one of those air fresheners? But that couldn't be right. It wasn't like her mom to tidy up downstairs or try and disguise the smell of the cigarettes.

The little girl felt even smaller as she stood alone in the kitchen: frozen like in a game of statues, sensing that something was wrong. Had someone been in the house? Maybe he's back and taken mom out but helped her clean up first. Her heart leapt. *He's been here.*

Anticipating a note in her bedroom, she virtually danced up the stairs, swinging the door wide open. Running around the side of the bed, she knocked over the delicate China ballerina on her side table, her most precious possession. She caught it just before it hit the floor. Her heart was pounding. But there was no note on her desk. As tears stung her eyes and their saltiness dripped into her mouth, that churning feeling in her stomach returned. The house was so quiet. *Think, think! He must have taken mommy out. She wouldn't leave me all alone, not leave without telling me where she was.*

The door to her mother's room was slightly ajar. At last the little girl allowed herself a half smile. Her breathing eased and she quickly wiped the tears from her eyes. She couldn't be seen to have been crying. *Of course, stupid girl, the note will be in there. Why didn't I check there first?*

She flicked the light switch gently, in case her mom was asleep, but the bed was empty. The rose coloured comforter was pulled taut. The room was perfect, everything in its exact place. The curtains were closed, but they were hanging absolutely straight, like they had to be. But there was no note, not on the bed, not on the dresser, not taped to the mirror.

Then she heard the sound, a sound that would haunt her waking hours for months and years to come. It was a whoosh, the sound of something falling into water. She froze in place before she let out a scream.

'Mommy!'

Her voice echoed throughout the house, but no one answered.

1

The summer night air was warm and there was only the slightest hint of a breeze. The fourth of July had passed and soon the last remaining firework displays would finish. The holiday traffic, busy and nose-to-tail would soon return to its normal level. But now, at this time of night, it was quiet. Angela Goodman sighed as she looked out of the car window. Although her marriage was over, their shared house remained her home and the tree lined street familiar. If only she could feel safe again. Then she might be able to relax, think about the future, about whether there could be another man in her life. There was still a lot to be grateful for: friends, people she could trust and a job that brought her the self-esteem she'd never achieved in her marriages. The car stopped in front of her drive, the automatic light triggered by its presence, illuminating the path to the front door.

'Thanks for driving me home Jim and thank Jackie again. I had a lovely evening.' As Angela opened the door, the car's interior light shone harshly on her face.

Your make-up could do with a retouch, thought Jim as he leaned across and gave her a kiss on the cheek. 'Always a pleasure. You're good company and we love having you round. Any time, you know that.'

'Thanks Jim, that means a lot.'

'Good night.'

When Angela stepped out of the car, Jim got a whiff of her perfume, mixed with the late night air. As he watched her walk up the path, his thoughts wandered.

You're still a very attractive woman, Angela, quite sexy. But you don't seem to be aware of it, although I can never be sure with you women. Do you know the power you have? Maybe you were a tease in your younger days, like those girls back in high school. The ones who used to ignore me, or worse still, laugh behind my back. Shit, how I hated them. Are you really just like them?

Now the suffused light from the hallway illuminated the front porch. Angela, silhouetted in the doorway, waved and blew Jim a kiss. Smiling to himself, he blew one back, before he revved the engine. He pressed the button on the car's CD player and turned up the volume. Maybe he wouldn't go straight home. Jackie wouldn't be waiting up. She never did. Although it was late, he needed to wind down and knew just the place to start.

Angela Goodman slipped off her coat and shoes, pausing momentarily to study herself in the full-length mirror. The lines were more pronounced than she would have liked. Did it matter? She would never do anything about them – besides, what for? Men couldn't be trusted: two disastrous marriages had taught her that one simple truth. It was a shame they'd taken their toll in the way they had. The second one was far from settled. This week would bring more angst, more legal correspondence, more hurt.

Tonight a nightcap was in order. Malt whisky, the one thing she never skimped on, to help her sleep. Lately, there was always a tumbler next to her bedside lamp. But before that, she would have to go through her elaborate checking routine to make sure no one had been in the house. It was downstairs where she'd noticed the first tell tale sign – an ornament moved just slightly on the mantle piece. No one else would have noticed, but she did. Then another time there were papers in the kitchen wastebasket that she didn't recognise. At times there was also a smell, a man's smell. You couldn't capture that in a bottle and have it analysed.

Mostly though, it was the way it made her feel – like she'd been invaded, her privacy violated. Then there were the memories it evoked, those alone made her shudder. When she'd tried to explain it to that detective last week, it had sounded so trivial. She'd begun to doubt herself, feeling quite foolish by the end of the interview. Each thing was small, but together, did they add up? Or was her mind playing tricks on her?

At least tonight everything looked in order – the ornaments, the one used glass, even the paper under the kitchen door, precisely where she'd painstakingly positioned it some five hours earlier.

Or was it? No, stop it!

The ice rocked in the glass as she climbed the stairs, cursing herself for having forgotten to replace the upstairs light bulb, which had blown earlier in the day. Now carefully skirting the storage boxes holding the remainder of her husband's things, she manoeuvred in the dark to her bedside table, switching on the soft, subtle light.

A shadowy figure sat in the corner chair, only inches from the doorway.

'Hi bitch, you've kept me waiting.'

Angela Goodman tried to scream but nothing came

out. The only sound was the glass dropping on to the wooden floor, the ice cubes slithering towards the cracks.

2

'Morning Scotty.'

Detective Annie Macpherson could feel herself bristle, although she was too professional to show it. Two weeks, two long and tiring weeks since she first met the Captain, Marco Franconi and she hadn't warmed to him yet. She expected she never would. Her Scottish Presbyterian background primed her not to suffer fools. Of course, he wasn't a fool, just a really irritating man who happened to be her sponsor, at least for the length of her six-month exchange. Franconi stood right in front of her desk, waiting for an acknowledgement and picking his fingernails – that annoying habit of his which inwardly made her cringe. The sooner she responded, the sooner she could get back to the file she was studying.

'Aye, morning Sir.'

'When Bronski gets in, I want to see the two of you in my office. We could do with catching up, so I can write my initial impressions of your exchange. What do you people call it? Um, an appraisal. I thought that's what they did to antiques.'

Annie forced a smile, although she wasn't amused by his joke. 'I'll pass the message on to Detective Bronski as soon as he gets in.'

'I guess I'd better tell them I can't understand a word you say.' With that quip, Franconi turned and headed into his office.

'Aye,' Annie murmured to herself, as her long blonde curly hair fell off her shoulder, thankfully blocking the look on her face from another colleague off to her left.

'Oh, we are privileged, aren't we?' Dave Ellison chided as soon as Franconi shut his glass door. Annie found her colleague's smile disarming and she'd warmed to him from day one. That would be as far as it would go though, given her simple rule never to get involved with anyone from work. It was still too painful to reflect on what happened when she broke it the one and only time. She enjoyed sharing the squad room with Ellison. His sense of humour more closely matched hers than any of the other colleagues she'd met so far. He had one of those lanky builds that Europeans associated with American basketball players.

'Shut up,' Annie said, just glancing his way.

'Temper, temper, now. Is this the fiery Scot we were told to watch out for?'

'Believe me, if you saw my temper, you would run a mile. That's right, you lot still talk in miles, don't you? Kilometres too complicated for you?' Annie pushed her chair back and grabbed her jacket. 'I might calm down if I have a coffee. You fancy one?'

'I never heard of coffee being something you fancy, but I'll have one if you're buying.'

There was that smile again, as Ellison closed his file and got up to join her.

The saving grace of the Westford Police Station was that a Starbucks coffee shop had opened in the last six months right next door. Ellison pushed the door open for Annie, as she reached into her handbag, trying to find her purse amongst the debris. Her desk was a sharp contrast to her handbag, neater than all the others surrounding hers. The worst was Detective Bronski's, her supervisor, whose desk was impossible to see for pieces of paper, files, unwashed coffee cups, who knows, maybe even a dead body. Her handbag, though, that was another story.

Luckily, they'd made it just before the mass of office workers started coming in, so the queue was bearable. That was another thing Annie had learned quickly, don't use the word 'queue'. The Yanks didn't have a clue what that word meant, neither could they spell it. As she waited her turn, she marvelled as she heard the people in front of her order the myriad variety of cups of coffee. It seemed so complicated and never ceased to amuse her. In her view, coffee was coffee, pure and simple. It woke you up, that was its function. But she would have the same as Ellison, it was easier that way.

Ellison went off to find seats. Scanning the coffee shop, he studiously avoided any of the other cops, so he and Annie could have ten minutes respite from the job. It wasn't long before she joined him.

'Two skinny cappuccinos and I've splashed out on two muffins. Can't have you believing all those stereotypes about my countrymen being tight with money.'

Annie slid herself along the bench seat, loosening her jacket and concentrating on placing the cups, muffins, plates and cutlery on the table.

'You'll make someone a good wife one day,' joked Ellison, while at the same time noticing how really blue her eyes were.

'How do you know I'm not doing that already?' retorted Annie.

'Oh, the obvious sign, no ring. More importantly, no husband in his right mind would let someone as beautiful as you out of his sight for six months.' When Annie winced, Ellison sensed it was time to change the subject. 'So, how's the exchange going so far? You enjoying yourself?'

Annie cut into her muffin before replying. 'Not bad. Bronski's quite straight with me. He doesn't want to mess up his first experience of supervising on the programme and wants to make sure I learn all I can. So far, it all seems routine, not much different from Stockport. I guess burglaries, violent assaults, surveillance, you name it, are pretty much the same wherever you are.'

'You mean you have robbers over there? I thought it was all quaint little villages, thatched cottages.' Ellison gave her a wink, as he took a drink of his coffee.

'Aye, apart from the big cities, the drug related violence, the little old ladies too frightened to go out at night and the rubbish strewn council estates. Oh, did I forget to include the terrorist attacks? Regrettably, we have everything you do, except us good guys don't routinely carry guns. I've only ever seen guns being issued to the Armed Response Team when there's a specific threat or intelligence. I certainly don't fancy wearing one of those shoulder holsters you're all so fond of.' Annie braced herself for a macho defence from her colleague: like in the documentary she'd seen some months ago about the constitutional right to bear arms, or some such crap.

'Too bad we need to,' he remarked.

'Anyway, Bronski sticks pretty close to me, knowing I'm unarmed.'

'I'm surprised they let an exchange go ahead with such a fundamental difference in the way our forces operate.' Ellison started on his muffin as well.

'I think it's a good thing that it's never been a stumbling block in the programme. Besides, you guys could learn a thing or to about how we talk ourselves out of situations, using our wits as a weapon.'

Ellison sat back, thinking about whether she would talk herself out of a drink after work, if he asked.

Detective Bronski was sitting at his desk when they got back and thankfully, she'd had the foresight to bring him a latte. As she bent over to clear a small space to set the coffee down, she thought she'd better speak first. 'Franconi wants to see us to discuss my first two weeks.'

The detective nodded, closing the file on his desk. 'I'll leave this to cool down, can't drink it too hot. Let's go.'

3

He received the call at the prearranged time.

'How did it go?'

'Fine, mission accomplished.'

'No loose ends?'

'Not that I can think of.'

'Good, it's been a long time coming.'

'Sure has.'

'Talk soon.'

He deleted the last number received in the call register as they had agreed. He wasn't expecting any more calls today. Now, he just had to sit and wait. Waiting was what he was good at – waiting, planning and thinking. The bitch got what she deserved. She paid all right. What was due. In fact, what was long overdue.

He realised how ravenous he was. It had been a long night. Later he would start the reconnaissance for the next task.

His only regret was that he couldn't do it all over again, but he had the next best thing. He could replay her pleading as many times as he wanted.

He played the recording.

4

Franconi was engrossed in a telephone conversation and Bronski hesitated momentarily before he rapped on the glass door. Without looking up, the senior detective waved them in. Only when Bronski and Annie had positioned themselves in the well-worn chairs did Franconi glance at them. He was busy scribbling notes on his pad.

From what Franconi was summarising, they began to glean part of what was going on. 'So the vic is in Westford Hospital now? Yeah. Right, only just arriving, but she's still alive as far as you're aware. The place is a mess. Yeah, I'll send a couple of my team down. Crime scene people been alerted? OK, OK, we're on to it.'

With the mannerisms Annie had already started to notice, Franconi put the phone down and simultaneously pushed his shoulders back and leaned hard against the back of his chair, as if he were trying to loosen some kink in his back. Then he began tapping the notepad with his pen. Both detectives waited for him to speak, although Annie could sense that Bronski was already on alert.

'The appraisal can wait, Scotty. I want the two of you on this case. So far it looks like attempted murder, but that could change. The victim is in a bad way. They're working on her now at Westford Hospital.' Franconi pulled his scribbled notes in front of him, using the pen to track through them. 'I'll start at the top, that way you'll know all I know. We've got a thirty-nine year old female named Angela Goodman, 388 Quaker

Lane Southwest, appears to have been brutally attacked in her own home.'

Annie felt her head spin, as she glanced over at Bronski. Had her supervisor recognised the name? When there was no sign from Bronski, Annie knew she would have to say something.

'Sir.'

Franconi shot her a look. 'Let me finish, Macpherson. Didn't they teach you anything over in little old England?'

'But Sir, I recognise the name.'

'What're you talking about? You've only been here ten minutes.' Franconi threw the pen on the desk and leaned forward. He wasn't smiling.

'Oh, damn, so do I.' Bronski turned to face Annie. 'That's the woman who thought she was being stalked. She came in last week. Your first interview, wasn't it?'

Annie looked from Bronski back to Franconi trying to gauge his reaction. 'I took all the details and reported back to Detective Bronski. We've been trying to locate the husband.'

Franconi stared at the two of them in disbelief. 'Tell me fast, because we've got to move on this one.'

Annie heard urgency, rather than annoyance in Franconi's voice and surmised that he'd be wondering if his team had screwed up. Bronski was more senior in this context, so Annie deferred to him, although she would have been quite happy to fill in the details. She'd a lot fewer cases cramming up her memory than Bronski, but she knew she had to bide her time.

'Angela Goodman came in early last week, reported that things had been moved in the house, just little things, an ornament, some papers, that sort of thing. She's going through a difficult divorce, nearly endgame and everything is being done through lawyers at the moment. No kids, just the house, but she wants it in revenge for the husband's philandering, as she put it.' Bronski had almost total recall of what Annie had reported back.

'Get to the point, Detective.'

Bronski's face reddened.

Annie realised that although Bronski was used to Franconi's abruptness, it obviously still affected him. It was time to butt in. 'She hadn't seen the husband in months. He's renting an apartment in New Britain, but she was convinced he was doing it – coming into the house when she wasn't there, trying to unnerve her.'

'So, she changes the locks. Tell me you at least told her to do that.'

'Already been advised to by the lawyer, even though the house is still in joint names until the settlement. When I interviewed her, she hadn't got around to it yet. Neither had she managed to get the keys off him.' Annie hesitated for a moment.

Bronski came back in. 'We went to his apartment to talk to him, but he wasn't there. The building superintendent said he was away for a couple of weeks. We told the guy to call us as soon as he's back. So far, no word, till maybe now?'

Franconi threw his pen down. 'Some calling card that's been left, isn't it? Get over to the house. See what you make of the scene. Then get over to the hospital and speak to the couple who found her. With any luck, they'll still be there waiting for news. If not, pay them a visit. Oh, and assess the situation at the hospital. She could still be in danger from the perpetrator if she makes it through.'

'Names, Sir?'

Annie already had her notebook out. If they'd made a mistake, she didn't want to compound it now. Most of all, she didn't want Franconi to start thinking she was incompetent, not when she'd graduated top of her cadet class and was considered a high flier back home. Here she was a nobody, an exchange of staff to enhance relationships, a nuisance, whatever the top brass wanted to think.

This rankled. Angela Goodman had presented as a highly-strung, nervous woman, frightened of her own shadow. It certainly seemed that she was imagining things, almost attention seeking. For once, the advice of Annie's father to always go with her instinct hadn't worked. A small part of her was relieved that he was dead. At least she wouldn't have to admit her mistake to him, if it came to that. Living up to his reputation as a detective while at home had been hard enough.

Franconi glanced at his scribbles again. 'Yeah, the couple who phoned it in – Jim Moorcroft and Jackie Winters. They live together, 88 The Gable, Westford. Moorcroft may have been the last one to see her, except her attacker of course.'

5

Bronski was unusually quiet as he retrieved his keys from his desk drawer. After quickly scanning for anything new amongst the debris on the top, he nodded to Annie, who already had her jacket on. Following his lead, she said nothing until they got to the parking lot and he unlocked the door to the car.

'So, what do you make of all this?' Annie watched the road, even though her supervisor was driving. She was still trying to get used to the rules of driving on the wrong side of the road. It was the rotary islands that confused her – roundabouts were a lot simpler. Annie knew that she'd have to rent a car soon, although she didn't need one for work. The unmarked police car was functional and Bronski was always happy to drive, like most men in her experience. Back home, she was an experienced police driver and served some time with the traffic cops before she joined the CID. But here, she was getting used to travelling on the bus to the station from her apartment in Westford.

'Not what I was expecting when we went in for your first appraisal. It annoys me that we hadn't had a chance to fill him in on the interview with Mrs Goodman before this happened. You were going to mention the case, weren't you?' Bronski glanced over at her while still concentrating on the road. 'This is all I need, us screwing up. Won't look good for the exchange.'

Annie decided not to comment on the exchange part, but was reassured that Bronski thought that they were in this together. He could have chosen to deflect the blame on to her, which wouldn't have boded well for the next five and a half months. 'I would have mentioned it, but I'm not sure that I was giving it much credence. It seemed more routine to me. I really thought it was all in her head.'

'Yeah, my first impression too, from reading your notes. Still, it looks like we blew it.'

'I've got that superintendent's number in my book. Maybe Mr Goodman did come back and he didn't bother to ring us.'

'You mean, 'Call us'? Americans don't say, 'Ring us'. Isn't there a saying about two nations being separated by a common language? Wasn't that Churchill?'

Annie realised that Bronski was tense. This was the first time he had corrected her language, unlike Franconi, who used every opportunity. She was tempted to say that the quote was usually attributed to George Bernard Shaw, but decided not to pursue it.

'Whatever. Anyway, back to the point – the superintendent?'

'OK, we'll swing by there as soon as we've checked the house out. If Goodman has beaten up his wife, then he'll be long gone now.'

Bronski was fiddling with the air conditioning setting, another sign to Annie that he was getting himself bothered about their encounter with Franconi. Bronski hated being in the wrong. She'd learned that much already. At the risk of annoying him even more, Annie had to disagree.

'But what if he's not?'

'OK, radio dispatch and tell them to send a patrol

car to check it out and make sure they get back to my cell phone.' The air conditioner was now blasting away.

The dispatch made, Annie concentrated again on the route. Westford had some really old, very beautiful properties with wrap around porches, which she'd only ever seen in the movies or on TV. Never having travelled to the States before, everything was a new experience. She was more used to spending her off duty time in her hometown of Huntly in Scotland or exploring parts of France or Italy. Truthfully, the only part of the States that had even remotely interested her before was Montana and the chance to fly-fish on the Yellowstone River. She'd nearly made it the year before when her local fly fishing shop offered her a place on an organised trip to Livingston, but her leave didn't coincide with the proposed date. To her great annoyance, she wasn't able to persuade any of her colleagues to swap leave with her. She doubted whether this exchange would afford her any time to arrange it before she went back. It was already early July and September was the best time to go: too soon for her.

Conscious that the silence was building up between them and not wanting Bronski to entertain second thoughts about her abilities, Annie decided to bring the discussion back to Angela Goodman. 'Aye, I thought she was just a bit on edge and probably attention seeking. I did tell her to get back to us if there was anything else suspicious and we tried to check out the husband. There wasn't a lot else to do. It was unlikely to be a stranger since there was no report of any forced entry. I'll have that bloody superintendent if Goodman came back and he covered up for him.'

Bronski was really concentrating now, trying to locate the street so he didn't respond to what she was saying. 'It's one of these on the right. Here we go.'

The police car was still parked out front and cars belonging to the forensics team were not far behind. Bronski manoeuvred into a spot just across the road. Neighbours were already milling around, trying to work out what was going on. Most of them had heard the ambulance an hour before and then watched as Angela Goodman was wheeled out on a stretcher. No one approached Bronski or Annie but instead talked among themselves. Annie heard one woman say, 'Such a shame.'

Although Bronski recognised the young rookie on the door, he still followed procedure and flashed his badge at Frank Petersen. Annie followed suit. Petersen nodded them through. To Bronski's knowledge, this was the second severe assault the kid had been 'first on scene' for in the last month. Probably having nightmares, thought Bronski. The other victim had died within twenty-four hours. Would Angela Goodman fare any better?

Annie had already observed that there was no sign of forced entry at the front door, her mind running through the list of possible explanations: Angela Goodman let her attacker in, the attacker had a key or another point of entry was used. But she kept her own counsel for now. Whoever assaulted Angela Goodman trashed her place while they were at it.

In the hallway, the two detectives were greeted with dried paint that had been thrown at the walls, but the scene in the living room showed the full effect of the rampage that had taken place in the house. Not only were the walls splattered with paint but the wooden floors were also littered with ornaments and framed photographs, which must, only hours earlier, have had pride of place on the mantelpiece. Angela Goodman's voice, describing how she checked those various pieces to see if they'd been moved, echoed in Annie's head.

The forensic team members were spread throughout the house and most just continued with their work as the two detectives passed by. One pointed the way to the Senior Scenes of Crime Officer. Glen Heaviley was still in the bedroom taking blood samples and he nodded to Bronski and Annie as they entered the room.

'Morning Detective Bronski, I don't think I've had the pleasure of meeting your colleague.'

As Bronski was absorbing the detail of the bedroom, Annie answered herself, 'Detective Macpherson, I'm on a six month exchange from England.'

'Yes, but not English. I believe that's a Scottish accent, much nicer than the English one.'

'Aye,' said Annie wanting to shift focus on to the job at hand without being impolite. 'So what can you tell us so far?'

'Well Detective Macpherson, as you can see, my team is gathering paint samples, fibres and prints from all parts of the house. I've been concentrating on this room, as it would appear to be where the main attack took place. From the state of the blood on these sheets, I would say she took quite a beating. I also found a tooth fragment.'

'Any evidence of a sexual assault?' Bronski was processing what he'd heard so far and Annie was taking notes.

'Too early to speculate yet. There is some staining on the sheets that isn't blood. Could, of course, have already been there. Depends what took place in this bed before the night of the attack and how often she changed her sheets. But that's your concern, not mine. I won't know what the other staining is for sure until everything is examined. You might want to ask them the same question at the hospital. I am sure they will have examined the victim for sexual assault, although the paramedic I spoke to was hoping she'd make it as far as the hospital. Apparently she was in a very bad way.'

Heaviley hadn't stopped what he was doing while he carried on the conversation and Annie watched as he labelled an evidence bag and passed it to the junior officer who had just come in. He then turned to Annie again. 'You've seen the state of the hallway, although unfortunately for us, by the time we exclude footprints from the two people who found her and the ambulance crew, we'll be lucky to find anything useful.'

'But you're convinced that the main assault was in this room?' Annie's eyes were taking in the whole scene again, after her first cursory scan. One wall in the room had been splashed with bright pink paint, almost making the room look like a brothel. The tasteful light blue walls had been transformed, although the wooden floor was relatively unscathed, except for the drips from the walls. Was the colour some sort of statement? The bedside lamp lay on the floor waiting to be dusted for prints and the same procedure would be applied to the top of the dressing table and the bedside cabinet. The young female crime officer was just getting to them, moving purposely, but unobtrusively around the room, careful not to get in between the detectives and her boss.

'Have you been into the other rooms yet?' Heaviley was now carefully collecting up the bottom fitted sheet from the bed, having labelled another large evidence bag.

Annie answered as she continued to scan the room. 'Only the hallway and the living room, so far. We'll do a walk through the whole house now. We wanted to speak to you first.'

'Can't enlighten you too much just yet, but if there is anything in these sheets we'll find it in the lab. I'll make a list when we've processed everything and then you'll know what we're examining.' It was clear that Heaviley now wanted to continue, free from distraction.

The rest of the house hadn't escaped attention. There was paint in the kitchen, dining room and the two spare bedrooms, each room a different colour, including black. Annie knew that paint samples could be analysed to reveal the brand. Even so, if it were a common one, they wouldn't find out a lot from this. The perpetrator wouldn't have been stupid enough to buy them all at once from the same store. More likely, this was planned and the paint collected over weeks, months, or even years: any follow up would probably be a waste of resources.

Annie also considered that the perpetrator would have had to carry a number of paint cans into the house.

She mentally reviewed the rooms again. There were at least five different colours. So even if they were small cans, the perpetrator must have been in the house for quite a while after the assault to carry out the vandalism. And could he, or she, have managed to carry all the paint cans into the house in one trip? What about levering them open? The perpetrator would have had to bring something with him to do that.

She nipped back into the bedroom and mentioned this to Glen Heaviley.

'Good point Detective, we'll check to see if there is anything still in the house that might have been used.'

Bronski was waiting for her to finish off the inspection. Perhaps the most significant thing they'd confirmed was that no one had forcibly entered Angela Goodman's house. Either she'd let them in or whoever attacked her had a key or knew how to pick a lock. Annie's instinct convinced her that Angela Goodman knew her attacker and that there was some kind of personal vendetta going on. But she had to keep an open mind at this stage of the investigation. Still, it was becoming more imperative to locate the husband.

6

The two detectives had been at the house at least an hour. As they walked out they spoke to the rookie cop, Frank Petersen, again. While they were in the house, another patrol car had shown up, at Bronski's request and the two cops had started interviewing the neighbours. Petersen nodded across the road and they turned to see an officer crossing over to them. Annie recognised him from the station but they'd never been introduced. The man was built like a Welsh rugby player – solid, broad shoulders, square neck – the kind of player you want on your side.

'Detective Bronski,' he said, before hesitating for a moment, 'and you must be our illustrious exchange detective I've heard all about.'

Annie shook hands with Officer Driscoll, his handshake matching his frame.

'So far, we've covered the right hand side of the road except for the people not at home and we're making our way down the other side now. Only thing so far is the report of a car around midnight. Apparently music was blaring as it left the house. No idea of make or licence plate, but you'll need to eliminate it. Maybe someone we haven't questioned yet has got more detail. The neighbours either side of her are out but they might recognise the car if it's been here before. Anyway, we'll finish what we can for now and come back later.'

'Thanks, Driscoll, see you back at the station,' replied Bronski.

The two detectives headed for Bronski's car. 'So, it's

the hospital next. Let's hope that couple ...'

Annie had her notebook open and filled in the sentence. 'Jim Moorcroft and Jackie Winters. Didn't Franconi say they telephoned it in, so they must have a key, mustn't they? Someone had to let the paramedics in. There was no forced entry.'

'Right, maybe we can account for one set of keys. Hopefully they knew her well enough to fill in some details. We'll also need to eliminate them as it sounds like they were first at the scene.'

As Annie reached for the door handle on her side, she had a sudden thought: 'Why would they return to the crime scene if they were involved?'

'Might be a good tactic – you know, to take suspicion off them – what we call the 'Good Samaritan' routine. I'm not saying that's what it is. Let's see what they have to say first. We'll need to interview them, just to eliminate them. Get back on to dispatch. We still haven't heard anything about the husband.'

Bronski was concentrating on the road, as traffic was building up now. Annie had to smile when Americans talked about traffic. None of them had experienced the M6 on a Bank Holiday weekend or the M6/M5 interchange. Now that was traffic.

Annie identified herself to dispatch and the message was negative. Mr Goodman hadn't returned as far as the building superintendent was aware. Mail was still piling up for him. The beat cop had left a report for them, including Mr Goodman's work address, car make and licence plate.

'Let's hope we get a break and someone noticed

more detail of the car from last night. Could be his. We better also pay a visit to his work address, see what they know.'

God, I hope it's not his, thought Annie. Then it would be our fault for not having located him in time. It was crucial either to get him eliminated or not. Right now he seemed as good a candidate as any. Annie reviewed the scene in the house again in her mind. The pink walls in the bedroom, they bothered her more than the rest of it.

Westford Hospital was busy. After showing their badges at reception, the two detectives were told that Angela Goodman was in surgery and they were directed to the waiting area outside the main operating room. Bronski wasn't prepared to waste time. 'Look, I'm sure the surgeons are too busy operating to take any notice of us waiting, so how about we speak to the admitting doctor in charge of the ER? It would help us to find out what their assessment of her condition was.'

'Hold on a minute.' The receptionist typed in a number and then suggested they take seats in the waiting area to the right of the reception.

They hadn't had time to sit down when a tall, black haired woman, dressed in a white coat and looking harassed, approached the desk. She nodded as the receptionist pointed out the two detectives. Without the hint of a smile, the woman approached them, hands in the pockets of her white coat. Annie noticed the dark circles under her eyes and wondered when this doctor last had a break. 'I'm Dr Cooperman, mind if I answer your questions in the canteen? I'm desperate for a coffee.'

The canteen had a Starbucks concession tucked away in a corner. Bronski stepped ahead as they entered. 'I'll get these, what do you want?'

After giving their orders, Annie pointed to a table away from the main crowd of staff that would afford them some privacy. The two women sat down.

'I've been on all morning without a break. Hope you don't mind talking here. We've had a really busy morning, which is unusual for a Monday. Caffeine keeps me going.'

'I know what you mean.'

The small talk ended when Bronski placed the tray on the table, together with three almond croissants, in addition to the coffees.

'Detective Bronski, you are a man after my own heart. Are you married?' But it was obvious to Dr Cooperman that she'd embarrassed the detective and so had to recover the situation. 'Sorry, just my sense of humour: take no notice. You have to have one to work in a place like this. So, how can I help you?'

Annie got out her notebook. 'Angela Goodman, thirty-nine year old woman, came in a few hours ago, appears to have been the victim of a vicious assault. Can you tell us about her injuries and more importantly, if she was conscious and said anything?'

Elise Cooperman sat back cradling her coffee cup, saving the croissant just for the moment. 'Vicious is a good word for it and no, she wasn't conscious. She had multiple bruising all over her body, a broken arm, severe facial injuries, broken cheek bone, black eyes, cuts, internal bleeding and the scan showed a blood clot in her brain. The best description I can give is that someone used her as a punching bag. Amazing that one human being can inflict that much injury on another, especially on a woman.' The pause allowed her to pick off a piece of her croissant, although it seemed to Annie that the doctor was just going through the motions of eating.

Annie was recording what Dr Cooperman was saying in her notebook. 'So, the operation she's having now?'

'To stop the internal bleeding, assess what damage there is to her organs: the spleen's probably shot. The head injuries will be assessed again in a few hours. She may be back in the operating room before the day's out, but the surgeons can give you more of an update. I wouldn't put my money on her making it, if you want the truth.' Just as she finished the sentence and lifted her coffee for another sip, her pager went off. 'I'm sorry, I'm needed back in the ER. Are we finished?'

'Just one more thing, was there any evidence of a sexual assault?'

'There were multiple contusions around the groin area and evidence of vaginal penetration. We used the standard rape kit. Sorry I should have mentioned that at the outset, so there will be samples of vaginal fluid, but if the attacker wore a condom, there might not be any seminal fluid. So I'm not sure how much help that will be for you. From a medical point of view, apart from the psychological impact of a rape and I wouldn't minimise it by the way, her other injuries are what is life threatening. This may sound harsh, but a rape would be the least of her problems.' The bleep sounded again. 'Now, I really must go. Thanks for the coffee.'

The waiting area outside the surgical suite was surprisingly crowded. A middle-aged couple were sitting comforting each other, the woman periodically wiping away tears. An elderly gentleman sat quietly reading a paperback book. Annie couldn't see what it was, but he was absorbed. In the far corner, two women talked in whispers. Another woman sat opposite. The man she was with was quietly pacing between the drinks machine and the far seating. He had a stocky build, about five foot seven, early to mid-thirties and receding hairline. Annie's bet was on these two.

'Excuse me, but are you Jackie Winters?' The woman nodded as Annie and Bronski pulled out their IDs. Annie guessed that she was in her early to mid twenties, with one of those slightly pointed faces, brown wavy hair and no make-up. She wasn't stunning, but attractive nonetheless. By now Jim Moorcroft had approached and confirmed his identity.

'Any news on how Angela is doing?' was the first question he asked.

By the time Annie and Bronski got back to the office, tiredness had set in. They had visited the crime scene, followed by the hospital, interviewed Jim Moorcroft, Jackie Winters, George Goodman's employer and the apartment house superintendent once again. Franconi had left for the day with a message that he wanted an update first thing in the morning. They'd also spoken to Angela Goodman's employer and verified that Jim Moorcroft, Jackie Winters and Angela Goodman all worked together and were friends outside the office.

Even Dave Ellison had called it a day. Bronski offered Annie a ride home but she was happy to catch the bus, allowing some moments of normality in what had been a difficult day.

7

As Annie unlocked her apartment door, all she wanted was a long hot soak in the bathtub, followed by a glass or two of red wine and some food. There was at least a portion of tomato sauce and meatballs left over from Sunday, when she'd made enough for several meals. Cooking for one was boring at the best of times and somehow didn't match cooking for two, so her policy was to make enough for leftovers and for the freezer.

It had been a good few months since she'd cooked for two and this exchange programme was a kind of healing process for her – six months away from the comments, the guilt and the hurt on both sides from the broken engagement. There had been a lot to sort out, or more precisely to cancel: the house purchase, the wedding and people making arrangements to travel up to Scotland. Yet that was the least stressful part of the whole thing. She couldn't think of Paul without picturing his face when she'd told him it was off, nor could she give him an explanation. She'd just known it wasn't right and that she couldn't go through with the wedding. She'd loved him, but not enough.

Just when it had become unbearable to be around everything that reminded her of the hurt she'd caused, her colleague Kim Littlemore found out that she was pregnant and the exchange she was due to go on was up for grabs. It had been a blessed relief at the time. Annie wondered if she would still feel the same in the next few weeks, especially with this case.

The scent from the candles was filling the bathroom,

the bubbles from the bath inviting, but just as her toes were halfway in, her cell phone rang. Luckily it was within reach.

'Macpherson.'

'Scotty, hope I haven't caught you at an inopportune moment.'

Annie had to smile in spite of her annoyance. 'Inopportune' wasn't a word she expected to be in Franconi's vocabulary. But she daren't say she was just about to get in the bath; no telling what kind of remark she might get out of him.

'No, Sir, I'm sorry we missed you. We got your message that you wanted to see Detective Bronski and myself in the morning. Did we miss something?' Annie shifted the phone to the other ear while she reached for her bathrobe, which was hanging on the back of the door. Somehow it seemed inappropriate to be speaking to her boss naked.

'No, I'm not calling about the case. I'll get briefed in the morning. There are some people I want you to meet. They live in your area back in England. How about I pick you up in an hour? I'm taking them to a little Italian restaurant, Mario's.'

Annie was too taken aback at the invitation to think of an excuse. An hour gave time for a bath and she'd find something in the closet to wear. Real food, how bad could it be? 'An hour is fine Sir, I'll be out front.'

Franconi was as good as his word. In one hour sharp he pulled up in front of her apartment house, on his own. The July evening air was just slightly cool and Annie had chosen a black skirt, black sandals and a smart white blouse with a purple fitted jacket. The outfit would do for informal or smart casual and set off her long blond curls. It was enough of a contrast from her black trousers and jacket – her staple outfits for work. Franconi leaned across the car and opened the passenger side.

'Evening, Sir, the others meeting us there?' Annie realised she'd no details of whom it was that Franconi was so anxious for her to meet: a man, a woman, a couple?

Franconi signalled and pulled out. The car was moderately tidy. Once he was on the main road, he glanced over at her. 'Dr Christine James and Michael Turner. They're a couple, but not married, although I'm thinking that part is only a matter of time. They've only been back in Connecticut a few weeks. She has a place near Manchester, England. I think it's called Didsbury. Starts with a 'D' anyhow.'

'I know Didsbury well. It's part of Manchester: a nice suburb, as suburbs go, full of students in big Victorian houses turned into student flats, good pubs and restaurants. In fact, I rent a flat in the next village, called Withington. She'll know it.'

'Good, so you should be able to relate to them.'

If only life were that simple, thought Annie: being able to relate to people just because you knew a restaurant or a pub or happened to live in the next village, but musings like that only brought her back to thoughts of Paul. They'd had a lot more than a shared love of food in common. They'd grown up together in the wilds of Scotland. He'd taught her to fly-fish for salmon near Huntly. They'd trained together at the Police Academy.

So much in common, more even than most married couples, so why wasn't it enough?

Franconi broke her reverie. 'I've known Michael Turner for a long time, used to be a cop, but he retired six, no seven years ago, after getting shot working undercover. But he's done OK for himself, runs Turner Security in downtown Westford. Divides his time between here and England now.'

Annie was intrigued; ex-cops always had some sort of story to tell. 'So what about the woman and the connection to England?'

'Yeah, well that goes back to a year ago last May. The body of a bag lady, that's a homeless person to you, was found behind one of the buildings covered by Turner's business. Turner came to the scene and we got reacquainted, let's just say. A few months later he meets Christine James through some friends of his and meeting her triggers a memory.'

'Which was?'

'Christine James and the bag lady who, thanks to Christine, was later identified as Maria Moretto, were best friends in high school. You don't have high school in England, do you?' Franconi glanced over at her again, as he prepared to pull into the parking lot for the restaurant. 'Let's get inside and order some wine and I'll finish the story. They should be arriving in about ten minutes.'

The description of the restaurant as 'little' was apt, thought Annie, but the atmosphere was fantastic. The smell of fresh Italian cooking permeated every inch of the place and the waiter greeted Franconi as a long lost friend. Even Annie got introduced, a first for her being introduced to a waiter in a restaurant. Along one wall was a set of booths while the rest of the restaurant had tables laid out in fours and sixes. Without a blink, the waiter led them to the furthest booth from the door. Annie got the feeling that this was Franconi's spot.

'Red wine OK for you?'

'Fine.' Although Franconi asked, the red wine appeared only seconds later along with olives and a basket of bread.

Once Franconi had downed his first mouthful, he said, 'Now where was I?'

'The two women having been best friends,' Annie prompted, still wondering where the story was leading.

Franconi continued the story. Annie was sipping her wine slowly, while she listened and nodded at the appropriate times. She didn't want to become tipsy in front of the boss. On Franconi's say so the exchange could come to a premature end and she was conscious that the two-week review hadn't happened yet. The matter of Angela Goodman had distracted them. She was glad she'd already cleared the air with Franconi about discussing the case. She knew it would be far better to go over things with Bronski there. Besides, she didn't want Bronski to think that she was going behind his back, even though she'd no way of knowing, when they parted a few hours earlier, that she would be sharing an evening with Franconi. If this couple hadn't had some connection to England, she was sure she wouldn't be sitting where she was. But now, she couldn't lose track of the story Franconi was telling.

Ten minutes later, the olives were nearly gone and Franconi had talked through two pieces of bread so far and Annie still didn't know if the murderer had been caught. She was just about to ask a question when she realised that Franconi had spotted his guests.

Franconi got up from his seat and Annie turned to see him hugging a very attractive blonde woman and then shaking hands with an equally attractive man. Annie's guess was that they were in their mid to late thirties; the woman probably a few years younger than the guy.

'Christine James, Michael Turner, this is Annie Macpherson, our exchange detective from Stockport.' By now Annie had also eased herself out of the booth, unsure who would want to sit where. Christine gave her a warm hug and Annie instantly took to her. Michael kissed her on the cheek before Christine motioned Annie back into the booth and then sat beside her. Michael took the seat opposite, next to Franconi.

'So I see Captain, you don't intend to drive home.' Annie could see that Christine and Franconi had some sort of love-hate relationship and Annie smiled to herself. She wasn't the only female who reacted to Franconi like that and she made a mental note to try and talk to Christine on her own, get more of the low down on her boss.

'They keep my car for me overnight and if I need them to, they'll even drop it back to my house in the morning. We're old paesans, you know that.' Franconi had taken Christine and Michael to the restaurant before. Franconi caught the eye of the waiter, who poured two more glasses of wine and put a second bottle on the table.

'To your health.' Franconi spent the next few minutes talking to Annie about his favourite dishes from the menu, complete with details of how each was prepared and served. Christine and Michael only half listened and Annie sensed they'd been through this routine before. Annie had to smile at Franconi's efforts – typical Americans, think people from Britain don't know much about food. There was a small deli in Withington, near Annie's flat that had the best Italian ingredients. After all, Italy was a lot closer to Britain than the USA. Still, she feigned interest so as not to upset him. It was obvious that he loved describing the food of his ancestors although Annie doubted he'd ever been to Italy himself.

With the orders taken, more olives and bread arrived to keep them occupied. As the three of them became engrossed in conversation, Annie's eyes wandered across the restaurant to the table of ten people nearby. They'd come in a few minutes earlier and the waiters had rearranged the tables to accommodate the party. One part of the group was talking animatedly but it was a woman near the end of the table who caught Annie's attention. Everyone around her was talking. She was the only one sipping her wine, on her own, no one paying her any heed. It was obviously a family group. Was she the unwanted one? Annie knew how it felt to be forgotten. Andrew, he had pride of place in their childhood household. Yet how could she be jealous of a boy, now a man, with Down's Syndrome? That was too selfish to contemplate.

She looked around the room. No one there knew that she was taking each of them in and trying to work out their stories. That was what being a detective was all about, wasn't it? Maybe Andrew was the reason for Paul. For once, Annie wanted to be special, have some of the attention. But that was sick, surely. Being jealous of a big brother with a severe learning disability who couldn't even tie his own shoelaces, whose speech wasn't intelligible to anyone who hadn't met him before, who at times forgot he needed the toilet and wet himself and wasn't even embarrassed. No, being jealous of Andrew was pathetic. Then nearly going through with a wedding just to feel special. Annie Macpherson, she thought, you are seriously screwed-up.

Franconi interrupted her ruminations. Time for Annie to tune back in. 'So tonight it's celebration time, thanks to the two of you and your testimony at the trial, alongside my brilliant detective work.'

'Not forgetting the forensic evidence and the alibis that didn't stand up as I recall,' Michael added pointedly.

'Yeah, yeah, OK Turner, but tonight we're all here and that bastard, even with the best lawyers money could buy, is starting a life sentence for murder, grievous bodily harm and false imprisonment.' Franconi was about to raise his glass for a toast, but somehow Annie sensed that Christine wasn't in such a celebratory mood.

'But not for sentencing a woman to a homeless life because of him, not for all the hurt he caused to Maria Moretto's family or the humiliation he's brought to his own family.' Christine was clearly still angry and Michael reached across and took her hand. It was a very touching gesture and Annie was moved by it.

Franconi put his glass back down on the table momentarily. 'Hey, I'm no fan of lawyers, but the prosecutor went for what they could prove and did a good job. Even if some of the stuff we knew he'd done wasn't admissible, we got him on the big counts. So, I reckon we need a toast to justice for Maria.' The other three all raised their glasses with him.

'Annie, you probably think we're rude, talking about something you don't know anything about.' Michael Turner still had his glass partly raised as he turned to look at her. Annie could instantly see the attraction of Turner. It was those eyes.

'I was just starting to fill Annie in about how the two of you led us to the identification of Maria,' said Franconi.

Between the three of them, Annie heard the rest of the story, noting that Michael and Franconi were perfunctory, sticking mainly to the facts, while any emotional context came from Christine.

'At least the Morettos felt that justice had been done and I take comfort in that.' As Christine finished with that statement, the main courses arrived and the conversation turned to lighter things. Annie heard about how Michael and Christine met, how Michael now divided his time between staying with her in England and carrying on his security business in Westford. Plans were advancing for Christine to leave England and return to live with Michael in Westford, where she was born, but that was still months off. Annie sensed that there was more to the background, which wasn't being said but she didn't pry. In her experience, people shared what they wanted to when they were ready.

When the coffee arrived at the end of the meal, Annie stirred hers and then put the spoon in and poured the cream over the back of the spoon allowing the cream to settle on top. Only Christine was used to this European way of pouring cream and she smiled at Annie, who again was transfixed by the next table. 'What's more precious than time?' one of the five men had asked. But the conversation from the table was too muffled for Annie to hear the reply. Soon after, the forgotten woman glanced over at her and smiled. Was there some mutual recognition, a shared loneliness?

Annie knew she had to stop this introspection. She didn't want to be one of those people who were lonely even in a crowd. As she tried to refocus on the conversation, she spotted two people at another table. Hardly a word had been spoken, both embarrassed by the silence between them. She almost wanted to go over to them, shake them and say, 'treasure what you have.' But then she realised that they could be what she and Paul might have become – two people with nothing to say to one another. When? In five years, or ten years? And what would she be like: feeling lonely in a crowded room, trying to be polite, but scared – scared to have his kids, knowing it wasn't going to last and not wanting complications, while at the same time Paul struggling to understand what was going on? At least she'd spared them all of that.

Annie was relieved when eventually the 'forgotten'

woman ended up engaged in a deep conversation with the man next to her. It didn't matter who the man was, at least she was involved, at last.

Back home, after being dropped off by Michael and Christine's taxicab, Annie fell into bed, exhausted from the day and the food and wine. She needed her sleep. Tomorrow would be a busy day.

8

Carol Wojinski tiptoed around the bedroom, trying not to wake her husband. The bedroom was at the back of the house, bordering on to the woods, so there was not much natural light. She didn't really need it. As always, her clothes were laid out on the chair in the corner of the room and she was used to dressing in the dark. Sometimes in the middle of winter, she wondered what it would be like to be blind and the very thought of it frightened her, especially the idea of not being able to see Gus's face again. She never tired of looking at her husband, his rugged features belying the gentleness of his character. When he found her staring at him, he would wink – letting her know that he was on to her – a signal between them that always felt precious.

Gus rarely woke with the sound of the shower and she knew from his breathing now that he was still deeply asleep. Smiling at his tousled hair, she remembered how it was the night before when they'd settled into bed together – five years and not one night apart. Long may it continue, she thought, as she fastened the last button of her blouse and quietly shut the door.

Over the last couple of weeks there had been a few moments of disquiet, the feeling that she was being watched, followed even. But she'd put it all down to her imagination running away with itself, as it had some months ago. She'd purposely avoided talking it through with Gus, knowing that it would unsettle him and just make him worry.

The warmth of the summer air hit her as she came

out of the house. There was no breeze to provide any relief. The routine was always the same: she used the remote control to open the automatic garage door at the side of the house. Then, in the car, the radio went on, but low at first so as not to disturb any neighbours. Reversing out, she paused to trigger the garage door shut.

'Take care today, as the temperature is set to hit ninety degrees. Don't leave any pets in your car. This is an announcement on behalf of the Animal Protection League.'

Carol smiled. Who would be so stupid as to leave a dog in a car with the windows closed? But you never know, perhaps one dog's life would be saved today because of the radio announcement, so who was she to complain? The announcer continued by saying that today's temperature was going to be the hottest of the week so far.

Right now, the humidity hadn't built up and that was a relief. Carol Wojinski hated feeling sweaty and her fingers moved automatically to the car's air conditioning setting. This was the best time of her day, the long drive to work made easier by the lack of traffic at this time of the morning. The town centre would be crowded soon enough and there were always people wanting to nip into her bookshop on their way into work. There were three or four orders to get ready for the early birds, but there would be plenty of time to do those and get the coffee maker on, before she opened the shop's blinds.

Talking to herself as usual, just above the voice of the man on the radio, Carol rehearsed what she needed to do as soon as she got into work. 'Now, I mustn't forget to switch the alarm off properly. No one would believe I've had the bookshop for six years, the way I still breeze in, flick the coffeemaker on and forget all about the alarm. Today I must be systematic. There's a lot to do.'

Glancing in her rear view mirror, she suddenly noticed the car behind. The driver, his face partly obscured by a baseball cap pulled low over his forehead, was starting to tailgate her.

'What are you doing?' she said loudly, panic starting to rise as she tried to accelerate away. But the car matched her speed. Cursing the driver, she tried to think how to take avoiding action. There was a blind bend just up ahead, so she didn't dare move into the oncoming lane, or she'd risk killing someone and probably herself as well, in a head on collision. Despite the air conditioning, her hands were getting clammy and the steering wheel felt slippery.

'Oh my God,' she screamed, as the pursuing car approached at an alarming speed. Her whole body jolted as the car took the full impact of the collision. With the car slithering sideways on screeching tyres, she frantically tried to steer clear of the edge of the road and away from the ravine. In that last instant, she caught a glimpse of the driver. It was the eyes she recognised.

The gully was steep and the VW Beetle rolled over several times before finally hitting the bottom. Within seconds it burst into flames, but it would be a few more minutes before the plume of smoke would rise high enough to be seen from the road. The other driver braked just in time, skilfully swerving to avoid the same fate as his victim. He checked his rear view mirror and scanned the road ahead. As expected, there was no one around. Within seconds, his pulse rate returned to normal. So far, everything was going to plan, but there was still a lot to do.

Carefully, he reversed his car, so that it was nearly parallel to where the VW had gone off the road. Parking, he got out, grabbing a backpack from the passenger seat and unlocked the boot. The racing bike had fitted in perfectly. Propping it up now against a tree, he lost no time in repositioning the car at the exact spot where the VW had gone over, easing it right to the edge. Sweat was now pouring down his face. Stepping out carefully from the precariously balanced car, he walked around to the back. Inside the cycling gloves, his hands were also sweating, but it wasn't much of an effort to push the car the last few inches, allowing gravity to take over. Momentarily mesmerised by the smoke and flames from the two cars, he allowed himself a few seconds to admire what he had done. A wide smile broke out on his face.

It would look very suspicious if he were to be found there now, so he had to sublimate his desire to linger over his handiwork. As the smoke and flames billowed further into the morning sky, he mounted the bike and coasted down the steep hill into town, nodding almost imperceptivity to Carol Wojinski's bookshop as he passed it. During his next hour of cycling, he reviewed his morning's work, concluding that it was as near to perfection as you could get.

9

Annie was first in, wanting to catch up on her notes and ensure everything was in order for the formal report back to Franconi. As she poured herself a coffee, she wondered whether the captain would mention anything about last night. He'd stayed for a nightcap with his 'paesans' after she, Michael and Christine had gone outside to wait for the taxi. Would Bronski think it should have been him at the meal? After all, she'd learned last night that he had been involved in the investigation, although he hadn't appeared in the witness box. Franconi had been the lead investigator, so he had taken the stand. Franconi could show off in front of her, but Bronski would already have known the whole story. Stirring her coffee now, she decided to play it by ear and let Franconi mention it, if that's what he wanted to do.

Reading over her notes from the file, a mental picture of Jim Moorcroft and Jackie Winters emerged; sitting quietly outside the operating room, while a friend of theirs was fighting for her life. If they hadn't let themselves into Angela Goodman's house, concerned that she wasn't answering her doorbell and was expecting them, who knows how long she would have clung on to life?

It became clear in the interview that Jim Moorcroft had known Angela for a number of years and all three were work colleagues at Westford Capitol Insurance. Angela was a team leader and both Jim Moorcroft and Jackie Winters were underwriters in her section. Jackie had known Angela for just over two years. Originally

Jackie had been a lodger in Jim's house, but they'd developed a relationship and were now partners.

Angela had spent the night of the attack at their house having a meal and Jim had dropped her home. The time he reported tallied with the neighbours' reports of a car and loud music. He admitted that he always played his CDs loudly and hadn't really considered the neighbours. Jim also insisted he had gone straight back to their house after dropping Angela off, although Jackie admitted that she'd been asleep and never heard him come in. Their stories seemed genuine enough and Annie and Bronski hadn't seen any need to get them to come down to the station. They could always be interviewed again if necessary. They also filled in details of their discovery of Angela. Annie remembered how Jackie Winters had cringed when she recalled Angela's almost lifeless form upstairs in the bedroom.

Annie next turned to her notes from the hospital. The doctors were not holding out much hope when she and Bronski interviewed them yesterday, following the surgery. Last night, just before Franconi picked her up, she'd heard a brief piece on the news about the attack. Obviously, one of the neighbours must have sought their fifteen minutes of fame. This morning, there was also a brief follow up on the radio. Annie decided that she would ring the hospital to verify the details in the news item. Better to have all the facts ready for Franconi.

'Westford Hospital.'

'Good morning, could you put me through to the Intensive Care Unit?'

'Hold on, caller.'

'Intensive Care.'

'Good morning, I'm Detective Annie Macpherson, investigating the assault on Angela Goodman. Could you tell me how she is this morning?'

The voice on the other end of the line, who had only identified herself by the name of the ward, hesitated for a moment. Annie could hear pages being shuffled. 'Mrs Goodman is alive but still in a coma, her breathing assisted by a ventilator. The next twenty-four to forty-eight hours will be critical.'

Annie let out a deep breath, relieved that she had confirmation that Angela Goodman had survived the night. 'Thank you. We'll need to know if there is any change.'

'There is a note in the file here to telephone either you or a Detective Bronski.' With that, it was clear the nurse felt she'd better things to do. Efficient, perhaps officious, or maybe Annie just had to get used to the cultural difference.

Bronski walked in just as Annie was hanging up the phone. 'Angela Goodman survived the night, but she's still in a coma.'

'So no chance we'll be interviewing her today then.'

'Would you like a coffee?'

As she was about to pour, Dave Ellison appeared with three cups of Starbucks coffee. He passed the first one to Annie. 'Just returning the favour from yesterday.'

'Much appreciated,' Annie replied.

Then taking the other cup from its holder, he passed it to Bronski. 'Oh and I saw you coming in as well, De-

50

tective. Latte, OK?'

'Glad you didn't leave me out, Ellison. I might have become jealous.' Bronski took the latte.

Ellison placed the last cup on his own desk and started to peruse the messages in his tray. But first he gave Annie a little wink.

Annie returned to her desk, knowing that Bronski would want time on his own to sort things out before they conferred, prior to reporting back to Franconi later that morning. Bronski would be at least half an hour if previous days were anything to go by. First she made a note of the phone call to the hospital in the time log and then turned back to the beginning of the file. She reviewed the interview transcript from when she'd seen Angela Goodman for the first time.

Looking at the date, she realised she'd only been on the exchange programme for three days and on the evening before, Bronski had said that he thought she could deal with any inquiries which came in from the desk first thing the next morning. He'd be late so she was covering. She remembered how she'd only just sat down and opened the bottom desk drawer to put her handbag in when the phone rang, startling her and then her relief when she heard Sergeant Patrick Owens' voice on the line, rather than a direct call from a member of the public. He was very accommodating and had told Annie on day one that if she'd any questions, just to ask him.

She recalled the conversation they'd had.

'Good morning Detective, hope you haven't gotten too comfortable upstairs while we do all the hard work down here. If you can drag yourself away from your coffee or whatever you detectives spend your time doing, I need you down here to interview a woman, a Mrs. Goodman.'

Annie warmed to the gentle ribbing. 'I think I could do that for you Sergeant, since you asked so nicely. Any idea what it's about?'

'Thinks she's being stalked. I said I'd get someone down to take a statement. Seems pretty stable,' he said, his voice slightly lower with the last remark.

'I'll be right down.'

Then just as Annie had reached for her notebook and pen, Franconi had come out of his room 'Got your first case already, Detective?'

'That was the desk sergeant, Sir. There is a woman downstairs wanting to report a stalker.'

'Well, I'm sure you'll handle that.'

'Yes, Sir.'

Annie remembered seeing Mrs Goodman sitting in one of the chairs in the waiting area. In fact she was one of three women sitting there that morning. Two of them looked like part of a pair, a mother-daughter combination, most likely. The younger one had obviously inherited the mother's genes as they both had ample figures and the same lank hair. The third woman was very attractive, if not pretty in the conventional sense. Her hair was meticulously cut in a dark brown fringe with longer sides just touching her shoulders. She was dressed in a crisp, light blue suit with a silk blouse, probably office attire. Annie thought she too would look better with a little less weight.

'Mrs Goodman?'

The smartly dressed woman stood up.

'Perhaps you'd like to come with me. I'm Detective Annie Macpherson.'

Mrs Goodman accompanied her without a word and Annie avoided any small talk on the way to the interview room. Unlocking the door, she gestured her to the seat at the opposite side of the table, furthest from the door. Cops were taught never to be the one furthest from the door. Of course, there were also alarms fitted under the table, if need be. But Mrs Goodman looked more like she might faint, rather than attack. But procedures were procedures. Annie remembered now that she'd come right to the point.

'Now Mrs Goodman, would you like to tell me how you think we can be of help?'

'I hope I'm not wasting your time. I don't really know where to begin.' Opening her handbag, the woman fumbled for a small, embroidered handkerchief, too prissy for Annie's tastes.

'Just take your time.'

'I'm going through a divorce, not very amicable, though I don't suppose many of them are. My husband left me for another woman. I didn't see it coming, felt like such a fool when he finally owned up. How could I have missed that one coming?'

'What is your husband's name?'

'George ... George Goodman, although his name is ironic. He's certainly not an angel, doesn't deserve that name. Sorry I'm nervous, I know I'm digressing.' Mrs Goodman put the handkerchief back in her handbag.

'That's fine, but divorce isn't a police matter, Mrs Goodman, so what is the problem?'

Angela Goodman shifted in her seat. 'I'm sorry. At work I'm the one in control. I'm the team leader in charge of a whole section. I don't know why I find other situations, like this one, so difficult.' Angela hesitated momentarily, continuing after a deep breath. 'The reason why I'm here is that I am sure someone is coming into my house during the day when I'm not there. It's just little things: ornaments moved slightly, less milk in the bottle, a drawer left open a fraction. Nothing major, but I'm very precise and I check things. I have to be precise in my job. I'm in charge of the underwriting section for Westford Capitol Insurance. Sorry, I've already told you that, haven't I?'

'Not precisely, but coming back to the things you've noticed, have there been any signs of forced entry into the house?'

'If you mean, have the windows or doors been tampered with, the answer is no.'

'Does your husband still have a key? Does he still have things in the house?' Annie was jotting down notes.

'Yes, but?'

'Have any of his things been removed? There may be a simple explanation for this.' Annie was trying to state the obvious, which people sometimes didn't see when they were upset. 'If things are being moved in the house and there is no sign of a break in, then it's likely to be someone with a key, isn't it? If I were you, I'd think about getting the locks changed.' Annie put her pen down for a moment.

'I know, that's what my lawyer advised. I haven't done it yet. Somehow I hate the thought of doing that. The house is still in our joint names, even though I have residency and I haven't checked whether all his things are still there. I find it too painful.'

'Then you'll need to discuss the residency issue with your solicitor, sorry, I mean your lawyer.'

'Yes, you're right of course. I feel a bit silly now. I guess it's just my nerves. I'm sorry I bothered you. I'll look into the locks today. And if it is my husband, I expect he will complain through his lawyer. At least that will set my mind at rest.' The woman reached for her handbag and pushed the chair back.

The interview lasted no more than ten minutes and when Annie showed Mrs Goodman to the exit, nothing more was said.

Now looking again at the transcript, Annie wondered what she'd missed. Maybe if she'd reacted differently that day, Angela Goodman would be at work now, supervising her staff. My first case and I've blown it already, Annie thought.

10

The news item was brief, but enough information for him. He knew what to expect when he answered the phone.

'I thought you said it was finished.'

'I thought it was, until I heard it on the news. I thought she was dead.'

'There's a big difference between being in a coma and being dead.'

'Hey, I wanted this as much as you did. It's all I've thought about.'

'You broke your promise.'

'I never break promises, especially to you. There's still time to rectify it.'

'So a promise is still a promise then?'

'I'll take care of it.'

Time now to consider how to remedy the situation. Planning was what he was good at. Why did the execution of the plan go wrong? At least his other plan had succeeded. Just covering tracks, that was important. That was what he had been taught and except for the one mistake, he had learned that lesson well.

He opened the diary and began to read that section once more.

11

Connie Lombardi decided that she couldn't leave it any longer – a whole week and still no word from her boyfriend. It wasn't like him, no matter what her mother had to say about it. But before she could take action, the phone rang.

'No mother, I haven't heard from him ... Yes I am very worried ... No, they say that there is nothing they can do: adults go missing all the time.' But she wouldn't give her mother the satisfaction of hearing the comment made by the insensitive officer, 'Perhaps he had a reason to disappear.' The remark had made her feel small, ugly. But she trusted Jason, knew there had to be a reason. He said he loved her and acted like he did. What more could she ask for?

Hanging up the phone, Connie Lombardi recalled the events of the past week.

Sunday: Jason never turned up to take her out for the meal they'd planned. Several phone calls to his cell, but every time it was on voicemail.

Monday: Waking up with a really bad feeling, she tried the cell phone again but it was still on voicemail. After work she went straight to the police. It didn't really help that she didn't know his address. Reporting him missing and not even knowing where he lived. No wonder they didn't take her seriously.

Tuesday: Too upset to go to work, she phoned in sick. Not a good move. Her mother's friend worked at the same place, so her mother got to hear about it and then harangued Connie for a good half hour on

Tuesday night. The search of all the places they'd been to together yielded nothing. It was starting to dawn on her how little she really knew about her boyfriend. He knew her body well enough and that thought both embarrassed and excited her. Once she'd loved his mystery. Now it seemed too cruel.

Wednesday: Back at work. His voicemail was full, so she couldn't leave any more messages and still no word. There were visions now of him lying face down in a ditch somewhere, never to return to her, not able to let her know where he was. The search along their favourite walk revealed nothing. Coming back to her bedroom she sat down and cried. A worn T-shirt of his, languishing in the laundry basket was all she had to show for months of a relationship she'd convinced herself would last.

Thursday: Over a bottle of wine, she wrote down every fact she knew about him. Sure she could describe his body in great detail, but the rest? Yes the rest escaped her. As she downed the last glass of wine, his favourite Pinot Grigio, the page remained mostly blank.

The rest of the week, indeed the whole weekend, was a blur: tears and tantrums, a long argument with her mother and cursing Jason for putting her through all this. Not even the task of telephoning all the hospitals on Saturday did much to cheer her up. There were no unidentified males in any of them. At least that was something. So here it was again, Sunday night. Just maybe the police would take her seriously tonight given that it had been a week. What else could she do?

12

By the time Franconi called the two of them into his office, Annie had convinced herself that she was going to get a dressing down. As usual he didn't look up at them until they were both seated. Franconi's body language didn't seem to bother Bronski but it annoyed Annie intensely. Who would have thought they'd shared a meal last night? Then, he was marginally more endearing.

'So what have you got?' Franconi wasn't wasting any time, sat back in his chair and starting to pick his fingernails.

Bronski had the file open on his lap, feigning finding where he wanted to start, although the two of them had it well rehearsed. 'Angela Goodman, thirty-nine year old female, currently living on her own, following her separation from her husband. The divorce is anything but amicable, as it appears that Mr Goodman has been having one affair after another.'

'How do you know that Detective?' Franconi was now staring at Bronski.

'Mrs Goodman reported to Detective Macpherson that the reason for the divorce was that her husband was having an affair. Jackie Winters, who found Mrs Goodman in her house following the assault, told us that Angela would have forgiven him the affair, until he told her that his current girlfriend was the third he'd had since their marriage.'

'Names, do we know who these women are?' Franconi was starting to shift in his seat.

'Jackie Winters said that she only knew the name of

the current one, Genevieve Montgomery. We've traced her: she manages a designer boutique. We're going to pay her a visit this afternoon. We still haven't located Mr Goodman but she may be able to help us. His employers only know that he's on vacation but didn't tell anyone where he was going. Apparently, he gets on fine at work, no complaints from his boss. Obviously keeps his private life separate. They knew he was married but not in the process of a divorce. He's due back at work on Monday.' Bronski paused in case Franconi wanted to ask anything else at this juncture.

Franconi nodded for Bronski to continue.

'Seems that Angela Goodman is well liked at work, very efficient manager, no complaints from her bosses. She unloads at work, though. Everyone we talked to knew about the divorce. Apparently she refers to George Goodman as *the bastard*.'

'Charming. What about the crime scene?'

Relieved to have skirted beyond the original interview, Annie was now anxious to take part in the briefing and when Bronski paused, she came in. 'There was no sign of forced entry. The locks were intact on both doors and no sign of any damage to the windows. So, either she let the attacker into the house or he had access to a key and let himself in, either before she got home or very soon afterwards. There was a lot of blood in the bedroom which forensics are examining, as well as finger marks, fibres and hair samples from the sheets in her bedroom. The house was trashed, paint strewn around the rooms, so he had to have been there for quite a while. There was one footprint left in some of the paint and one glass on the draining tray, which is also being examined for prints. Nothing of value seems to have been taken: TV, jewellery, but of course, we can't be sure of that, because without Mrs Goodman to tell us, we don't really know what might be missing.'

'But you're thinking the motive wasn't robbery or a random attack?' Franconi was tapping his pen against his notebook, his other habit, marginally better than the fingernail picking.

'There was too much damage in that house for me, well for us,' Annie glanced over at Bronski who nodded in agreement, 'to think it was random. It seems that it was someone who wanted to attack, not only Mrs Goodman, but her sanctuary, the place she came home to every night where she should have been able to feel safe.'

'Hmm, seems that way, doesn't it? But spare me the sob story, Detective. You'll soon discover that not many houses over here offer much sanctuary.'

Annie recoiled a bit, but hoped that she didn't show it. That remark wasn't called for, in her view.

Franconi continued undeterred. 'So nothing from her job that would seem to lead to the attack. You don't think it's random, or a robbery. So, if I hear you right, the only one in the picture so far is the husband, who's conveniently out of town. Well, we can't wait till Monday, so get on to the mistress and see if she knows where he is. My guess is that she knows. Also, see what you can find out about the previous ones.' Franconi paused but he was obviously still considering the information. 'What about the car the neighbours reported?'

This time it was Bronski. 'Jim Moorcroft dropped her home about midnight. She'd spent the evening with him and his partner, Jackie Winters, the same couple who found her.'

'He check out so far? Maybe he circled back and let himself in. They have a key, didn't you say?' This time Franconi was still, the pen on the desk lying beside his notebook.

'They do but from the state they were in at the hospital, I wouldn't think they'd be involved. They were both very distressed at having found her like they did. They thought she was dead at first and are so relieved that she's still alive. Jim Moorcroft says he came straight back home after dropping her off and didn't notice any other cars or anything suspicious. Said he'd waited for her to let herself into the house. Jackie Winters can't verify his alibi as she said she went straight to bed, leaving the cleaning up until the morning. Never heard him come in.' Bronski nodded in agreement. Neither detective had considered the couple as suspects after they'd spoken to them.

'OK, but let's not rule him out just yet. What about next of kin?'

Bronski looked at Annie again.

'The hospital confirmed from her records that the husband is still listed as her next of kin and at her current address, but it also lists her brother, Captain Charles Hegarty. Jackie Winters said that he is on a tour of duty in Afghanistan at the moment, but that was due to end last week sometime. She didn't know the exact detail, only that Angela is expecting him to visit imminently. I'm waiting for the Department of Defense to get back to me with contact details since the hospital record is out of date.' Annie realised as she said it that she would have to get back to the government agency again, as it was over twenty-four hours since she'd left the first message. 'I'll follow that one up again today.'

'Right, keep me posted.' Franconi shut his notebook, signalling that he was finished with them for now. He picked up the phone and started punching numbers in before they were even out of the room.

13

Annie waited until they were back at their desks. 'Well that wasn't as bad as I thought it would be.'

Bronski was sifting through messages and didn't look up. 'Generally his bark is worse than his bite.'

Annie knew that Bronski was really sensitive to any criticism from Franconi and she vowed not to put him in that position again. 'So what's next? We've got a couple of hours until we pay Genevieve Montgomery a visit. Maybe I'll get back on to the Department of Defense. They're not exactly prompt in getting back to us, are they?' Annie was double-checking her own messages, in case a reply had come back and she was maligning them unnecessarily, but there was nothing. However, before Bronski got a chance to answer, her phone rang.

'Detective Macpherson, I have a Captain Hegarty on the line for you.'

Annie cupped the phone and half whispered to Bronski: 'speak of the devil.' Then she replied to the receptionist: 'Put him through please.'

Bronski watched as Annie nodded and replied 'Aye' as the person on the other end was clearly establishing whom he was speaking to and trying to work out why he had been given a message to telephone the police.

'Sir, where are you telephoning from? I see and when are you expecting to be back in Connecticut? I am about to explain that.' Annie was shifting in her seat, sitting now with her elbows on the desk, adopting a more formal posture to deliver some sombre news, never easy over the telephone, or in person for that matter. After a deep intake of breath, she continued: 'I am sorry to have to tell you that your sister, Angela Goodman, was viciously attacked in her home two nights ago. She's in Westford Hospital, in a coma, in a very serious condition.'

There was a pause and Bronski saw Annie cupping her elbow as if she were uncomfortable with the conversation. 'I can't tell you that Sir, the doctors are doing everything they can. I'm sorry, I know this news is shocking.' Annie leaned back in the chair now but was still taking notes. 'So you will let us know when you get in. I'll give you my cell phone number as well.'

When she finally hung up the phone, Bronski was waiting to hear the details. 'Well, he left Afghanistan at the end of last week and went directly to Colorado and then on to Montana to a fishing lodge. He was having a break before coming back here to spend a few weeks with his sister. He sounded quite shocked at what has happened. He's going to try and get a flight back today if possible, but will keep us informed.'

'Good. We'll need to interview him and see how much he knows about his sister's life. Let's hope he can fill in some more background. Let me know when he calls you. Now, why don't we head up to the Westford Mall, grab a bite of lunch and then check out Miss Montgomery?'

'Aye, but I hate the brother already.'

Bronski gave Annie a quizzical look. 'What the hell?'

'It's only because he's doing what I want to be doing, fly fishing in Montana.'

Bronski laughed, 'Never took you for a fisher.'

'It's in my bones, being from one of the fishing meccas of the world. You have heard of salmon fishing in Scotland, I hope?' Annie grabbed her jacket and followed Bronski out of the door.

Just under two hours later, they entered the First Class Dress Boutique. Annie homed in on Genevieve Montgomery immediately, even though there were three assistants in the shop. There was something about her, a predatory, 'I'll take what I want' kind of attitude. Annie knew other women like her and it was the aspect of sisterhood she could never understand. Bad enough if a man succumbed, but for a woman to actively chase another woman's husband was something Annie considered unforgivable. She thought about Angela Goodman and how she looked in the hospital. What if this woman had wanted her out of the picture?

The dyed brunette approached them, dripping with jewellery, acrylic nails painted a deep red and matching lipstick. 'How are you today? Is there something I can help you with? Our sale has just started and there is an additional 20% off anything you see in the store.' It was the usual sales patter and it was obvious that she took them for a couple.

Bronski smiled and produced his badge, 'Detective Bronski and Detective Macpherson. We're not here to shop; we're looking for Genevieve Montgomery.'

The woman was clearly taken aback. 'I am Ms Montgomery. Is this about that attempted burglary last month?'

Bronski didn't answer her question directly, simply adding, 'Is there somewhere private we can talk?'

The small office at the back of the shop doubled as a storage room, but as Genevieve Montgomery ushered them in, Annie noticed that there were three seats. Genevieve Montgomery took the one at the far right corner, right next to a mannequin whose features were strikingly similar to the woman herself. Annie nearly smiled, but stifled it just in time.

'So what's this all about? Is it to do with the attempted burglary or not, only I haven't heard any more about it from the security staff.' Genevieve Montgomery folded her arms across her chest, a simple movement signalling that she was a woman who didn't like to be trifled with. A simple movement that also accentuated her cleavage, which Annie found distasteful.

'No, we don't know anything about an attempted burglary. Ms Montgomery, do you know a George Goodman?'

'What if I do?'

'Could you please just answer the question?'

'I do know George Goodman, but why are you asking?'

Obviously Ms Montgomery wasn't going to be helpful unless she absolutely had to be. Annie didn't like the woman's attitude. It was as harsh as the makeup she was wearing. Bronski was being more patient than she knew she would be herself, if she were leading the questioning.

'We need to get in touch with Mr Goodman as a matter of some urgency. We have reason to believe that you know Mr Goodman very well and may know where he is. You may have been in contact with him over the last few days.' Bronski wasn't letting up.

'I have already told you that I know George Goodman, but what leads you to believe that I am party to where he is, or even if I did, that I would tell you that information, which surely is private?'

Now her coyness was really beginning to annoy Annie. She didn't want to upstage Bronski, but she'd had enough. 'We have reason to believe that you are in a relationship with Mr Goodman and are, in fact, cited in his wife's divorce proceedings. As my colleague has said, we need to interview Mr Goodman urgently on another matter and thought that you would be willing to help us with our inquiries. I am sure that you would not withhold information that is needed as part of a police investigation.'

Montgomery fixed a stare at Annie. 'I don't know where George ... Mr Goodman is. He's on vacation, but told me that he needed some time to clear his head. His wife has not taken the divorce well and he has been feeling quite stressed about it. He's only phoned me once, last night, to say that he will be back at work on Monday and will see me Monday night. Now, that is all I know. I don't pry, unlike his soon to be ex-wife.'

'So, you have no idea where he was calling you from?' Annie wasn't convinced.

'I have already said that. I don't see how I can help you further. I have a shop to run now, so if you don't mind.'

Bronski pulled out his card. 'If you hear from him

again, tell him I want to speak to him. Tell him he would be better coming into the station himself, or we will be turning up at his work place on Monday. He might save himself some embarrassment.'

'And what do I tell him it is about?'

Annie folded her notebook and started to follow Bronski out. 'I'm sure that both of you read the newspapers.'

Genevieve Montgomery stood up, pulled her tight skirt into place and smiled.

The youngest of the shop assistants was approaching the boutique carrying three cups of coffee and a brown bag just as Bronski and Annie got to the next store. Annie recognised the young woman immediately and acted intuitively. 'Excuse me, I'm Detective Macpherson and this is Detective Bronski. Just before you go back in, can I just ask you a couple of questions, just routine?'

The girl looked startled and glanced towards the boutique window. Then she stepped back so that the three of them were out of sight of the shop. 'I don't know how I can help,' she murmured, shifting uncomfortably on the spot. It was obvious that talking to the police was the last thing the young woman wanted to do but Annie didn't give her a chance to refuse.

14

'Good work, Detective.'

'I knew she was lying. It was that knowing smile she flashed just as we finished the interview. Not seen him, oh aye. So why was she off work for two days then at short notice? I'll take great pleasure in charging her for obstruction, once we prove she knew where he was.' Annie looked across at Bronski, just as he was opening his car door. 'So what now, get on to dispatch?'

'No, somehow I don't think we're going to need that. My guess is that Genevieve Montgomery is on the phone to him right now and that we'll hear from him quite soon. Let's just be patient and she'll do our job for us.' Bronski was behind the wheel now, negotiating his way out of the mall parking lot where every bad driver was absent-mindedly reversing without looking.

Annie knew he was right but she was still angry with Montgomery. The boutique owner reminded her of some of her mother's friends – haughty, know it alls. 'So where to now?'

'Why not another visit to the hospital? We need more on Angela Goodman's prognosis. See if we can pin down her doctor. If she comes out of the coma, she might be able to give us information on her attacker.'

'That would save us a lot of trouble.' Inwardly Annie thought how much of an optimist Bronski was but kept her own counsel. It wasn't the first time she'd dealt with someone in a coma. Although it was possible for someone to come out of a coma spontaneously, she also knew that the longer the coma lasted, the longer any predicted recovery time would be. Somehow, instinctively, she felt that sometime soon, a decision would have to be made about turning off the life support system. She also knew that when that decision came, her own guilt for her part in the life and death of Angela Goodman might overwhelm her.

Ten minutes later they were at the nurses' station where they were informed that Angela Goodman had two visitors, Jim Moorcroft and Jackie Winters. We haven't cleared those two yet, thought Annie, but they'd seemed genuine enough that first time they'd met. Still procedures were procedures and Franconi did mention it this morning. The nurse went into the room first, asking the other two visitors to leave, as the hospital had a strict policy in the ICU.

Bronski and Annie were waiting by the door as Jim and Jackie came out with the nurse. They both nodded as they saw the detectives and hesitated just outside the room.

'How is she?' Annie was trying to gauge their reaction to their friend's predicament.

'It's so awful seeing her like this. She's normally so full of life. Never sits still. I find it unbearable seeing her like that. She'd be so angry.' Jim Moorcroft nodded as Jackie hesitated. 'They won't really tell us anything, but I guess they don't need to. You only have to see her attached to those machines to know it must be touch and go.'

'I'm sure she appreciates you sitting with her.' As usual, Bronski was trying to say the right thing. Annie thought she could learn a few lessons in tact from her supervisor.

'We came over from work. Everyone is so concerned. The whole department is upset. Some of the others want to come but we're not sure if that would be allowed. We keep everyone informed.' This time it was Jim speaking and Jackie nodding. 'Anyway, you'll see for yourself. We better leave you to it.'

But before they left, Jackie turned back momentarily, 'I don't suppose you can tell us if you've found out who her attacker is yet?'

'We still have a number of inquiries to make.' Annie replied and then because of Franconi that morning, she added, 'We are still working on the timeframe from when you dropped her off, Mr Moorcroft, until you both found her. In fact, we may need to ask you some more questions in the next couple of days.'

'Of course, we want to help in any way we can. Whoever did this needs to be caught.' By now, Jim had Jackie's elbow in his hand and was directing her to the exit. 'You have our contact number.'

Before they went in, Annie reminded Bronski about getting an officer posted outside the door. As Bronski went off to arrange it, Annie took the opportunity to ask the staff nurse whether there had been any other visitors. Jim Moorcroft and Jackie Winters were the only ones. Each time their visit had been timed and they were asked to leave when the allocation was up.

The nurse had no concerns when Annie mentioned that an officer would be posted outside the room. 'You'll need to inform the hospital vice president. He will want to alert our own security.' Annie nodded and made a note of the vice president's name. Annie was surprised when the nurse added, 'Just so you know, the nurses are far too busy to get coffees for your officers, so if you could make that clear.' With that, the nurse answered a phone call and Annie took it as a signal to leave.

No matter how many times Annie had seen people in similar situations to Angela Goodman, entering that room still gave her a shock. It was clear that the woman was barely clinging on to life. Her bruises looked far worse than the last time they'd seen her. Partly it was the noise, the whirring, the beeping and the rhythm of machines doing for a human being what the body does naturally for itself. Annie wondered what it would take to tip the balance. Again the thought struck her that someone was probably going to have to make a decision about when to switch off the machine. Given the situation with the husband, she hoped that the law wouldn't allow him to do it. Perhaps the brother would decide.

Bronski joined her a few minutes later. Annie sensed that was he was uneasy too. It wasn't long before he whispered, 'There's nothing to be gained from staying in here. Let's see what the doctors can tell us.'

Annie felt a bit disrespectful leaving so soon. Angela Goodman didn't deserve to be lying there. The guilt came back. She should have taken that interview more seriously. She looked at her supervisor.

It was as if Bronski read her mind. 'Hey, you're not responsible for this. Don't worry, we'll get the bastard.' Annie wondered if Angela Goodman would process that piece of information, but there wasn't even a flicker of reaction from her.

Bronski opened the door for them to leave. They had a couple more people to see in the hospital.

A half hour later they were in the car again. The doctor they spoke to hadn't held out much hope. He was more interested in the issue of next of kin and Bronski and Annie had cautioned that the husband might have to be displaced as next of kin and that the legal department in the hospital should be looking into it. They'd also seen the hospital vice president who agreed for the officer to be posted outside the door and asked that they liaise with his head of security. It was the last thing they did before they left the building.

'There's not much more we can do today. Want me to drop you home?'

'Actually, I'd like to go back to the station for a while and write up my notes. I'll get the bus or a taxi home, but thanks for the offer.'

'The station it is, but don't stay too long or you'll make me look bad, partner.' Annie laughed. Bronski hadn't called her that before. Perhaps she was starting to fit in.

Dave Ellison was the only one still in the squad room. Even Franconi had left for the day. 'Hi stranger, no Bronski?'

Annie smiled as she pulled her chair out, just in his line of vision. 'He's just dropped me off. I wanted to write up a few notes while it's still fresh.' Her knee was resting on the chair, but she hadn't sat down as yet.

'How long you staying?' Ellison was leaning back in

his chair, tapping his pen in his hand.

'Don't know, maybe a half hour, max.'

'I've got a bit more to do. How about grabbing a bite to eat when we're both finished?' Ellison hesitated. 'Not a date you realise, just I suspect we're both hungry and I don't have anything at home. I was thinking of going down to that Mexican restaurant a few blocks over. Want to join me?'

'You have such a way of making a girl feel wanted. How can I resist?' Annie laughed and sat down to start her work.

As Annie put the key in her lock three hours later, she smiled at how she'd managed to resist Dave's charms. She'd made her excuses after the meal and one drink in the bar and then caught a taxi back, refusing the offer of a ride home. At least she didn't have to prepare any food. That was a bonus, but she still went straight to the refrigerator and got out the half empty bottle of white wine. Pouring herself a drink, she noticed that the answer machine was flashing.

'Hello sweetheart, only me. We'll probably be in bed by the time you get this. Why don't you email me so I know you're all right? We love you.' Annie smiled at her mum's voice and the use of the 'we'. She knew her mother wasn't getting any younger and one day she would be put in a position of having to decide Andrew's future. Margaret Macpherson would keep her son at home until her dying day. The level of care her brother required had already seen her dad dying before his time.

Switching on her computer, with wine glass still in

hand, Annie checked her inbox. She had an email from Rob, one of her detective colleagues back in Stockport. He was relaying the latest office gossip. The two of them had clicked immediately, both being foreigners in Stockport. Rob was from London and had a really strong cockney accent; the strength of accent only matched by hers. When the two of them talked in the squad room, no one else could fathom out what they were saying. As usual in the email, he ended with his favourite line about still being available and saving his well toned body just for her.

Annie smiled, feeling quite nostalgic for home. Although this exchange was a great opportunity Annie still wondered if she'd done the right thing accepting it. When the chance came up all those months ago, she'd been at her lowest ebb with the wedding called off and the backlash from everyone. You'd have thought she'd committed a crime, rather than owning up to her true feelings before it was too late. But now, she worried whether what had happened to Angela Goodman was down to her. What if she hadn't been on the exchange? Would someone else have treated the interview differently? Annie knew the animosity that divorce can bring. She'd been through it with enough of her friends, but none had ended up in physical violence. If it turned out to be Mr Goodman, her worst fears would be confirmed.

The ring of her cell phone brought her out of her reverie. 'Macpherson.'

'Hi partner, guess who just called?'

'Mr Goodman?' Annie felt her heart beating faster.

'The very one. It seems he's cutting short his vacation after I mentioned what the urgent matter was that we needed to discuss with him.'

'And I wonder how he knew to give you a call.' Annie smiled.

'Funny that he didn't elaborate. Just said he'd heard from a friend. Anyway, he's travelling tonight and says that he'll come in to see us in the morning, about ten. I think he's anxious to be eliminated from our inquiries.'

'And have had time to build up his alibi.' Annie was pacing the living room. 'Do we need to warn the hospital he might visit, let our officer know?'

'I'll do that as a precaution, but I don't think he's planning on doing that. He explicitly said he isn't going to visit her. He made it clear that he's moved on with his life and she isn't a part of it anymore, but I'll brief people in any case.'

'Aye, just in case he's the one trying to make sure she isn't part of it anymore. So we're seeing him in the morning?'

'Yeah, I've let Franconi know. We've got interview room one booked at ten and we'll see Franconi after we finish. Anyway, see you in the morning.'

When Annie finished the call, she went back to her computer and started a new document with a list of questions she had for George Goodman.

15

'We don't get many cyclists in here. You training for something? Not one of these famous Olympic athletes, are you?'

He wasn't in the mood for shooting the breeze with the motel desk clerk. What he wanted most was to get up to his room and shower. The cycle ride had taken a couple of hours and he was starving. But her observation made him realise that his plan wasn't as faultless as he thought. A cyclist was more memorable than a car driver. Stupid mistake.

'Just keeping fit, that's all.' His tone remained calm as it had to and he never gave her any eye contact, simply filling out the registration form as he had practised. Three identities but he managed to keep them all straight.

The receptionist wasn't as oblivious as she seemed, as she took the hint, hurried up the registration process and handed him the keys.

Walking the bike to the back of the building, he carried it up the stairs. No way was he leaving an expensive bike in the parking lot, even though it was sheltered from the road and this looked like a decent neighbourhood. Besides, he was sure he hadn't been spotted, but you could never be absolutely certain. The miles between him and the scene of the accident should be enough. Tomorrow he would be back in his apartment, but now there were things to do.

First of all, he closed all the curtains in the room. Then he laid out his backpack on the second twin bed.

The one he was going to sleep on had already been decided and he left that perfect. The laptop was placed on the desk, although that was a generous description of a table with a less than comfortable looking chair, but it would do. Then he laid out the fresh clothes: jeans, a T-shirt, a light jacket, all casual and unremarkable. The cycling shorts had started to chafe his skin and he felt relief as he peeled them off. Rivulets of sweat poured down his chest. Walking into the bathroom, he filled the sink with water, adding the concentrated washing liquid. Peeling off the cycling top, both items went into the sink to soak.

Looking at himself in the mirror, he smiled a self-satisfied grin. This one had gone well, very well in fact, except maybe for the bike. That might have drawn some attention. On the other hand, many people would come and go today and one cyclist would leave hardly any impression at all. Even if it did, it didn't matter. There was nothing to link him to a crime scene over thirty miles away.

Running the shower, he waited until the steam filled the room and the heat was at its most intense. Every pore of his body needed cleansing. The water was soothing against his skin and he couldn't decide which sensation he felt more, hunger or tiredness. But it was afternoon now, no wonder he was so hungry.

16

Annie was the first one in. The sun was out and shining into the squad room, giving it a more cheerful appearance than it actually deserved. Annie looked around, not believing the chaos on everyone's desk and wondered how anyone managed to get anything done. Looking over at Dave Ellison's empty desk, she was pleased that nothing had happened between them the night before. She knew he'd wanted it to and she'd been tempted herself. But today would have been awkward and she didn't need complications. Best to keep it friendly. Besides, what if she'd missed that call from Bronski. That could have been embarrassing.

Just as she placed her jacket on the back of her chair, the phone rang.

'Detective Macpherson.'

'Hi Detective, it's Courtney, one of the technicians from the lab. The finger marks from Mrs Goodman's house have been processed and the results are ready to be picked up. I'll leave the envelope at reception.'

Annie headed down the corridor to the stairs and ran up the two flights, arriving a bit breathless at the lab window. There was a bell to ring for attention. Same the world over, thought Annie. The frizzy haired lab receptionist who slid the window open looked about twelve and turned out to be a stickler for procedure. Annie had to show her ID and sign a form before the young upstart reluctantly deigned to release the report. Not as friendly as the technician who telephoned, thought Annie. I wonder if the technicians realise what their receptionist is like? But there was no point antagonising anyone.

As tempted as she was to read the report right then and there, Annie knew that it was only fair to let Bronski have first sight. After all, he was leading on the case. Besides, the envelope was sealed, so any attempt to look at the results would have been obvious. The lab receptionist had also put her off. She took her time walking back down the two flights of steps.

Bronski was by his desk when she arrived back, just putting his jacket on the back of his chair. He stood there, rolling his sleeves up. Annie had a quick flashback to Sunday mornings when she was growing up. Her father performed an identical procedure when he was just about to sit down at the breakfast table. Annie remembered the strong forearms and his commanding presence.

'Morning. I have the lab report on the finger marks. It's the only report done so far.' Annie proffered the file to her supervisor.

'So, anything interesting?'

'I guess you'd better tell me. I haven't looked yet. Thought you deserved first honours.' Annie smiled, while Bronski sat down.

'Very considerate, Detective, I'll note that in your report.'

Annie felt a slight twinge of guilt, remembering how tempted she'd been, only stopping short because the envelope was sealed.

Bronski had the packet open in seconds, concentrating on the printout. He rubbed his chin, looking quizzically at the report. Then he looked over at Annie who was now at her desk. 'The prints on the glass match Jim Moorcroft. I thought he said he just dropped her off, never went in the house.'

Annie opened her notebook, taking a few seconds to find the right part. 'That's what he said.'

'Maybe he had a drink when he went to pick her up, not when he dropped her off.'

'That's possible, no note of it in here though.' They both looked at each other, neither one wanting to acknowledge they might have made an error. 'Perhaps we need to check him out some more.'

'Get Ellison to run him though the computer: he's a whiz at it. If he's not the upstanding citizen he comes across as, Ellison will find out.'

Annie was relieved that Bronski was focused on the report, even as he gave the instruction. She felt like she was blushing at the mention of Ellison's name and she certainly didn't want Bronski to get wind of their meal last night. But her relief was short lived, as just as she was making a note, Dave Ellison opened the squad room door.

'Just the man.' Bronski was watching the younger and fitter man approach his desk. 'Detective Macpherson wants a word with you.'

Annie felt herself tense up. Ellison was going to take this the wrong way.

'She can have a word with me anytime.' Ellison was smiling at Bronski, no sign of being ill at ease.

Only Annie felt embarrassed, but she kept her cool. 'Detective Bronski says you're the best with the databases. We need to see if Jim Moorcroft has any previous as his finger marks were found at Angela Goodman's house.'

'I'm on it.' Ellison winked at Annie, but luckily Bronski missed it. He was still concentrating on the rest of the report.

'There's other finger marks but no match to anyone on our database. So that's not much help at the moment.'

The silence lasted only a matter of moments. Dave Ellison was typing away and staring intently at the screen. Then he leaned back, folding his arms behind his head, looking as if he were just about to put his feet up on the desk. When he eventually had both Bronski and Annie staring at him questioningly, he said, 'Very interesting; your boy has got previous.'

Ellison proceeded to scroll down the screen, periodically clicking the mouse. Annie pulled a chair up beside him, careful not to get too close, afraid that touching him might trigger off a sensation she didn't know if she was ready to handle again. Bronski leaned over the back of her chair. Ellison read aloud from the screen. 'So, he was arrested and charged with aggravated assault ten years ago, domestic violence, beat up his wife. Let's see ...' Ellison clicked on another link. 'No, never went to court, the wife dropped charges.' Ellison clicked the mouse again. 'Traffic offence four years ago, paid a fine.' Ellison continued to scroll, with all three staring at the screen, but there was nothing further for him to read out.

'We need the wife's details, must be his ex now, as

he's living with Jackie Winters. Let's talk to her, but we'll get him in first.' Bronski glanced up at the squad room clock. 'But it will have to wait. Mr Goodman is due in less than an hour and we need to plan the interview. Thanks Detective, good work.'

Annie and Bronski spent the next half hour discussing their approach to George Goodman, but the news about Jim Moorcroft was still reverberating in her head, making it hard to concentrate. What if another mistake had been made? Annie hadn't lacked confidence during an investigation before. Maybe it was the cultural differences or disparity in procedures. Whatever it was, she didn't like the feelings this investigation was beginning to engender in her. Perhaps she was simply homesick. She knew she needed ten minutes on her own before George Goodman arrived and at a suitable point told Bronski that she was going to the restroom.

Looking at herself in the mirror, Annie was surprised at how tired and washed out she appeared. Perhaps it was the time of the year. All the locals in the office were tanned while her pale Scottish skin and fair hair made her stand out. But was it only that? Splashing water on her face and a touch of lipstick brought some much needed colour. Get a grip, she told herself, as she pushed the door open and headed back into the squad room.

'He's here. Are you ready Detective?'

'Yes Sir,' Annie replied with more confidence in her voice than she felt inside.

George Goodman wasn't someone Annie would have

described as handsome. She remembered an expression her mother used to say, 'He has a lived-in face.' That seemed to fit the man before them. His face had almost the consistency of leather: too much sun and too little sun protection. The lines on his face were worn, almost carved out and in a few more years, he would look chiselled. But he had a full head of dark brown hair, greying a bit at the temples. Annie could see how Angela Goodman would have been attracted to him a few years ago, but not necessarily how he was still managing to attract other women. What else did he have to offer, she wondered. He wasn't much taller than Bronski, maybe five foot nine or ten and he could use some fashion advice.

When they entered the interview room, Bronski put a tape in the machine with George Goodman's agreement, since it had already been made clear to him that he wasn't under arrest. George Goodman sat back in his chair, keeping a distance from the table and straightened the cuffs under his sports coat. He seemed to be going through some sort of ritualistic behaviour to prepare himself. Annie noticed he repeated the cuff straightening and also flicked a bit of fluff from his trousers. His body was turned very slightly so that he was at an angle to the two detectives and his head had to turn in their direction as he was asked to state his name.

Annie had seen this preening behaviour before with a paedophile she'd interviewed a year or so ago. In that case, the man's demeanour never changed, even when the evidence from his computer was being placed in front of him. Annie remembered how sick she'd felt having to look through the photographs on his PC.

Then there was the look of horror on his wife's face when she realised what he had been doing. She could still picture the woman drawing her children close, perhaps wondering if they too, had been victims without her knowledge.

Bronski started the interview. 'So, Mr Goodman, when was the last time you saw your wife?'

Again, the imperceptible shift in body posture and the pursing of the lips indicated that George Goodman considered that all of this was beneath him, an inconvenience to be gotten over with as soon as possible. Goodman took a smartphone out of his chest pocket and keyed into his appointments calendar, scrolling down the pages as if he had all the time in the world.

'Thought so. It was the 29th of May at 7:30 pm. We met at the house. We had some things to discuss and I wanted to pick up the last of my belongings. I think, from memory, I was there about an hour.'

'And how was your wife on that occasion?'

'Her usual vindictive self. She spent most of the conversation blaming everything on me, failing to see herself for what she was.' The words were uttered with no emotion, as he carefully put the phone back in his pocket.

'And what was she?' Bronski was leaning forward attempting to engage with the man on the other side of the table. Annie kept her distance, feeling as if her distaste for Goodman would leak out if she were any closer. Annie also noted his use of the past tense.

'A selfish, loveless woman, who wants the world to be perfect, yet won't make any attempt to create that world. One of life's natural takers, rather than givers, if you know what I mean.'

It sounds like you are describing yourself, not your wife, Annie thought. You take what you want, when you want, with no thought of the consequences. Annie felt herself to be a good judge of character and Angela Goodman hadn't struck her as being anything like that.

'And you haven't seen her since that night?'

'No, and that is by choice. Everything's to go through my lawyer. I expect I may have to see her one last time in court, to finalise the divorce, if it comes to that.' Playing the victim thought Annie. But she ruminated on the last few words 'if it comes to that.' Did he mean, if it came to the divorce going through, or if she died and that was the end of it? Annie wanted to explore his meaning, but Bronski didn't pick up on it.

'Do you know the conditions of her will?' Bronski continued.

'I know the conditions of the joint will, which should still be in place. I've asked my lawyer to have it revoked, but Angela has to agree to it. I don't know whether she has done that or not. I haven't heard back from my lawyer about that. If she hasn't, I guess the will is as it was.' Goodman had still not chosen to face them and this disdain was now getting on Annie's nerves. She didn't like people sitting side on; it was distracting.

'Which was?'

'The standard: everything left to each other, like most married couples. I wanted it changed. The house is part of the divorce settlement and I only want what I'm entitled to, nothing else. So if you're trying to imply that I would have a motive to harm her before the will is changed, you're way off base.' This time the straightening extended to his lapels and then the cuffs again.

'So what can you tell us about the assault on your wife?'

For the first time in the whole interview George Goodman paused, then shifted in his seat to face Bronski full on, placing his palms flat out on the table. It was clear that Bronski had hit a raw nerve.

'Nothing for God's sake! What do you take me for? I know absolutely nothing about it. Nothing, zilch, less than nothing, if you want the truth. Is that clear enough for you? You should be out there finding whoever did this. Not for my sake, but for hers. As much as I am pleased to be divorcing the woman, that is as far as it goes. I wouldn't wish her any harm.'

It was obvious Goodman was riled and the goodwill of the interview process was slipping away. Annie wasn't sure if her own approach would have been different, but instinctively she felt that Goodman, for all his flaws, had nothing to do with the assault on his wife. Then again, she'd felt that Jim Moorcroft was an upright citizen.

The interview ended ten minutes later. Goodman reported that he had been in Boston the night of the attack, but was staying alone in a motel. His alibi was weak, but they would check it out. Maybe if they hadn't seen Genevieve Montgomery first, Goodman and Montgomery might have concocted a better alibi together.

There was nothing more to be gained at this stage by keeping Goodman at the station. Bronski did ascertain before the interview finished that Goodman was going to telephone the hospital and ask for his name to be taken off the next of kin information. He'd made it clear that he wouldn't be making any decision about his wife's life support, if indeed that decision had to be taken. He also implied that he wouldn't give the police any cause to think he would be happy to gain from his wife's death.

No pleasantries were exchanged as Annie escorted Goodman out of the station, noticing that it was Genevieve Montgomery who was waiting for him in the parking lot.

17

Before he got dressed in the clothes he had laid out on the bed, he finished washing the cycling shorts and jersey and hung them up in the shower. It would only be a matter of hours before they were dry and ready. After dressing, he looked around the room one last time and then walked to the local diner. The menu wasn't inspiring but typical and a burger and black coffee met his needs.

Walking back was pleasant. The summer air was warm and he felt himself starting to sweat again after the air-conditioned diner. But it didn't matter too much. In minutes he was back in his room and the first thing he did was to turn up the air-conditioning.

Turning on the TV, he switched over to the local station, waiting for the news to come on. Going over to the other side of the room, he took the three cell phones out of the safe where he had left them just over an hour ago. Turning on the first one, he smiled. There were missed calls after missed calls. He decided to listen to the messages. It had been just over a week and before now he had resisted the temptation, but he thought that by now, she would have given up and taken the hint. There was nothing she could do about it. He was out of her life and that was the end of it. He smiled as he listened to the pleading, begging him to telephone her.

Then he took the sim card out and smashed the phone on the floor grinding the plastic with his foot. Carefully, ensuring that he picked up every last bit, he placed the remains in a bag in the backpack to throw in a dumpster tomorrow, a long way from there.

The second cell phone had only one message, which he listened to and smiled. The voice always made him feel better. He wanted to talk but it was too risky to return the call: they both knew that. Besides, they had talked last night. He deleted the voicemail. Soon though, it should all be over. He checked the balance on the third phone and the battery. No telling when he would need that one. Both phones went into the back-pack.

Before he stretched out on the bed to relax, he put out the 'do not disturb' sign. Tonight would be an early night. Tomorrow, he had arrangements to make and more travelling to do. Just as he was drifting off to sleep, the local newsreader's voice intruded:

'Police are investigating a two car crash on the mountain road leading into ...' Get on with it, he thought. 'They have not yet released details of the identification plates as both vehicles were so badly damaged in the fire. So far all the police spokesman has been able to tell us is that one body has been found. Police will continue the search for the second body tomorrow. We will bring you an update when we have more. In other news ...'

Rolling over on the bed, he smiled again. You'll be hard pressed to find that second body, he thought, as he used the remote control to switch over channels.

18

Dave Ellison could see from the look on their faces that the interview hadn't gone particularly well. Annie only glanced at him briefly, not wanting to say anything unless Bronski decided to discuss the interview with him. But Bronski chose not to. Instead he just summed up the next steps.

'Well, I'll do a file note on that one and I'll check out his alibi. The motel should confirm if he was where he said he was. Still, he could have left the motel in Boston, driven to Westford, committed the assault and then driven back to the motel. I'll make some calls, but first some lunch. It might be best if we grab a bite and then stop by and pay Mr Moorcroft a visit at work. Let's see what he has to say about what we found in his record.'

Annie wanted a break, but not necessarily to join Bronski for lunch, but she felt she'd no choice since it would mean that he would have to come back to the station for her in order to go and see Jim Moorcroft. It was a pain not having a car and she knew she would have to see about renting one soon. She wanted a quiet word with Dave Ellison too, about last night, but that would have to wait.

'Sure, let's go,' she replied, hoping that she sounded more enthusiastic than she felt.

Bronski finally turned round to Dave Ellison, just as they were going out: 'We'd invite you along Dave, but we're going on from lunch to pay Mr Moorcroft a visit.'

'That's OK, I know two's ...' Ellison started to quip back, but the door shut before he could finish.

In the packed diner, the waitress nodded to Bronski, indicating a booth by the back window. Annie suddenly realised that she was starving and the burger with fries proved irresistible. Bronski ordered the clam chowder and half pastrami on rye with coffee. Annie noticed for the first time that Bronski was ill at ease in a social situation. At the station he was more confident but he looked awkward sitting across from her in the booth.

He wasn't at all like Franconi, who commandeered every situation and was equally at home in a restaurant as he was in the station. Annie thought back to that meal with Franconi, Christine James and Michael Turner. She'd taken an instant liking to Christine and knew she would enjoy seeing her again. Although Christine had given her their phone number, without a car, Annie felt awkward suggesting they meet up. Still, she would get around to that in good time.

'So, Detective, how are we going to handle Mr Moorcroft?' Annie felt she had to get Bronski on to safe territory.

'What would you suggest? How would you play it?'

'I've been known for my direct approach,' Annie laughed.

'I've noticed that.' For the first time that day, Bronski smiled.

Annie felt slightly embarrassed but continued. 'I would start by going over his alibi again and then mention the glass to see if he has a reasonable explanation. Depending how he responds, I'd then venture on to the previous.'

'Sounds like a plan. You can lead this one.'

That was just what Annie wanted to hear. The coffee arrived, giving her some time to think up other topics of conversation. She was still curious about Michael and Christine, wondering whether to bring them up or not. Bronski might feel affronted that Franconi had invited her out for a meal with them and not him but she decided to chance it.

'I met some people the other night, from one of yours and Franconi's cases.'

'Who was that?' He obviously hadn't heard about the meal out.

'Michael Turner and Christine James.'

'Hmm, interesting case. Turner used to be one of us: did you know that?' Bronski paused for a minute while his clam chowder was set down in front of him and the waitress topped up Annie's water.

'I think it was mentioned.'

'I never worked with him. He left on medical grounds just as I came on board. By all accounts he was a good detective. Shame about getting shot and not being able to return to active duty. But who knows, if he stuck out the office work, he might have been fit enough one day. But some guys can't wait. He and Christine James gave us the breakthrough we needed on the case. You know they identified Ruby?' Bronski broke the crackers into his soup.

Annie looked puzzled. 'I thought she was called Mary or Marie or something.'

Bronski laughed. 'You were paying attention. You nearly got it right. Her name was Maria Moretto Marshall. Ruby was the name we gave her before we got the identification. We always name dead women, who are unidentified, by the names of jewels. We don't like to have them being nameless while we try to find out their identities.'

'I approve of that.' Annie picked up her glass. She loved the American habit of getting ice water with the meal.

Bronski paused for a moment while he finished the last spoonful of the clam chowder. No sooner had he put his spoon down, the waitress reappeared to take it away, but not before asking if he wanted a refill. He just waved a 'no' at her.

'Where was I? Christine James. Now she's an interesting character. Did you know when she identified Maria, she was only back in Westford because she was recovering from her husband's death. She'd been living in England with him.'

Annie was surprised. 'No, that hadn't come out in the conversation.' Annie realised now that this must have been the missing link she'd been wondering about and it cleared up the UK connection in her mind.

Over the next few minutes Bronski gave her a brief overview of the whole case. Then over the last refill of their coffee, he refocused on the afternoon's task. 'So, as far as we can ascertain, Jim Moorcroft is in work today. It will be interesting to see how he reacts to seeing us again, won't it?'

A half hour later, they had their initial answer. Jim Moorcroft rose immediately from his chair on seeing the two of them enter the open plan office. His was the third desk in the row nearest the window with a clear view of the whole room. It only took seconds for him to reach them. His colleagues, although curious, seemed too absorbed in their tasks to take that much notice.

'What's happened? Angela? She's not ...' Only one woman looked up, anticipating an answer.

'As far as we know, Mrs Goodman is still in Intensive Care. We just want to ask you some more questions. Is there anywhere quiet we can go?' Annie nodded to the woman as she said it, wondering why there wasn't more interest being shown about their presence.

Jim Moorcroft's immediate concern turned to finding a quiet place to talk, away from all the cubicles. Eventually finding an empty interview room, he appeared ill at ease, fussing about the seating arrangements and wanting to break the silence.

'Jackie and I saw Angela again last night. God, she looked awful. That's why I thought the worst when I saw you. I don't cope very well with being there at the hospital. It's the sound of those machines, you know what I mean? You get so you start to count the bleeps, start to imagine that some are too long, that the frequency is changing. They say to talk to her, but I'm not convinced it helps. Her face is so swollen: how would you even know if it moved slightly? Jackie is better at sitting with her then I am. She can really focus her attention on Angela. I'm sure she's willing her to pull through, that she's trying to get on to her wavelength somehow.' Jim Moorcroft paused, realising that the two detectives weren't really listening to what he was saying.

It was Annie who spoke when he stopped. 'Mr

Moorcroft, have you any objection to answering some questions for us? You are not under arrest but you could have a lawyer present if you wished to do so. Or we could do this down at the station, if you prefer.'

The statement stopped Moorcroft in his tracks but his indignation was palpable. 'I don't understand. I want to help in any way I can. Angela is a very close friend. I will tell you anything you want to know. I have nothing to hide.' He shifted in his seat trying to get comfortable.

'Mr Moorcroft, you told us before that you dropped Angela Goodman off at her house around midnight.'

'That's right.'

'And you didn't go into the house with her?'

'No, I waited for a minute or two until she opened the front door and switched on the hall light. She turned and waved to me and then I pulled away. I told you all of this before.'

'Tell us again about when you picked her up. Did you go into the house at that point?'

'No, I pulled up in front of the house and she came out.' A look of indecision passing across his face, he continued before Annie could respond. 'At least I think she did. Actually, I can't be definite now that I think about it again. I might have gone into the house to wait for her.'

'Would you be likely to forget that you went into the house, if you did?'

Jim Moorcroft had picked the skin on one of his nails until Annie could see blood on his finger. It was obvious that his self-assurance was fading rapidly. 'I don't know. I pick her up a lot. I mean I did pick her up a lot. She was always coming over to our place.'

Annie wondered if she'd perceived something in that last comment. 'Was that a problem for you?'

Jim Moorcroft was clearly taken aback. 'No, and I don't know what you think you are implying. Of course not, it's just that I might have mixed up the last time I picked her up with the time before. I can't remember now that you're asking me again.' Jim Moorcroft got up and started to pace around the room. 'What's this about anyway? What does it matter if I went in or not?'

Annie and Bronski looked at one another and left a gap of a few seconds, before Annie faced Mr Moorcroft squarely. 'Your finger marks were on a glass by the sink, which puts you in the house at some time near to when the assault took place, unless Angela Goodman was in the habit of leaving glasses out for days at a time. And we matched your prints to the glass because your prints are on file for a previous arrest for aggravated assault.'

Jim Moorcroft looked as if he was going to be sick. He stopped dead in his tracks and glanced through the glass door at his co-workers in their cubicles, just on the other side of the interview room. The bloodied finger was now in his mouth and he was biting down at it, until he winced. His voice dropped to nearly a whisper. 'I could lose this job if that becomes common knowledge. You have no idea how long it took me to get this job. No one here knows except the personnel officer.' Again he glanced through the glass, checking that no one was walking past. 'My arrest was unfair. I found my wife in bed with another man. I just lost it and I nearly lost everything. She dropped the charges, but to some people,

I'm still guilty.' He was grabbing the back of the chair he had been sitting on, his knuckles starting to go white.

'But you didn't think of telling us or that it might be important that the last person to see Angela Goodman and the person who found her had a record of arrest for criminal assault?' Annie was getting angry now, but trying to stay calm.

'I didn't think it was relevant. It's nobody's business.' The pacing started again.

'I'm afraid you're wrong on that one, Mr Moorcroft. It is very much our business.' Bronski had butted in for the first time, but Annie didn't lose any momentum.

'Were you and Mrs Goodman more than just good friends?'

'This is too much! I'm not prepared to answer any more of your insulting questions. A close friend of mine, who you didn't even know existed until a few days ago, is critically ill and someone, not me, is responsible. I suggest you go looking for that person. If you want to ask me any more questions, you can arrange it through my lawyer. I'm done here.'

Annie watched as Jim Moorcroft stormed out of the office, past the cubicles and to the exit. Now his colleagues took notice. When the two detectives went through the door a couple of minutes later, all eyes were on them. They didn't leave immediately, however. Their next stop was at personnel, where the senior personnel officer was a lot more helpful. They also learned more about Angela Goodman's work record and periods of leave for depression. Annie wondered just what she'd been like to live with.

'I'm calling it a day. What about you? Want me to drop you back at the station?' Bronski was just starting the car engine.

Annie was fastening her seat belt, neither detective in a good mood after striking out twice. They seemed no further forward than a few days ago. Annie decided to comment on the day first, rather than the question she'd just been asked.

'Aye, I know how you feel, but I still can't get a sense of what happened to Angela Goodman. It seems a case of no one's in the picture or all three of them – Goodman, the mistress or Jim Moorcroft – are all in there somewhere.' Annie paused to give Bronski a chance to respond, but he was concentrating on the traffic or maybe he didn't rate her detective work so far. It was time for her to start proving herself. She decided to make a suggestion.

'Don't you live in the vicinity of Mrs Goodman's?' The question seemed to surprise Bronski, who looked over at her quizzically.

'Not too far away, about five minutes in the car. Why? Is there something on your mind?'

'Aye, I'd like to go back to the house. I want to just sit there for a while, look again at her things, try and get more of a sense of her and whether this was random or provoked. Know what I mean?'

Annie realised that this would have been the advice her father would have given her: know the victim and you learn about the perpetrator. Some days, more than others, she wished she could hear his voice again. That strong Aberdeen accent, the no nonsense approach to his life, to his work. Annie knew that to him, they were part of the same thing. She could still see the smile on his face when she told him that she'd passed all the exams to be a detective and had been offered a position. It was what he had wanted for her, what he had wanted for himself and what his own father had wanted for him. Three generations of detectives. Still, she suspected that if her brother hadn't been born with Down's Syndrome, the expectations would have been for him, not her. She didn't want to be a disappointment to her dad, even though he had been dead for two years.

Bronski took his time answering. 'Sure I do, but I don't think it'll help much. But if you want to, you'll need a key. Radio dispatch now and get a patrol car over with it. We'll meet them there.'

It was the same rookie cop, Frank Petersen, who had been on the scene that first day who pulled up in front of the house minutes later. He nodded to both detectives as he got out of the squad car and after handing the keys to Bronski, he took off.

'So, you want me to come in with you, or what?' Bronski asked, taking a quick look down the road.

Annie guessed that Bronski would be wondering what the neighbours would be thinking. 'No, I'm fine. I'll call a cab when I'm finished. Should I keep the keys or drop them back at the station?'

'Bring them back tomorrow. I'll see you in the morning, then.' Bronski started to walk back to the car, but then turned around. 'Look why don't I just come in with you and then drop you home.'

'Sir, I would like to do this on my own, if that's OK with you.'

He tried one last time. 'Are you sure you're OK with this?' Bronski was still lingering.

'Aye, I'll see you tomorrow.'

Annie was pleased when Bronski finally took no for an answer. She wanted to use the instincts she knew she had, but felt she'd demonstrated little of lately. That was why she needed to look and listen to what this crime scene was telling her, alone.

Once she saw his car turn the corner, Annie let herself into the house. She felt herself starting to retch as she shut the door behind her and walked up the stairs. From experience, she knew that the scene would be as bad on the second viewing as it had been on the first, but the reality this time was that it was worse. Scrapings of blood and paint had been taken and somehow that compounded the original violation of the hallway and the bedroom – the marks left behind, the bed stripped bare. This was no longer a place to come home to and Annie shuddered as she sat down on the bed. What were they missing? What had Angela Goodman done to provoke such a vicious assault? This was no random attack.

At times like this, Annie knew she had to go back to basics. Walking back down the stairs, she attempted to recreate what they supposed Angela had done: placing her coat on the coat rack, maybe looking at herself in the mirror. Annie hesitated for a moment at the mirror, taking stock of what she saw, realising that she herself was looking fraught and then chastised herself.

Get on with it. Slowly she opened the door into the kitchen. The glass from the drainer had been removed for evidence and Jim Moorcroft's prints confirmed. How does someone forget to mention they were in the house? Her eyes scanned the whole room. Angela Goodman was meticulous. Apart from the chaos wreaked by the intruder, each cupboard, when opened revealed a truth about the owner. Everything was in place, jars in neat rows, labels all facing to the front. Every cup had a handle facing in the same direction. No wonder she could be so accurate about things being out of place. If Annie had seen her at home, rather than at the station, she might have taken the whole thing more seriously. Would that oversight cost Angela Goodman her life?

The living room was the same. Minus the vandalism, the couches were tasteful: red background, small yellow flower printed pattern and each had a beige throw on it, to be pulled down and used to protect against any chill. The coffee table had remnants of fingerprint dust and the magazines had been moved, but the stereo system was intact and the CDs lined up perfectly. Not only were the CDs in alphabetical order, they were also in sections. Annie realised that most were easy listening and female artists. Did these belong to Mrs Goodman, or her soon to be ex-husband? It was hard to tell. There was a standard lamp to the side of one of the couches, the type of lamp that is left on when someone goes out for the evening, but wants to make it look as if they are at home. Had Mrs Goodman come in here and turned the light off before going upstairs? Annie noticed some dust left behind by the forensics team. They'd obviously thought of that and would eliminate her prints.

The dining room had not escaped the paint and Annie still couldn't get a sense of what the vandalism in each room meant. The bedroom made some sense, but the other rooms? She walked over to the liquor cabinet. The whisky bottle had been taken away for evidence and Annie remembered that the report didn't mention Jim Moorcroft's finger marks on the bottle. Maybe, only Angela had touched the bottle. Moorcroft hadn't poured himself a nightcap, at any rate.

The small study off the dining room was the least damaged of all the rooms, as if the perpetrator had decided that enough was enough. Or was there something different about this room? Maybe Angela didn't even go in there that last night, but Annie still went in wanting to get a feel of the room. Mostly it was bare and Annie suspected that this wasn't Mrs Goodman's study, but maybe George Goodman's. The desk drawers were empty and there was nothing on top of the desk, not even a lamp. The lighting in the room wasn't very bright, so a desk lamp would have been needed. Did the perpetrator turn this on for some reason and then take it with him? But why, especially if he was carrying paint cans?

There were three filing cabinets, seemingly labelled with household information. Annie opened the first one and flicked through the manila files. Someone, Mr or Mrs Goodman was meticulous about saving receipts. The vacation file revealed that they'd been to the Bahamas, Puerto Rico and Mexico in the last five years. Annie couldn't find her marriage certificates, which was unfortunate as it would be useful to check out the first husband and see how amicable or not that divorce was. A further filing cabinet, unlabelled was locked. Annie looked around for the key, but couldn't find it in the room. She made a mental note to look around for it upstairs.

After shutting the filing cabinet, Annie walked slowly up the stairs, instinctively switching on the hallway light, just as she suspected Angela Goodman would have done, especially if she was carrying a drink with her. But the light bulb had obviously blown. Annie stopped at the top of the stairs trying to recall whether she'd made a note of the light not working when they'd made their first visit to the house. The upstairs landing didn't have any natural light so was considerably darker in the late afternoon. Annie surmised that it would have been nearly pitch black when Mrs Goodman walked up those stairs.

Putting on the bathroom light, Annie stepped back into the hallway to examine the light. It was one of those glass bowl type fixtures, which would have to be unscrewed first to get to the light bulb. It would also take a ladder to reach the fixture. It could have been out for weeks, or if the perpetrator wanted the darkness on the stairs, he could have unscrewed the bulb while he waited for Angela Goodman to come home. At least that was what Annie surmised had happened. The perpetrator must have already been in the house, unless it was someone she knew and she'd let him in and he'd forced her upstairs. But then why the glass, upstairs on the floor? It seemed more likely that the perpetrator was waiting for her in her bedroom. Annie switched off the bathroom light.

Stepping back into the bedroom, Annie reached for the wall light in the room and then opened her notebook. For the second time, she felt as if she might be sick. It was the pink paint, brash paint, paint that made a statement. Sitting on the bare bed, she closed her eyes and tried to imagine what had happened in this room.

There was only a mild breeze in the air, not enough to cool the oppressive humidity of the late afternoon. This was a necessary stop, but not the last task of the day. The man got out of his car and walked slowly up to the headstone, looking like any other visitor, nothing to make him stand out. Pausing, he read the whole inscription. It was simple enough, but said it all. The grave wasn't exactly neglected, although there were no fresh flowers. The basket he was carrying would make a welcome addition and show how much he still loved her.

But there was also the guilt. He hadn't yet achieved what he had set out to do; what he had promised her all those years ago when he stood at this same place, what he had planned so meticulously.

The job was only partly done. True, he had made her suffer. He had even made her admit that she'd lied all those years ago. They'd always believed her and because of that, his life and that of those around him was ruined. How could she have done that and still slept nights? He hadn't slept. All those nights in that cramped cell and for what? For a bitch that couldn't get enough of him until she changed her mind and wanted someone else. Nothing he did for her then was enough. He thought of all those times he'd told her how he felt about her, how much he wanted her. Then there were all the gifts, but it was never enough. Why didn't anyone see her for what she was?

No, instead they misinterpreted everything he did. But now it was almost over. He wouldn't fail again.

Annie froze as she heard a key turn in the lock. For a second she wasn't quite sure what to do. Who could it be? If it were Bronski, he would have called her to say he was on his way, but then she realised that her hand-bag was downstairs in the hallway, with her phone on vibrate. Had he tried to call her? As far as she knew she had the only available key, since Jim Moorcroft and Jackie Winters had handed theirs into the station. But surely, Bronski would shout out. Heart pounding in her chest, she looked around the room for anything to pro-tect herself with, but there was nothing.

Slowly, she approached the bedroom doorway, hop-ing that the floorboards wouldn't creak and give away her position. For now she was still hidden from view. In the poor light, she screwed up her eyes trying to see who had let themselves in. Whoever it was had enough illumination from the outside to realise that the hallway was like the scene out of a movie.

'Christ, what the hell?'

Before he could say anything else, Annie appeared at the top of the stairs and started to walk down.

'Who the hell are you?' The words were firm but the accent was one she remembered from a few days ago. The man wore an army uniform and Annie could just see that his badge said Capt. Hegarty. He was about six foot three and considerably younger than Angela Goodman. The front door remained open and Annie could see that his bags were still outside.

'I'm Detective Annie Macpherson from the Westford Police.' Annie showed her ID, as she reached the bottom of the staircase. 'We spoke on the phone yesterday. I was expecting you to telephone to let us know you'd arrived back.'

'I just got in from Montana. I rented a car at the airport and came straight here. God this place looks awful.' He couldn't stop himself staring at the hallway and then opening the door to the living room. 'What bastard would do such a thing?'

Annie followed, keeping her counsel as he made his way into the kitchen.

'Where was she attacked?'

'Look, why don't we bring your bags into the hallway? I'd like to shut the front door, if you don't mind. Then I can fill you in with more details.'

Mrs. Goodman's brother brushed past her and picked up two very heavy looking duffle bags and deposited them in the hall.

Annie shut the door. She was sure that he would've seen worse than this scene in combat, but this was his sister's house after all, so the emotional impact would be severe. She wanted him to take his time to digest the state of the downstairs before he had to face the bedroom.

They stood awkwardly in the hall before he broke the silence, repeating his earlier question. 'Where was she attacked?'

'The main crime scene was in the bedroom.' Hegarty hardly looked at her as he rushed past up the stairs. Annie followed but missed his initial reaction to seeing the bedroom. His distress was obvious as she reached him seconds later. Annie remembered her own reaction seeing the bedroom the first time. At least he was spared the blood on the bedclothes and the complete disarray.

'Was she raped?' he mumbled, as he tried to take in the bedroom scene, mesmerised by the paint on the walls.

Annie hesitated. What brother wants confirmation that his sister has been raped? 'We're still awaiting test results from the hospital but it seems likely.'

'Have you seen her? The hospital told me she's in a critical condition.'

Annie decided she would have to be frank with him. 'I saw her yesterday and spoke to her doctors. She's in intensive care. They are doing everything they can, but the assault was vicious.'

'I need to see her.'

'Of course. I could come with you, if you want.'

But Hegarty was too distracted to take in what Annie was saying. 'I need to book myself a room. I can't stay here like Angie and I had planned. There is a motel near the hospital. I need a shower and a change. I've been travelling for hours.'

Annie realised that he was just stating the plan, not reacting, just saying what the drill was. She had seen other people in shock and knew she would have to state the options for him to decide. 'I don't have a car, so I could come with you and wait while you get ready and then go with you to the hospital. Do you want me to do that?'

Hegarty picked up his duffel bags. 'Let's just get out of here.'

Annie picked up her handbag and then checked the kitchen light was off before locking the front door. By then Hegarty had put his bags into the boot of the car.

While Hegarty had a shower and changed out of his military uniform, Annie telephoned Bronski at home to let him know that she was with Angela's brother and would accompany him to the hospital. Annie wanted the opportunity to find out more about Angela Goodman's background, although she wondered how forthcoming Hegarty would be. There was something off hand about him that Annie couldn't quite put her finger on. But then, of course, there was the shock of seeing his sister's house in such a state. Soon he would be seeing her, which would be even more traumatic.

22

Gus Wojinski was having his second cup of coffee and contemplating the tasks he had promised to do. The first was mowing the lawns. Then he needed to check the filtration system on the outdoor pool. Last night Carol had said that the chlorine seemed too concentrated. She would know, using the pool every day as she did in the summer. 'My little dolphin' was his term for his wife.

When the phone rang he knew it would be her, checking that he was out of bed and focused on the day's chores. 'Hi sweetheart', he said as he picked up the phone.

'Hi Gus. Gee, I wish my husband picked up the phone with that greeting for me,' said the familiar voice.

Gus laughed. 'Sorry Sandra. I was expecting it to be Carol, checking that I'm doing the chores, but I'll have a word with Pete if you want.'

'Yes please,' came the quick reply.

'So, what's up? Don't tell me Carol has forgotten the keys again?' Sometimes Gus was surprised at how absent-minded his wife could be. He anticipated having to look for them in the house and then driving to the bookshop.

'That's just it, Gus, she's not here. I was wondering if she'd decided on a sleep in and was coming in later.'

'She's not there yet? She must have set off at the usual time. I was still asleep, but she left a note.'

'Perhaps you're right. Maybe she did forget the keys and has had to drive back home.'

Gus looked at his watch. 'But she would have been

back here by now.' As he held the phone, he walked into the living room to have a look out the window. 'I can see our whole road from the window and there's no sign of her.'

'Hmm, she would have got back to yours by now, wouldn't she?' Sandra replied.

'I would have thought so. But the traffic would be worse coming in our direction.'

'That's true. Look Gus, I don't want to alarm you but I hear from people passing the bookshop that there has been an accident on the road into town. I passed the fire crews and the police cars myself, but didn't really know what was going on. Some others are now saying that two cars went off the road and down the ravine. I didn't think any more about it until I got to the bookshop and it wasn't opened up.'

'Oh my God, you don't think ... ?'

'Gus, I don't know. I haven't any details. Should I call the police from here?'

'No, tell you what, why don't you go over to the coffee shop. Make sure she hasn't just gone out to get you both a drink and call me back as soon as you've checked it out. I'm going to get in the car and start to drive her route to work. I'll take my cell phone. Call me on that if I need to turn back.'

'OK Gus. I'll be ten minutes at the most.'

The next couple of minutes were a blur to Gus. Finding his car keys became a major task as he couldn't think straight with worry. He tried to convince himself that there was an innocent explanation. The coffee shop was his best guess. Carol was always doing stuff for people.

23

Annie pointed to the right as they got out of the lift. There were two nurses at the nurses' station as they approached. Only one looked up and she recognised Annie.

'Good evening, Detective.' Annie was grateful for the greeting. Perhaps that would demonstrate to Hegarty that she had been checking on his sister. Anything would help.

'Good evening. This is Captain Charles Hegarty, Mrs Goodman's brother.'

'Good evening, Captain. Good to have you Stateside again. Your sister's room is just down the hall. I'm afraid there is no change in her condition and the doctor won't be back again tonight. I am sure you have lots of questions. We can arrange an appointment for you to see her surgeon in the morning.'

'Thank you, I'll need all the information I can get.'

'Captain, can we take details of where you can be reached?'

It was another few minutes while Hegarty filled in the contact form and then Annie walked him down the corridor. As they approached Angela Goodman's room, Officer Tully stood up. Annie was again relieved that she knew the officer stationed outside the room: two pieces of luck.

'Officer Tully, this is Captain Hegarty, Angela Goodman's brother. He's on leave from Afghanistan.'

The officer put out his hand and Hegarty shook it. 'Welcome, Sir. I'm sorry the situation isn't better for you. I expect you have seen enough of injury to last you a lifetime.'

'What's your role here, Officer? The detective didn't tell me there was a guard outside my sister's door.'

Before Tully could answer, Annie replied. 'I'm sorry, Captain Hegarty. We don't want to take any chances, as we suspect that the perpetrator didn't expect your sister to survive. We need to ensure she is protected until we make an arrest.' Annie tried to sound reassuring but was convinced from the expression on Hegarty's face that she was pretty wide of the mark.

'I see,' he said. 'I would like to go in now and see Angie, alone, if that's OK with you.'

Annie knew that he wasn't exactly asking her permission, so she just nodded.

When the door to the room shut, Annie turned to Tully, who ventured his opinion. 'Hard for him, eh, coming back to this?'

Annie nodded. 'It's an awful shock.' Then turning her head towards the door, she added, 'I wonder how he will take seeing her as she is.'

'Not what he was expecting, at any rate,' Tully replied as he put Hegarty's name in the logbook alongside the time.

'Has she had any other visitors?'

Tully looked at the top of the page where the day's entries had been recorded, his pen still poised in his hand.

'Let's see. Today, Jackie Winters came early afternoon, 1:30, stayed about twenty minutes. Then an hour ago Father Loftus, one of the Catholic priests, visited for about ten minutes. I was on duty for that one.'

Probably touting for last rites business, thought Annie, but who was she to judge? Her Presbyterian upbringing had lasted until she turned eighteen and then her choice was to leave religion behind. The last time she'd been in a church was for her father's funeral.

'And Jackie Winters was alone?'

'I wasn't on for that one but she's the only visitor listed. Of course, there have been nurses in regularly doing observations. We've noted those down as well, although I don't think they like that.'

Interesting that Jim Moorcroft hadn't come. Annie wondered if he'd told Jackie about their talk earlier in the day, or even if Jackie knew about the domestic violence in his past. She made a note in her book to question Jackie further, to see if anything was forthcoming. Maybe he was still at it and she too was a victim.

'When do you finish?'

'I should be relieved in another half hour.'

'Do you want a coffee, I could get you one?' Annie offered.

'Thanks Detective, that's the best offer I've had all day, but I'm going home from here, so I'm OK.'

'Right, I'll be in the waiting room. Please let Captain Hegarty know when he comes out, or pass the message on if you change shifts before then.'

Tully nodded and closed the logbook.

Annie took a seat in the small waiting room. She was the only one there. Everyone else was visiting respective rooms. The magazines were weeks old and besides she wasn't particularly interested in the latest celebrity gossip. She hated the concept of 'celebrity' – so false and not good role models either, in her view. Annie often thought that the real role models were people who worked with her brother and other people with disabilities – staff who were caring and compassionate. They deserved the money, not these 'fifteen minutes of fame' types who had more money than sense. Their weekly wage could keep Andrew in supported accommodation or what the Americans called 'an assisted living facility' for a year. So the magazines remained on the table and instead she got out her notebook. She wanted to review everything, as she knew Hegarty would have more questions for her as well.

About a half hour later, Hegarty came into the waiting room, clearly distressed. Annie still had her notebook open. Rather than taking a seat, he chose to stand. They were alone in the room.

'This is your fault.'

Annie was momentarily taken aback by his tone. 'Sorry, what do you mean?'

'She went to you for help and you turned her away. So what did you put her down as, eh? Was she neurotic, paranoid, a fantasist, or an attention seeker in your view? If you had only listened, maybe this wouldn't have happened.'

Annie went quiet. Hegarty was expressing what she'd been musing about for the last few days. What had she really thought of Angela Goodman? But the woman herself seemed to be satisfied with the actions Annie proposed, so what made her brother come out with that remark?

'Did Angela tell you about our interview?'

'Yes, in her last email to me. See for yourself.' Hegarty paced around the room while he scrolled through the messages on his smartphone. 'This is it, sent last week.'

Annie took the device from him and read the screen:

Charlie

Don't know where you will be when you get this. You may still be in the air or perhaps you've already arrived in Billings on route to Livingston. There'll be several trout with your name on them waiting for you. At least I hope you're there. I still can't bear thinking about you being in Afghanistan. I know you can't give me specifics of your travel, but we families do worry about you guys.

Speaking of worries, don't want to burden you, but we need a talk when you get here. I'm being spooked in my own house, things being moved, strange smells. I think it's George, but I can't be sure. I even decided to report it to the Westford Police a couple of weeks ago. Saw a Scottish lady detective, Annie Macpherson. I could tell she thought I was a nut case, a time waster. She's not even a proper member of the force, just on some sort of exchange. You know how I get, never been the assertive type. God knows if I were, George wouldn't have walked all over me, but enough of that. Anyway, I went out of the station with my tail between my legs. But I know things aren't right. Anyway, we'll talk when you get here.

You know there are things you don't know about me, reasons why I get nervy and stuff I've never told you. Maybe when you're here we can have a good heart to heart.

It just seemed such an age gap when you were younger, but now you're a serving officer, fighting for our country. There are things you need to know about my past so you understand me better, little brother. But all that can wait until you have your dream vacation. I don't mind taking a back seat to the Yellowstone. Just watch out for those black bears, or is it grizzlies?

Let me know when you expect to arrive. Tight lines, Love Angela xxx

Annie felt a pang of guilt. She hadn't thought she'd come across like that to Angela Goodman, but clearly she had. If the case was going to get anywhere she had to know more about the woman and Hegarty was key to that. She didn't want to come away tonight empty-handed. What would Bronski say in the morning? After their earlier phone call, he was expecting some background details. If she couldn't establish a rapport with Hegarty, then Bronski would have to and she didn't want to have to hand over that responsibility. She certainly didn't want Franconi to consider that it might be better with her off the case. That decision might even jeopardise the future of the exchange programme.

24

Gus Wojinski's mind was working overtime as he got into his car, first checking that his cell phone was getting a signal. No return call from Sandra as yet. As he started on the route he knew his wife took into work, he was so intent on searching for any signs of her car that he noticed things he'd never observed before, like small side roads and a scenic overlook. His mind returned to why she'd disappeared. Maybe she'd had a flat and turned off the road somewhere, but surely she'd have phoned him.

He couldn't bear the thought of anything happening to Carol. They'd been trying to start a family and she was a few days into a missed period. In fact, tonight she was going to use one of those home pregnancy tests and he had planned a romantic meal for that evening, whatever the result was. They would either celebrate or commiserate and keep trying. Although at her age, time wasn't exactly on their side.

In desperation, Gus tried Carol's cell phone again, but it wasn't connecting. She should have been at work for a good hour by now. Perhaps he should try the bookshop again. Why wasn't Sandra calling him back? Surely she'd been to the coffee shop by now.

Twenty minutes later, he saw that a diversion was in place and the car in front took the diverted road. Gus pulled over, much to the annoyance of the State Trooper.

'Sir you can't stop here. You'll be holding up traffic.'

'But I'm worried about my wife. This is her route

into work and her colleague has called me to say that she hasn't arrived. I'm worried she may have been in an accident. Her cell phone has lost its connection.'

'Pull over to the side here, please Sir.'

While Gus tried to tuck in as far as he could, he noticed that the Trooper was motioning other traffic forward and through the diversion. He stepped out of his car and approached the young officer. By then there were no more cars in view.

'Name, Sir?'

'Gus Wojinski.'

The officer took down the details and ran through more questions. Within a few minutes he had all the details of Carol's car, relevant telephone numbers and her place of work. Then he radioed in to his colleagues further up the road at the scene.

Gus paced back and forth trying to ascertain as much as he could of the conversation on the radio, but it was difficult and it was clear that the Trooper was trying to keep as much of the detail to himself as possible. Not repeating the information he was being told, as it was said to him. Finally he said, 'I'll advise him to do that.'

Gus waited expectantly as the Trooper firstly motioned another car forward and then walked back to him.

'Sir, the best thing you can do is to continue into town and go to your wife's shop. Then have a look around town and if you don't find her, report into the local police station and give them all the details you've given me.'

'That's it? That's all you can tell me? Surely you know what cars have been involved in the accident?'

'The fire crew are sifting through the wreckage. They haven't got a make and model for either car as yet, so there really isn't anything else I can tell you right now. Report your wife missing if you don't find her in town.'

With that last piece of advice, the Trooper went back to directing the traffic and reluctantly Gus reversed his car and followed the diversion into town. Just as he got on the main road his cell phone rang.

25

'Listen, I am really sorry that I gave your sister that impression. I thought she was satisfied when we finished the interview and we were pursuing her husband for questioning when we found out about the assault. I also suggested she get the locks changed.' It didn't seem a lot now that Annie was justifying it, but Angela Goodman had no hard evidence of any crime being committed.

'I can't believe this is happening. She's all the family I've got.' Hegarty was still pacing.

Annie felt she needed to offer some comfort or some relief, but she also needed to explore more about the past Angela alluded to, finding out whatever Hegarty could tell her. She wasn't sure how much to push it tonight. After all, in the last two hours, the man had seen his sister's house in a shocking state and had just spent time with her, not being able to communicate, seeing her lying there helpless.

'Should we try and see if we can talk to one of the doctors? Someone must be on duty tonight, rather than you having to wait for morning. I could have another word with the nurses.'

'No, the nurse has my cell phone number now and has promised to call me if there is any change. I've just spoken to her again. There isn't a whole lot else I can do right now. The doctor is back in the morning and I'm seeing him at nine.'

'Are you sure? If you want to stay longer with her, I can find my own way home.' Annie got up as she was talking, putting her notebook in her jacket pocket at the same time.

'No, I'd be better just coming back in the morning.'

'OK. Do you want to go somewhere, maybe get something to eat?' Annie wanted the opportunity to question him.

'I haven't eaten all day. I guess I should have something.'

'I noticed a steak house next to your motel. How about going there?' Annie didn't exactly invite herself, but unless he objected, she intended to join him. He didn't and they left the hospital after Hegarty stopped once more at the nurses' station, just to double check the appointment time in the morning.

Annie was relieved that they were seated at a table away from one of the overhead fans. She found their motion distracting, but at least they provided less of a chill than the air conditioning, which she found overpowering in most restaurants. Rather than bringing relief, she ended up chilled to the bone. The restaurant was quiet and although it looked like one of those that would be popular with families with its 'all you can eat' salad bar, it was late in the evening for small children to be in the restaurant. They were in a section with only one other set of diners and the people at that table looked as if they would be finishing soon.

Just before he sat down, Hegarty excused himself for a moment, saying he wanted to wash his hands. As he walked away from the table, Annie noticed again how tall he was, with that walk of the military about him. He was also very good looking, deep brown eyes with contrasting blond hair, obviously bleached by the sun in Afghanistan. The powder blue short sleeved shirt he was wearing set off his tanned skin, just the opposite of her fair Scottish, maybe even pasty looking, complexion. She never tanned, just burned which was even more unattractive than being pale. She remembered blistering once as a child when they had an unusually hot summer and her dad had taken her to the beach as a treat. Mum and Andrew had stayed home, as Andrew was in a bad mood for some reason and mum and dad weren't sure how he'd behave. Andrew was the reason they did so little as a whole family when she was growing up, although it wasn't until she was much older that she realised that. In some ways, she didn't care. She loved being on her own with her dad. He would always tell her stories in the car and he always talked about granddad. She never tired of listening to him and having their special time together.

'Have you decided what you're having yet?' Hegarty asked as he slid into the booth. He opened his menu but only glanced at it, obviously familiar with what the chain of restaurants had to offer.

Annie opened the menu again. 'Just the salad bar for me and the appetiser portion of the shrimp. I find the entree portions too big.'

The waitress approached with water just as Annie finished her sentence and took their orders right away. They both went up to the salad bar together. Hegarty finished before Annie, but politely waited for her before they walked back to the table together. More polite than Paul ever was, she thought, fleetingly.

In the meantime, the waitress had left a Coors Light for Hegarty and a glass of white wine for Annie. The first moment or two was awkward. Annie wasn't sure how to get into a conversation with him. It was less formal than an interview and certainly not a meal out between two friends. Her purpose was to obtain information, but in the kindest way possible. In the end, Hegarty broke the ice.

'I must apologise for my rudeness back at the hospital, Detective Macpherson. It was the shock of seeing Angie like that. She's my big sister, always capable, always in charge. Our dad died when I was really little and I only knew my mother and Angie growing up. Well mostly it was Angie, to be honest. Mom never got over dad's death and was often depressed, taking to her bed for days at a time. Angie got me ready for school, made sure I got there safely, cooked our meals. In some ways she was more of a mom to me.'

Annie didn't say anything, willing him to continue.

He hesitated as he ate some of his salad, 'I didn't realise how hungry or how thirsty I was.'

'Me neither. Look why don't you call me Annie. Detective Macpherson sounds too formal.'

'As does Captain Hegarty. Everyone calls me Charlie. And now that we're on first name terms, can I order you another glass of wine when the waitress comes back? I'll be ready for another beer by then.'

'Aye, I could drink another,' replied Annie as she picked up her wine glass and enjoyed the crispness as it went down her throat. She was warming to Captain Charles Hegarty.

An hour later, Charlie opened the door of her taxi. 'Should I call you tomorrow after I've seen the doctor?'

'The station number and my cell are on the card. I'll be in the station early. Good night Charlie.' Annie put her seat belt on in the back of the taxi and gave her address to the driver. Ten minutes later she put her key in her apartment door.

26

'I can't believe they just came into work like that, bold as brass and interviewed me. What are they playing at?' Jim Moorcroft was sitting at the kitchen table while Jackie served up spaghetti bolognaise. He hadn't been in the house ten minutes and had poured them both a glass of wine before the meal. As usual, he and Jackie hadn't travelled home together.

'I never saw them come in, but then again, I was working in the claims section today. No one said anything there, so it obviously hadn't got around the building. And that's why I was home earlier than you, for a change.'

'I know, I know, but Jack, you should have seen how everyone in our section looked at me. I know what they were thinking: What have you done to Angela? Shit, she's my friend, more like a sister than anything else. I feel so angry.' He distractedly put too much Parmesan on his meal.

Jackie knew that wouldn't help and she wasn't surprised when he pushed the plate away. She could feel herself getting tense, wondering if he would just take it to the sink and put the whole thing down the garbage disposal. It wouldn't be the first time that a meal she'd prepared became the butt of his anger and then the rest.

Fortunately, Jim pulled the plate back and picked up his fork.

'What exactly did they ask you?'

Now Jim had to be careful. Jackie didn't know about the arrest or any of the details of what he went through.

She knew he'd been married but he always played that down, never going into detail. He just said they'd grown apart. Yeah sure, grew apart, when he couldn't bear looking at her, knowing she was sleeping with someone else. What a bitch. Deserved what she got from him. 'They just went over what they'd already asked me, but it was the tone and the fact that I was the last one to see her before the assault. And they found my finger marks on a glass in the kitchen.' Jim was only playing with the spaghetti being more interested in the wine.

'Did they? So, did you go into the house when you dropped her off or when you picked her up? You and I are there so much. I bet my prints are all over the house too. Surely, they can't make much of that.'

'That's just the thing. When they asked me, I said no. But now that I think about it, I probably did go in when I picked her up. I think I had some water, but like you said, we're there so much I couldn't quite remember. And it was their tone. It got me confused. I know I didn't go in when I dropped her back, I'm sure of that.' The wine glass was in his hand again.

'Maybe you satisfied them. I bet you don't hear from them again.' Jackie started on her meal, hoping her words would have the desired effect.

'I bet they interview you again, though, to try and take my alibi apart. They'll want to know when I got home, whether I seemed distracted or not, that kind of thing.'

Jackie was surprised. 'But don't you remember? The first time they talked to us in the hospital, I told them that I'd gone to bed before you were back. I can't change the story now Jim, without it looking suspicious. That might be even worse for you.'

'What do you mean, it might be worse for me? You don't really think I had anything to do with Angela's assault, do you? You're looking at me like that bitch of a detective did today. I've had enough.'

The noise of the wine glass smashing as he threw it against the wall drowned out Jackie's attempt at a reply. He slammed the door as he stormed out.

As usual, she was left to pick up the pieces, wondering how much more of this she could take.

27

Gus frantically answered his cell phone, not even glancing to see who the caller was. 'Carol?'

'Hi Gus. Sorry, it's me, Sandra. Where are you?'

'Have you found her?'

'Not yet, but I've only been to the coffee shop. Fiona has just come in, so I thought that when you get here we could have another walk around town.'

'I'm just on the main road now: should be with you in about twenty minutes. There's a roadblock because of the accident. I'll tell you about it when I get there.' Gus had to pay attention to his driving now, as his nerves were really getting to him. All he could say was: 'Please God, please,' which he repeated over and over in the car.

Sandra put the shop phone down and Fiona looked at her quizzically. 'I have an awful feeling about this.' But before Fiona could respond, a customer came up to her with a question. Carol was a stickler for the customer coming first and had drilled into both of them that any conversation between them ended when a customer approached.

Sandra made her way into the small back kitchen, labelled Staff Only. As she made herself a coffee, she wondered if there were any problems in Gus and Carol's marriage. Carol had been behaving a bit strangely of late. What if she had decided to go missing on purpose? What if she simply wanted to start again some place else? But then she questioned whether she was reading too much into this. After all, the thought had only occurred to her because of a programme she'd seen on TV weeks back about adults who go missing and start new lives somewhere else. Something about that had appealed to her as she watched the documentary. Frankly, she would be jealous if Carol succeeded in doing it. Sandra's reverie was broken by the door opening. It was Fiona.

'So what's going on? Do you think it was Carol's car in that accident?'

'I don't know, but let's not speculate in front of Gus. He sounded in a state of panic on the phone. I'm sure the police will have more information. Someone in the coffee shop said she'd heard there were two cars, but how people know that, I have no idea.'

'I haven't heard anything,' Fiona said, as if she was always missing out on something.

'Anyway, like I said, Gus will be here soon. Are you OK if we leave you here while we take a look around town, see if anyone has seen her this morning?' Sandra didn't want any hassle when Gus got there. Fiona was only a student on her summer vacation, working in the bookshop to get some money for next term. Not the most reliable summer help they'd had, either.

'Sure, but it's not like Carol not to be here. She's the most conscientious person I know. I think something's happened to her.'

'Well, keep that thought to yourself, whatever you do,' Sandra answered.

It was nearly a half hour before Gus arrived, breathless. 'There was nowhere to park. I'm three streets over on a parking meter. Any news?'

Sandra and Fiona just looked at him. Neither had

seen someone so flustered before.

'No, but let's take a walk around. We're bound to bump into people who have seen her, if she's been in town today.' Sandra grabbed her handbag before Gus had a chance to answer and nodded to Fiona on the way out. 'If you need me, call my cell.'

Their first stop was the coffee shop again, at Gus's insistence. He knew that his wife was a creature of habit. Sandra slightly resented him not taking her word for it, as she'd already questioned the staff who knew both Carol and her by name.

'There's a small dress shop she often mentions,' said Gus on the way out. 'Hanbury's?'

'It's just around the corner.' Sandra led the way and Gus peered into all the other shops as they passed. The view into most was pretty good, but Sandra knew that it was a pointless exercise. From their conversations, Carol mostly shopped outside town in the large shopping mall. Sandra thought it a bit hypocritical that Carol expected people to frequent the bookshop to support local shops but used the mall herself. So, not surprisingly, they drew a blank. Gus was getting more and more agitated. They tried three more shops in the promenade before making their way back to the bookshop.

'I'm going to the police.'

'Do you want me to come with you?' Sandra wasn't sure what she could add, but felt that she had to offer.

'Thanks, but I'm sure they'll contact you if they need to know anything about her work that I don't know. I'll keep in touch if I find out anything.'

As Gus left the bookshop, he couldn't help but

think how differently this day was turning out from the one he had planned. He had a further thought on the way to the police station. He stepped into the pharmacy and enquired as to whether a woman had purchased a pregnancy kit that morning. He didn't want to, knowing how she valued her privacy, but he used Carol's name. The girl behind the counter knew his wife and confirmed she hadn't sold her one. Then discreetly she questioned the other assistants who hadn't either. Another blank and he had run out of ideas. Now he feared the worst.

The desk sergeant showed him into a small interview room. As he waited for one of the officers to interview him, he felt like the walls were closing in on him. He had all he could do to keep it together. Only once had he ever been in trouble with the police. As a teenager, he had stupidly tried to buy beer under age and the liquor storeowner called the cops. Even now, he shuddered remembering how scared he was when his dad came down to the station. The roasting he got from him was worse than from the cops. Thankfully, he didn't have long to wait.

'Mr Wojinski, I'm Officer Brent.' The man offered his hand and Gus shook it.

'I understand that your wife has not turned up for work and that you have been looking around town for her.'

'Look, I'm frantic. I can't get a hold of her on her cell phone. I have heard that there was a major accident of some kind on the route she takes to work and I am petrified that she was one of the cars involved. I've driven the route myself and the State Trooper I spoke to over an hour ago said to come here and report her missing, if I couldn't find her in town. I just want to find out what cars were involved in that accident so I know whether my wife is alive or not.'

'Let me take a few details.' After making a note of Carol's name, their address her place of work and the car details, the officer added: 'If you wait here, I'll see what I can find out.'

28

Annie woke suddenly, unsure whether she was dreaming or a phone was actually ringing. She stretched out an arm, groping for her cell phone. Eyes barely open, she couldn't see the caller ID.

'Annie?'

'Mum, what's the matter? What time is it?'

'Sorry, dear it's just after ten in the morning here. I keep forgetting we're so far ahead of you.'

By now Annie had switched on the table lamp and had swung her feet over the side of the bed. Her heart was pounding. She knew if her mother was so distracted as to forget the time difference between the two countries, then something was seriously the matter.

'What's wrong, Mum? What it is?'

'I'm in the hospital, dear, Andrew is being admitted. I had to call an ambulance a few hours ago. I heard him fall out of bed. He had another one of his fits, but he didn't come out of it like he usually does and had a second one.'

Annie interrupted her mother. 'Mum, what are the doctors saying?'

'Nothing as yet. He had another major one in the ambulance and is still unconscious. They're trying to control it.' Her voice broke and the sobbing started.

'Mum, is anyone with you? What about Auntie Lil?'

Margaret Macpherson didn't cope well with stress, even though she had taken care of Andrew his whole life. Annie knew she never really slept through a night and was always half awake listening out for Andrew, almost like a new mother. Thirty-five years of listening out for him would be enough for anyone, but Margaret was too stubborn to consider Andrew going into any form of supported accommodation. 'As long as I can take care of him, I will' was her view. She wasn't getting any younger, but Annie knew that it was no good starting on that conversation now. Besides, they'd had that discussion too many times in the recent past. Annie had harboured the constant fear that there would be some trauma while she was in the States and too far away to be any use to her mum.

'She and Uncle Alasdair are on their way now. She'll stay with me tonight if I need her to. I don't think Andrew will be coming out today, although I haven't spoken to the doctor yet. I'm sorry, Annie, I shouldn't have called you until I knew more. I just didn't know what else to do.'

Annie could hear the sobbing again.

'Mum, try and stay calm. The doctors will need to talk to you. You did the right thing calling the ambulance. He's in the best place. Let them take care of him.'

'I know, dear, but I couldn't bear to lose him, not after your father.'

'Mum, don't do this. Andrew is a fighter; he's come through worse than this. I'm more worried about you.' It was true, Annie sometimes thought she was going to lose her mother as well as her father. His death was so sudden and unexpected and yet her mother was the one who was slowly being worn down from all the years of taking care of her son. 'Please Mum, you have to think of yourself too. Go and have a cup of tea and something

137

to eat. I'll call you back in about an hour. Auntie Lil should be with you by then.'

'Aye.'

'But Mum, call me before then if you speak to the doctors.'

Annie put the phone down and looked at the alarm clock. It was just past five. Exhaustion hit her again and she put her head back on the pillow. Two hours later, the sound that awoke her was the alarm clock going off. Her first thought was guilt that she could have gone back to sleep after the distressing call from her mother, but then fear that it had been two hours and she'd said she would ring back in an hour. What if the worst has happened?

'Mum, it's me. What's happening?' But it was her Aunt Lil who answered. Annie swore that the two women were interchangeable on the phone, same accent, same inflections.

'Annie, Alasdair and I are having a coffee. Your mother is with Andrew now. She asked me to take her phone, as she was expecting a call back from you. He's regained consciousness but the doctors are still concerned. They want to keep him in a few days and do some more tests. They think his epilepsy medication needs reviewing, but he seems to be over the worst of it, thank God. Your poor mother, how she suffers with all of this.'

'I know, thanks for being there, Aunt Lil. I appreciate it. Tell Andrew I said to stop scaring Mum, will you?'

Her aunt laughed. 'Since when has something you've said frightened your brother. He'll just laugh when we mention you.'

Annie smiled, that much was true. Andrew still liked to pat her on the head and give her a bear hug. Whatever else, he was still her big brother. 'Tell Mum, I'll call her later when I get into work and give Uncle Alasdair a hug from me.'

For once, Annie was the last one in. Bronski and Dave Ellison were at the computer. They both looked up as she walked in.

Bronski sensed something was wrong. 'What's up? You look like you haven't slept. Did Captain Hegarty keep you up late?'

'There's some problems at home. My brother's in the hospital, so I had some early morning calls from Scotland, but I think he'll be OK. I'll fill you in on Captain Hegarty when you two are done.'

'If you're sure.' But even as he said it, Bronski sensed that it wasn't the time to ask any more details about her brother. He seemed to recall something about him having some sort of disability, but he would find out more later.

Annie wanted to focus on business. 'So what are you two up to?'

'We've got the original statement from Mr Moorcroft's ex-wife and an address. We're just running it through the computer to see if she still lives there.'

Ellison moved the mouse and clicked on the next page. 'There you go – Linda Moorcroft. Her name's the same, so it looks like she never remarried.'

Bronski made a note of the address. 'Perhaps we'll pay her a visit later. She's not too far from here.'

'Sounds good to me. Moorcroft gives me the creeps. I've also been wondering if we need to have another word with Jackie Winters. Maybe she's incurring his wrath as well. Trouble will be getting her on her own. She works and lives with him, so it won't be easy. Come to think of it, I didn't see her there yesterday when we went into his section. Thought they both worked there.'

'Maybe that section has more than one office. I might call her first. Ask her to come down here to speak to us. But now, let's get ourselves some coffee and catch up on Captain Hegarty.'

29

'Do you want to tell me about your brother first, get that off your mind?' Annie and Bronski were sitting in the interview room, away from the noise of the office. The coffee tasted good for a change; someone in the office knew how to make decent coffee. Annie was never one to bring personal problems to work, but somehow this seemed different. Bronski was easy to talk to and she knew she could trust him not to think less of her for getting this out in the open.

'Andrew is thirty-five, has Down's Syndrome and severe epilepsy, still lives with my mum. Last night he had a fit and fell out of bed and then had a second fit, so my mum telephoned for an ambulance. He had another seizure in the ambulance. Anyway, he's regained consciousness but is being kept in the hospital. The doctors want to review his medication. The problem is he really can't tell us how he is, as his speech is so limited. I'll ring my mum later to get an update, but so far, the worst seems to be over.'

'Is there anyone with your mother?'

'My Aunt Lil, mum's sister and her husband Alasdair. They're really close. They'll look after her.' Annie sipped her coffee, willing the coffee to wake her up some more.

'You thinking of going back?' Bronski sounded a bit concerned now.

'No, there isn't a lot I can do. Andrew's had problems all his life, as you can imagine. I love him, but practically, I'm not as much use as my aunt will be. I just need to stay in touch with them, if that's OK.' Annie put her cup down. She wanted to go back to being a detective.

'Fine by me. So, tell me about Captain Hegarty.'

'He's on leave for another six weeks and was going to split the time between Montana and here, staying with his sister. We obviously cut the Montana time down with our phone call. There's quite an age gap between them. He was just a kid when she left home and joined the army herself. She was going to train as an army nurse, but he says that she came back home within two years. He never really understood why she left the service. They've never talked about it. Maybe we should do some digging, look into her army career.'

'OK, we can do that. I presume she was Angela Hegarty then?'

'I checked that out. They are brother and sister, same parents despite the age gap. I wondered at first if they may have had different fathers, but no, she was a Hegarty, like him. She married her first husband about six months later. He remembered the exact date, as his dad died a month later, so he and his mom were then left on their own. It sounds as if the mother never got over her husband's death and Angela stayed close by and was there almost every day getting him ready for school, before she went off to work.' Annie hesitated for a moment, remembering that the next piece of information had been difficult for Charlie to say.

'He doesn't know for sure, but thinks that that was probably what broke up her first marriage. It didn't last two years at any rate. I got the name of the first husband, Dennis Cullen. Charlie says that Angela has never talked about him and he was too young when they got divorced to appreciate if they had any problems. Do you think we should check him out anyway? When you think back to the viciousness of the attack, it does make you wonder whether there has been a growing resentment for years, maybe something from the past that was never settled, going back even further than George Goodman. What do you think?'

Bronski had been nodding throughout. 'I think you've got a point. Too bad Captain Hegarty was so young at the time, but this is good. Anything else?'

Annie had been going from memory so far, but she got her notebook out now. When she'd arrived home the previous night, she'd written everything down while it was still fresh in her mind, surprising herself at how much she and Charlie had talked about. What she hadn't recorded was how fascinated she was with him.

'Let me see. He was in high school when Angela met George Goodman. Charlie thought at first that they were good for each other. George was more outgoing, more confident apparently, than he remembers Dennis Cullen to have been. But again, Charlie was a lot younger when he knew Dennis Cullen, so those observations may have been clouded by a child's view.'

'So, had Hegarty changed his mind about Goodman?

'He said at first Angela seemed really happy. He knew that she really wanted to get pregnant and had heard Angela and their mom discuss it from time to time. He then enlisted when he was eighteen and went off for basic training. So he lost the day-to-day contact,

143

but they kept in touch through their mom and directly. The mother died a few years ago. Charlie didn't go into any detail and I got the feeling that it wasn't straightforward. Maybe I will get some more if it seems relevant later on. I didn't want to push things last night.'

'But what was your impression?'

'He didn't say it, or I guess even really imply it. It was more what he didn't say. If I had to guess, I would say she committed suicide, but don't quote me on that. Let's see, what else?' Annie was scanning her notes again as her cell phone rang. She looked at the caller ID, then at Bronski. 'It's Captain Hegarty.'

'Take it, let's see what he has to say.' Bronski sat quietly, while Annie answered.

'I'm really sorry to hear that. When will they decide? I see, so you will be there the rest of the day, you think. Hmm ... I can ask about that, I'm not sure. I will check with Detective Bronski. If you are going to be there we may come by the hospital later ... We'll find you.' Annie clicked to end the call.

Bronski was waiting for the gist of the call to be relayed. Annie looked pensive. 'Angela Goodman has taken a turn for the worse. There is swelling in her brain. The doctors are deciding whether to operate later today. They want to do a few more tests first. Charlie is staying put at the hospital as he will have to sign as next of kin for the surgery.'

'Sounds bad, my guess is that this woman isn't going to make it and that we will soon be investigating a murder. What was it you were saying you need to check with me?'

'Charlie wants to know when he can stay in the house. He's asking if we have searched it enough for evidence, whether it is still a crime scene.'

Bronski looked quizzically at Annie. 'Strange that he wants to stay there, don't you think? Can't be short of money. I wouldn't think a few days in a motel would be out of his price range.'

'I don't think it's that. He strikes me as one of life's natural problem solvers. He wants his sister to pull through and the most practical thing he can do is to get the house back in order for her. My guess is that he'll want to repaint those walls.'

'You really think that's all there is to it?'

Annie nodded.

'OK, I'll check with Glen Heaviley and with Franconi. Meanwhile, write up your notes and then we'll pay the ex-Mrs Moorcroft a visit and then circle around to the hospital. I'd like to touch base with Captain Hegarty myself. I see that you are already on first name terms with him.'

Annie wondered if she should have referred to Charlie as Captain Hegarty as she was reporting back to Bronski. But he had asked her to address him as 'Charlie'. Perhaps she should have told Bronski that, but then decided not to make an issue of it.

30

He recognised the caller ID, the one they'd agreed on.

'Hi.'

'This waiting is getting to me.'

'I know, me too. I thought I'd got it right to start with. I should have used the knife. It's not like I don't know how to.'

'So, what's next? Keep waiting or what?'

'I've been doing some reconnaissance.'

'And?'

'Surprisingly easy to play being a priest and the hospital are pretty gullible. Meet your new Catholic chaplain.'

'A priest, eh? Never quite pictured you as that, I must admit.'

'Best way of getting past the cop outside the door. They must all be Catholics. Never even checked my ID. Just saw the collar and waved me through. I was tempted to bless the young officer and you'll love this next part.'

'What's that?'

'I gave her a blessing while I was in there. You know, like the one Father O'Brien used to give after confession. I got it down pat. Impressed myself.'

'Too bad your audience didn't appreciate it.'

'Maybe she will the next time.'

'So that's the new plan, is it?'

'I know it will work, just have to be sure to go when it's not visiting time. Wouldn't do to run into any visitors now, would it? Might ask me questions.'

'Guess not.'

'Let them all have another few days, she's not going

anywhere.'

'As long as you have a plan, I can wait a little longer.'

'Besides, He might do it for me and save me the trouble.'

'He?'

'God, of course, my new boss. I wish you could see me in the outfit.'

31

Surprisingly, the ex-Mrs Moorcroft hadn't changed her name, which Annie found a bit strange. Seemed that most women were going back to their maiden names after a divorce, at least most of the women she knew. Maybe it wasn't the same in the States. The woman who answered the door was pretty much as Annie had expected of a woman who had lived with an abuser. Her long brown hair looked as if it could do with a shampoo and her eyes narrowed as she opened the door. Her frame was willowy and even from the restricted view Annie had of her, she wondered whether this woman suffered from an eating disorder.

Although she'd been expecting them, she wouldn't open the door fully until she'd checked out both of their IDs. Annie thought she noticed a bit of a shake as she passed the IDs back and carefully opened the door to let them in. Without shaking hands or offering a drink, she led them into the living room of the house and motioned to them to take the two over-stuffed single chairs while she sat alone on the couch. She tucked her legs underneath her before she spoke a word and Annie thought she really just wanted to curl up in the foetal position and let the couch envelop her.

'So, you didn't explain a lot on the telephone, Detective Bronski, what do you want to know from me that isn't already on the record?'

Annie knew she might warm more to a woman asking the questions, but it was Bronski's turn.

'We appreciate that you might find it difficult talking about your ex-husband, Mrs Moorcroft.'

'Linda, please. I use the Mrs as little as possible.'

Bronski shifted slightly and then continued. 'We need to find out more about Mr Moorcroft's background. What he was like with you, the marriage ...'

The woman didn't let him finish before she cut in. 'So if I just say that he was a bastard and if I never saw him again it would be too soon, is that sufficient for you?' Linda Moorcroft folded her arms as she spoke and looked at Bronski with an intensity that was frightening. It appeared that she'd learned to be aggressive, after years of having aggression thrust upon her.

Women should judge whom they needed to direct that aggression at, rather than targeting the male population in general, thought Annie.

Bronski didn't acknowledge the question with an answer. 'The assault he was arrested for, was this out of character for him?'

Linda didn't answer him, instead turning directly toward Annie and fixing her with a stare. 'What do you think, Detective?'

Annie knew what Linda's game was. 'I expect it was a repeated pattern,' she found herself saying, more to lessen the hostility against Bronski, but also because in her experience these situations were never a single isolated event, no matter what the guy said. She thought back to the interview with Moorcroft and his indignation when the arrest was brought up. Annie knew then that this guy would make it a habit to abuse a woman like Linda Moorcroft. Had she detected any such signs with Jackie Winters? That would need to be explored further.

Linda unfolded her legs and leaned forward. Her elbows were resting on her knees, her hand rubbing her face, coming to rest over her mouth, as if she were willing her lips not to move, but at the same time wanting to get the words out, wanting desperately to purge herself of the memories.

'It started the first day of our honeymoon. The lovely sweet husband of the day and the night before, the man I had been engaged to, the man who was the love of my life, woke up as if he were a different person. Nothing was right, not with the motel room, with the food, with the sights we were seeing, or with me. Yes, mostly with me. I couldn't work out what I had done wrong. Of course, I convinced myself that it would be OK once we got back to our own apartment, once we started our married life, but it wasn't that different. Some days were OK while others were a nightmare. The abuse started in subtle ways: nothing physical at first, just me constantly trying to please him. Anticipating anything that could go wrong and trying not to let that happen, just so he would be in a good mood. It was as if I was on a tightrope with very little room to manoeuvre. I had to have everything so carefully balanced or something disastrous would happen and there was no safety net, believe me, nothing to catch me.'

She looked at the two of them and smiled. 'Actually when I think back on it now, that subtle abuse was worse than the physical abuse. When he started to hit me that felt better. It was more out in the open. It seemed logical somehow, like I really deserved it. Once

I got a good slap, it would then be OK. I was punished and it was over for a while. There were longer good periods in between the abuse, longer good periods than when the abuse had been more subtle. It was as if the physical abuse gave him a break and I convinced myself that if I could just get things right for him, it would all stop.' Linda hesitated for a moment, lost in thought. 'Once he went six months without hitting me and I got complacent.'

Annie knew how difficult this was for her. 'Can I get you a glass of water or anything?'

But it was as if Linda Moorcroft didn't hear the question. 'I should be OK with this by now. It's been nearly eight years. Just when I think I've moved on, it all comes back.' Linda Moorcroft buried her head in her hands and started to whimper gently.

Annie got up and went into the kitchen, coming back with a glass of water and a box of tissues she'd found on the side. She placed the water and tissues on the coffee table and sat down next to Linda Moorcroft, placing her arm on the woman's shoulder. It was the right thing to do in the circumstances and Linda Moorcroft didn't flinch.

It took another half hour to hear the rest of the marital history and how in the end Linda Moorcroft summoned up the courage to report her husband. Bronski was careful with his questions, but also thorough. Eventually, he extracted an admission of repeated marital rapes, which hadn't been reported before and for which Jim Moorcroft had never been charged. But Linda Moorcroft wasn't about to press charges now, just as she hadn't all those years ago. Tearfully she admitted that her husband had found her in bed with another man, just as he had told them. But unlike in his version, the adultery made sense, after a long history of abuse. Of course he had left all of that out. She'd taken the option of dropping the charges, as she knew Moorcroft would play the victim and more than likely get away with it. At least she'd had the courage to defy him and finally leave the marriage.

Annie and Bronski stopped for a sandwich on the way back to the station and decided to eat in the car, neither wanting to take the time to wait to be served.

'I don't know about you, but that bastard is certainly in my sights as Angela's attacker. It would explain the lack of a forced entry, the finger marks on the glass, the attentive visiting, maybe even the destructiveness. He sounds like a man who's filled with rage against women. The attack on Angela could be a repeated, much more destructive and violent part of his pattern,' Bronski offered.

Annie looked out the window. 'I see all that and I have seen it before. Men who move on to victim after victim, but something doesn't seem right for me and I'm not even sure what that is.'

Bronski looked over at Annie. 'So you don't think it's Moorcroft, then?'

She turned back to face him. 'Don't get me wrong, not that I don't think he's capable of it, but in this case it just seems too convenient. If he did it, he'd know we'd be able to trace his record and find out about the previous. I don't know, I just don't see him doing it. They were friends: there's no suggestion that there was anything more to it. What would be the motive?'

'You mean besides having a pathological hatred of women?' Bronski remarked.

'There is that.'

32

Gus had nearly lost it when the officer left the room, but he knew he had to stay composed. Finally the door to the interview room opened and Officer Brent came back in, followed by another man.

The second man held out his hand, 'Mr Wojinski, I'm Detective Malin, I'm investigating the crash this morning. I understand you are concerned that one of the cars might be your wife's? Could you please confirm the make of your wife's car?'

'A Volkswagen Beetle, cream coloured, two years old, good condition. She's a very safe driver.' Gus couldn't help but put up a defence of his wife and her driving skills.

Officer Brent looked at Detective Malin, waiting for him to explain what they knew so far.

'Mr Wojinski, both cars were burned pretty badly in the crash and we are still trying to identify exact details, but as you know, the Beetle is a distinctive shape and yes, we believe that one of the vehicles was a VW beetle. We also found the remains of a woman's body in the car.'

Gus Wojinski went very pale and his shoulders started to shake. He tried to speak but found that he couldn't. Describing his beautiful wife as 'remains' was more than he could bear.

'Sir, we can't be sure, but we will do everything we can to let you know as soon as possible if the victim is your wife. It would help if we could access her dental records.'

Gus found that he couldn't reply. He tried to say

something but no words came out.

Three hours later, Gus poured himself a large scotch in their kitchen. Carol's parents were travelling down from Maine and his mother had booked a flight for the next morning from Florida to be with her son. He kept trying to convince himself that it was all a mistake, but the reality was that it had to be Carol in that car. There was no other explanation as to why she wasn't there with him on the day they were waiting to learn if they were going to be parents.

33

The hospital parking lot was nearly full and Bronski knew he was lucky to get a space with afternoon visiting in full swing. Officer Collins was sitting outside Angela's room as the two detectives walked down the corridor. Although he knew both detectives by sight, he nevertheless asked for their IDs. Annie was impressed with his thoroughness. It might be needed.

'So who's been here today?' Annie asked, as she nodded at the closed door of Angela's room.

'Captain Hegarty is in there now. He arrived at ten and has been here most of the day. Doctors and nurses have been in and out. Jackie Winters was here this morning for about an hour.'

'On her own?' This time it was Bronski.

'Yeah and no sign of the other guy, Jim Moorcroft. But I understand he's been banned from visiting, that right?'

Bronski nodded. 'For now, at any rate.'

'Oh, and that new priest, Father Loftus, was here again, his second visit. Only stayed a few minutes. He told me on his way out that he was praying for her. Captain Hegarty missed him by a minute or two. He'd gone for a coffee. I asked Father Loftus if he wanted to meet Mrs Goodman's brother, but he said he had a number of other patients to see.'

'Is that the same priest who was here the other day?' Annie recalled previous mention of a visiting priest and she couldn't help thinking that Angela Goodman needed a miracle, never mind a priest giving her a blessing or whatever he did.

'Yes, I was on duty then as well.'

'Good. Keep up with the running log of everyone who enters this room. We still don't have her attacker yet.' Collins nodded and Annie and Bronski knocked softly and then let themselves into the room.

Annie introduced Charlie to Bronski and the two men shook hands. Charlie looked physically more tired than the last time Annie had seen him and she felt concerned about the strain this was having on him. Bronski appeared uncomfortable in the room. Annie had to admit that the noise of the machines was distracting and Angela looked worse than the last time they'd seen her. In this room, Annie was reminded that her brother Andrew was also lying in a hospital bed. If he woke up attached to lots of monitors and wires, he would start to pull them out, no matter how ill he was. Usually they had to keep him heavily sedated to prevent that. What would it be like for Angela Goodman if she came out of the coma?

'Have you heard any more from the doctors?' Annie asked, just as Charlie got up from his chair and offered it to her. She put her hand up to signal that she was OK standing. Bronski too was standing but Annie noticed that he was shifting uneasily on the opposite side of the room.

'They are waiting for some more test results but they are hoping to reach a decision late this afternoon about whether they will operate again or not. They are going to discuss all the options with me, then I will have to decide, as her next of kin, what to do.' Charlie hesitated for a moment before continuing. 'I told her once that if I was ever sent home in that kind of state and she had to make a decision about me, just to let me go. I said I wouldn't want to be kept alive artificially or end up in a persistent vegetative state. I said to tell them to switch off the machines.' He was speaking in a very low voice and Bronski moved closer to hear him.

'What did she say to that?' Annie found herself asking.

'Something like she could never make a decision to let me go, that she had promised my mother that she would always take care of me, that she would get another opinion, but she never said what I should do if it was the other way around.' Hegarty looked at them both, but neither detective knew what to say in reply.

The three of them stayed quiet for the next few minutes, Charlie lost in his own thoughts and Annie and Bronski feeling responsible for Angela lying there and determined to find her attacker.

Finally Annie broke the silence. 'Officer Collins said that Jackie Winters was here this morning.'

'She's been here every day. Takes some the burden off me, although I don't suppose Angie knows that either one of us is here, but the doctors keep saying to talk to her. I only saw Jackie briefly. I went down to get us both a coffee and then she joined me in the canteen for a few minutes before she left to go back to work.'

Annie saw that his eyes were filling up. If Bronski hadn't been there, she would have touched his arm but felt too embarrassed in front of Bronski. Yet, she knew she had to pursue something with him, in as gentle a way as she could.

'Has Jackie mentioned anything about Jim Moorcroft?'

'What do you mean? She lives with the guy, works with him. What are you asking exactly?' He was paying close attention to her now and Annie didn't want to make him suspicious yet. She wasn't sure what Jim Moorcroft might have said to Jackie about being banned from the hospital room.

'We're just trying to understand a bit more about the relationship between Jim Moorcroft, your sister and Jackie Winters.'

'What's to understand? They're all friends. Jim was the one who introduced Jackie to Angie. He was friends with Angie first, friends with both her and George. But I think Jackie is closer to Angie now. Sometimes they seem to me to be like sisters.'

Annie didn't pursue the matter any further knowing that Charlie had a difficult night ahead of him. But she knew that she wanted to talk to Jackie Winters again and find out whether she was another victim of Jim Moorcroft's.

Just as they were leaving, Charlie called after them. 'Have you heard when I'll be able to move into Angie's?'

Annie looked at Bronski, but he waited for her to reply. 'We're still waiting for clearance from Glen Heaviley. Oh, and when we get it, we can put you in touch with a specialist cleaning company.'

'Thanks, that would be a help.'

34

As the two detectives walked out of the hospital, Annie suggested one more stop before they returned to the station. Bronski was sceptical. 'She won't want to see us at work. He's in the same section, isn't he?'

'But they live together as well, so I think work is a better bet. I'll telephone ahead and ask her to meet us in their canteen. She'll have to think up some excuse to tell him, unless she wants to tell him the truth.'

As she'd suspected, Jackie Winters wanted to speak to them privately and suggested that they meet in the local mall after she finished work. She and Jim travelled to work in separate cars, so it wasn't unusual for her to do some shopping on her way home.

Annie and Bronski were already in Starbucks when Jackie Winters walked through the door. For the first time, Annie noticed how slender she was; one of those women who looked like they needed to be protected by a man. It also stuck her, how alike Jackie Winters and Linda Moorcroft were physically. Annie wondered whether Jim chose that body shape on purpose. Jackie's long hair was pulled tightly back into a ponytail, which made her look even younger. But her face was tense and Annie sensed that she would rather be anywhere else but meeting with them.

Bronski stood up as she approached the table. Five minutes earlier, Annie had selected the table with care, set back in the corner of the room, a fair distance from the next couple three tables away. It was important for them to be able to speak in relative privacy.

'Can I get you something?' Bronski enquired and Jackie noticed that the two detectives already had their coffees.

'A skinny cappuccino, no chocolate on top,' came the reply, as Jackie Winters slid the chair back.

Annie thought she would try and break the ice. 'Nice mall: it's the first time I've been here. I don't recognise most of the women's stores. They're different from the ones I'm used to, although there are a few universal chain stores.'

'I wouldn't know. I have never been outside the US. I have no desire to travel to Europe either, so I will have to take your word for it.' Jackie hadn't so much as looked at Annie as she said those words, keeping an eye instead on Bronski as he approached their table with her drink. She also seemed to be scanning the whole coffee shop, perhaps anxious that one of their colleagues might be in there or pass by and see her.

'One skinny cappuccino, hold the chocolate.' Bronski placed the drink in front of Jackie who barely nodded a thank you. Bronski glanced at Annie to see if any start had been made, but her face indicated that he should take over.

'Thank you for agreeing to meet us. We just had a few more questions to ask you, Ms Winters.'

'I prefer to be addressed as Jackie.'

'OK, Jackie, we interviewed your 'partner', if that is the correct terminology for Mr Moorcroft?' Bronski faced her directly, but Jackie's eyes were still scanning the room. She just nodded, so Bronski continued. 'He may have told you that we found his finger marks on a glass in the kitchen.'

'So what? Jim and I were always at Angie's. We probably saw her once or twice a week. Both our finger marks will be all over her house. That glass could have been there for days.'

Annie felt that Jackie was getting overly defensive. Bronski was simply stating evidence found to date, so Annie decided to make an observation to test Jackie's reaction. 'Somehow, I doubt that, seeing how meticulous Angela Goodman was.'

'So you knew her, did you? Seems to me that you are covering up for not believing her in the first place. If you had taken her seriously then maybe none of this would have happened. I certainly wouldn't be sitting with you now.'

Annie knew there was an element of truth in what this woman was saying, but that wasn't the point any more. The point was to find her attacker.

Bronski stepped in again. 'Did he mention to you that he went into the house when he picked her up or when he dropped her off the night she was attacked?'

'I can't remember that we talked about that specifically but I think it is one of those things. We go in her house so often that you forget if you did it that one night or not. I remember he was running late that night because he was helping me get the meal ready and also had to pick Angie up. Sometimes Angie is waiting by the door and comes out just as you pull up in front of the house. Other times, you go up to the door. I know I have done both but I can't say what Jim did that night.

It wouldn't surprise me if he couldn't remember. It's a bit like going out your door and forgetting if you locked it or not. Then if someone asks you directly, it's even harder to remember. But surely, if he attacked Angie he would have been careful not to leave his finger marks behind, wouldn't he?'

'Maybe he would simply have said that he's in her house a lot and that his finger marks were likely to be all over the house. And you would have corroborated that?' Bronski was not giving up any ground.

Annie could tell that there was something about Jackie's tone that Bronski didn't like either. She felt it would be more fruitful to get into Jackie Winters' relationship with Moorcroft and she was waiting for an opportune moment to bring that up. But for now, it was still Bronski's interview.

'Tell us again what Mr Moorcroft was like when he came home.'

Jackie straightened up in her chair. 'I told you already, Detective. I was asleep. I loaded the last few things in the dishwasher and got myself ready for bed. I fell asleep as soon as my head hit the pillow. I'd had enough wine.'

But Bronski interrupted her. 'What time was that then?'

'I don't know the precise time. I wasn't exactly keeping track. I guess it was well past eleven. From the time they left the house until I fell asleep was probably less than twenty minutes. I was too tired to do more than I have just told you.'

'And you didn't wake up when Mr Moorcroft came

in?'

'No, he has a routine. Often he has another drink downstairs, puts some music on low. Doesn't switch on loads of lights. I hardly ever hear him come in, if I go to bed when he's out. I'm a deep sleeper.'

Annie decided it was time to change tack. 'He sounds like a very considerate man.'

Jackie turned to her. 'What is that supposed to mean?'

'Most considerate men don't have tempers.' Annie was trying to see how Jackie would respond.

'Are you giving me a lesson in men, Detective? Only I haven't come here for that. If we're finished, I have some shopping to do and I'd like to get started.' Jackie appeared to be reaching for her handbag.

'Just a couple more questions, so we don't have to disturb you at work again.' That got Jackie's attention. 'What is Mr Moorcroft's temper like?'

'I never said he had a temper and I don't know what you are implying.' Her tone was getting indignant.

'What I am getting at is that we know Mr Moorcroft has a temper and that he has used it in the past. But maybe you didn't know about that. Maybe he hasn't shown it to you, or maybe it's only a matter of time. I presume you know he was married before.'

'He told me that soon after we met. But they split up a long time ago. He has no contact with her now. I don't even know her name. He never talks about her. What are you saying? Is there more to it?'

'He was arrested for an assault on his ex-wife. It would be in your interests to tell us if he is hurting you.' But before Annie could finish her sentence, Jackie Winters grabbed her handbag and left without another word.

Neither detective tried to stop her.

'Well, what do you make of that?' Bronski asked, as he took the last swig of his coffee.

Annie pushed her cup away and commented, 'I suspect she tries very hard not to be on the receiving end of his wrath. My bet is that she's a victim too.'

'I'll drop you home unless you want to go back to the station for anything,' said Bronski as they got up to leave.

'Thanks. I'll take you up on the offer. I need to contact my mum. It's close to eleven pm in Scotland now. Hopefully she'll be at home, not still at the hospital. She won't mind if I wake her.'

Annie realised she'd been distracted most of the day and hadn't given a lot of thought to Andrew. But she knew if there had been a crisis, her mother would have found a way of getting a message through to her, so no news was good news. Yet, she still had that pang of guilt about not being closer to home, even though Stockport, where she lived in England, was a good five hundred miles from her mum and Andrew in Huntly. She also wondered if her ex-fiancé Paul might have been at the hospital. Sometimes it upset her how Paul stayed in touch with her mother. It was as if she couldn't move on with her life, without him always being in the background. And she knew that her mother still hoped the two of them might get back together again.

'So tomorrow we need to summarise where we are

for Franconi. You still having doubts about Moorcroft?' Bronski glanced at her while still watching the traffic.

'Still that nagging doubt, but I'm not sure why. Wish we got more out of Jackie. Did you notice how similar she is body type wise, hair colour and hair style to Linda Moorcroft?'

'Now you mention it. You think he goes for a certain type, sort of fragile looking?'

'Something like that.'

By the time they reached Annie's place they'd decided how they were going to approach the review with Franconi. It still bothered them that a week after the assault they were no closer to charging anyone.

35

Jackie Winters was too angry to go straight home. The shopping had been a ruse to get out of Starbucks. In some ways, she didn't care if she was going to be late home. She was sick of having to be good and fed up trying to please a man who could be so utterly selfish when he wanted to be. She opened her cell phone in the car and went to the contacts list. The phone answered on the third ring. 'Hi, it's Jackie. How are things? Is there any news?'

'Still waiting for the doctors. Should be within the next half hour. Were you thinking of coming over?'

'I can if you want me to. I'm at the mall, but I can be there in twenty minutes.' Once they agreed, Jackie closed her phone and then opened it again. She composed a text message to Jim; no point in antagonising him unnecessarily.

Jackie checked her cell phone as soon as she parked. His return text was abrupt, simply telling her that he would be out and not to wait up. That was a coded message that he was getting up to his usual tricks. She switched off the phone and locked the car, her mood getting darker by the minute.

Arriving on the ward, one of the nurses recognised her. 'Captain Hegarty is in the staff room with two of the surgeons. The meeting has only just begun.'

'Thanks' said Jackie. 'Can I wait for him in Angie's room?'

'Of course.'

Jackie nodded to the officer outside the room and he

put her name in the book. He knew it by now.

Sitting down beside Angie, Jackie tried to second-guess the doctors and the conversation they would be having at that very minute with Charlie. It didn't look good. She almost felt that it would be better if the machine just went wrong and all this could be over. She had the weirdest sensation that she should simply switch off the machine. Then Charlie wouldn't be in this difficult dilemma, wouldn't have to make a decision that he would have to live with for the rest of his life, blaming himself, when he was the least to blame of anyone. Would the machine have to stay off long she wondered or would it be enough to switch it off and then switch it straight back on? But the action wasn't hers to take. She knew that, no matter what, it wasn't her action to take.

She suspected Charlie wouldn't be long. She'd grown quite fond of him over the last few days, so different from Jim. Charlie was the kind of guy every woman wanted: very good looking and caring, loyal, but there was no point. They were in different leagues.

A few moments later, the door opened, bringing her out of her reverie. Charlie was ashen and she knew from the look on his face that the news wasn't good. Jackie stood up, not knowing what to say, suddenly feeling awkward.

For what seemed like minutes, Charlie stood at the end of the bed, his gaze focused intensely on his sister, lying there so helplessly. Then he put his hands to his face and his shoulders started to shake. Without hesitation, Jackie got up and put her arms around him, while he fought to hold back the tears.

The canteen didn't offer a lot of privacy, but there were so few people around, they managed to find a quiet section. Jackie came back with two coffees and a sandwich for Charlie. She knew from his brief comments that he hadn't eaten since lunchtime. She placed the coffees and the sandwich on the table. He had managed to compose himself by the time they'd gotten to the canteen. He looked at the sandwich briefly but then pushed it to one side.

'I'm sorry, I don't think I can eat. You have it, if you want.'

Jackie leaned over and put her hand on his. Charlie didn't pull away, like Jim usually did. Everything was always on his terms. 'Tell me what the doctors said,' Jackie whispered, not moving her hand until he looked at her.

'They want to operate again. They think it's her only chance. The tests show that the brain has been swelling. If they do nothing, the chances of her surviving are virtually non-existent. But the operation is also extremely risky. Essentially she could die on the operating table. But even if she survives the surgery, it could still be days before we know whether she will come through or not. I have to give them an answer in an hour. They'll perform the surgery tonight if I'm prepared to sign the consent form.'

'Charlie, I'm so sorry. I don't know what to say. Have you made a decision?'

Charlie shut his eyes and rubbed them with his hands. 'When I was little, she was like a mother to me. Our mom was never well. Some days she never got out of bed. After my dad's death, she lost the will to go on.

Not even two kids who depended on her could make her get out of bed some days. Angie was my mother for all intents and purposes. She dropped me off at school and then went on to the high school. She sometimes skipped her last class to get back in time for me. She missed out on so much: after school activities, sports, you name it. She had responsibilities no kid that age should have. It was only when one of my aunts moved in with us that Angie was set free. Then she joined the army and I didn't see her for six months while she was on basic training.'

'She never told me any of that, just talked about how much she loved you. She's so proud of you.' Jackie was holding her coffee but hadn't yet taken a drink from it. Charlie hadn't touched his either.

The canteen was starting to fill up now, the night shift coming on duty, grabbing a sandwich for later and a coffee for now. Charlie was momentarily distracted and reached for his own cup. When he placed it back down, he said to Jackie: 'What would you do?'

Jackie didn't answer right away, mulling over the question in her mind. 'I can't answer that. I don't think from what I know of Angie that she would want to remain like she is now. She wouldn't want to be dependent. I guess you need to think about whether you believe the surgery can change that or not.'

'I'm sorry, I had no right to put you in that position.'

'Charlie, I'm her friend and although you and I have only just recently met, I feel like I've known you for ages. Angie talked about you so much. So you have every right to ask me what I think. I just can't give you an answer.'

'I'm going back to the ward now. Are you staying or leaving?'

'I'll finish my coffee and follow you up and then sit with you for a little while.'

Charlie left the canteen without another word. When he was out of sight, Jackie opened her cell phone.

36

Mrs Wojinski was fussing around Gus and it was starting to get on his nerves. He began to feel that maybe he would have been better off on his own. After all, he was going to have to start getting used to that. The thought brought on another bout of crying and he stepped out on to the porch so her solicitations would be left back in the room. It was just starting to get dark and he noticed the fireflies lighting up the bushes. Memories of the many nights that he and Carol had sat out on this porch overwhelmed him. Slamming his fists against the railing he nearly screamed. But what good would that do except to bring out more of a reaction from his mother? Hearing the phone ring, he rushed back into the house.

His mother was standing at the kitchen counter with the phone in her hand. 'Yes Detective Malin, this is Madeline Wojinski, Gus's mother. Yes, he is right here. I'll pass the phone to him.'

Gus had all he could do not to grab it off her.

'I wondered if I could come over to your house, only some jewellery has been found at the scene which is still recognisable. We wondered if you might be able to identify it. Would now be convenient?'

Gus placed the phone back in its cradle.

'Detective Malin is on his way. They've found some jewellery and want to see if I can identify it. I need a few minutes on my own. Do you mind?'

'Of course not. I'll get some fresh coffee on for Detective Malin.'

Maybe I can do something useful, thought Gus, as

he went into their bedroom. Carefully he took Carol's jewellery box out from the top drawer of the chest of drawers and placed it on the bed. Not having seen her leave for work that last morning, he couldn't be sure what jewellery she was wearing, so he scanned the box to work out what was missing.

Touching various items made memories come flooding back of times she'd worn the pieces. Concentrate, he said to himself. Then he noticed that the gold necklace with her birthstone was not in its usual place. It was one of her favourites. Also missing was her gold watch, his first Christmas present to her after they were married and of course, her wedding ring. She never took that off her finger, insisting that it was bad luck to remove it. Earrings, yes the ones that matched the necklace were also missing.

Shutting the box, he put it back in its place and went into the bathroom. Looking in the mirror, he hardly recognised himself. Dark circles had started to form beneath his eyes and they were red from the crying. Pull yourself together man was all he could say to himself. He had to face this next bit – maybe it wasn't Carol, after all. But that thought only comforted him for a second. If it wasn't her, then where was she?

When the doorbell rang, he let his mother answer it.

Detective Malin took a seat at the breakfast bar opposite Gus. Mrs Wojinski busied herself serving coffee.

'I'm sorry Mr Wojinski, I know this is difficult. The body we found in the car was moved to the ME's office this afternoon for examination. The jewellery was removed from the body. I'm afraid it has to remain in the evidence bags, but I wonder if you recognise any of the pieces.'

Malin carefully placed the four bags on the Formica surface of the breakfast bar, studying Gus for any reaction. Picking up the bag with the birthstone necklace first, Gus rubbed his fingers over it as if that might somehow bring his wife back. But when he touched his wife's wedding ring, he felt his stomach lurch. Rushing out of the room, he only just made it to the bathroom.

Mrs Wojinski took her son's place at the breakfast bar and touched each of the bags in turn. 'I remember her opening up the box at Christmas and how happy she was with this watch. It's inscribed on the back.' Then, as she lined it up with the other items, Gus came back into the room. Without comment, his mother slid off the stool to allow her son to take his seat again.

Gus touched each of the bags again and then finally commented. 'All of these items are my wife's, Detective. Will I be able to have them back at some stage?'

'Just as soon as I can release them. I am so sorry for your loss Sir. We will do everything we can to work out what caused the accident.'

Mrs Wojinski showed the Detective to the door. By the time she returned to the kitchen, her son had retreated to the side porch again and she heard the sound of the swing seat. By now it was very dark and she knew he needed time on his own. When the phone rang, she went to answer it. It was Carol's parents, who had just settled into their motel room. It was left to her to tell them what had just transpired. At least they had each other for comfort.

37

Annie noticed the light blinking on the answer machine as she shut the apartment door behind her. The shock on her face was visible when she heard Paul's voice. 'Annie, your mum asked me to ring as she doesn't want to leave Andrew. He's better and the doctors think he will wake soon. Your mum wants to be there when he does.' There was a slight pause. 'I guess it's about five-thirty for you. I'm leaving the hospital now. I have to get back to Stockport. I was home for a few days seeing my folks when I heard about Andrew so I came over to see if I could help. Your aunt is with your mum.' His voice became more hesitant and Annie found that she was holding her breath waiting for him to continue. 'Your mum says you like the placement, um, Annie, I miss you.' And there the message ended.

As the last few words were said, Annie realised she'd begun to cry. Right now she could curl up beside Paul and be perfectly happy, but she knew it wouldn't last and that he deserved better. Hearing his voice again, hearing him say that he missed her brought back all the emotion, the trauma of the cancelled wedding. What would have happened if she'd been at home and answered the phone? She wasn't sure she would have coped with talking to Paul.

She wandered aimlessly into the kitchen, not sure what to do next. There was no point in trying to ring her mother, as she knew that her phone would be switched off. And it sounded as if Andrew would pull through. She was tempted to replay the message again but what good would that do?

As she opened the door of the refrigerator, she was startled by the sound of the phone. She picked it up and without thinking, blurted out 'Mum?'

'Annie, it's Dave. Sorry, are you expecting a call?'

'Sorry Dave, I just had a message on my machine from a friend. My mum is at my brother's bedside. I just thought she might have taken a break to give me a ring.'

'So I guess you want to stay put, in case she does try, but have you eaten?' Ellison's voice was comforting.

'No, I was just trying to see what I had in to throw together, but I'm not inspired.' Annie felt herself relax.

'How about I pick up a pizza and swing by. I could be there in half an hour; that way you can stay by the phone.'

Annie's instinct told her this wasn't a good idea, but after the day she'd had and the lack of sleep last night, she wasn't in the mood to argue. 'Thanks Dave, that would be lovely. I'll see you in half an hour.'

*****

Charlie spent another twenty minutes with the doctors and gave them his decision. He wanted the surgery. He wanted his sister back. If there was even the slightest chance that could happen, he couldn't deny her that. The doctor said that he would schedule it for later that evening and advised Charlie to have a break; it was going to be a long night.

Suddenly Charlie felt like eating something decent, not a hospital sandwich. As he passed the waiting room, he spotted Jackie flicking through a magazine. He had forgotten she'd said she would wait. She looked up as he stopped at the door. 'Surgery is later tonight. I'm going to wait in Angela's room, but first I need something to eat. Have you got to get back or can you join me?'

The diner was only a block away so the two of them walked in the warm night air. 'It feels good to get out of that place, if only for a short time. I'm not used to sitting around.'

Jackie smiled. 'No, a regular action man, aren't you? Someone used to being in control, knowing who the enemy is.'

'I wouldn't go that far,' Charlie quipped as he opened the door of the diner.

Once their orders had been taken, Charlie took a sip of his beer. 'I needed that.'

'I guess you must be really worried. What do the doctors think the outcome will be?'

'You know how cautious doctors are, but they think she'll have a better chance than if they don't operate. Look, could we talk about something else while we're eating. I won't be able to hold it together otherwise.' And with that, he picked up his glass and finished off his drink. The waitress noticed and asked him if he wanted another. 'Why not, it's going to be a long night.' The waitress smiled, no doubt envisaging a much better night for Charlie than it was going to be.

'I could stay with you, you know, wait for the news.' Jackie reached over and touched his arm for the second time that evening.

Charlie glanced down at her hand but didn't attempt to move it. 'Thanks, Jackie, but I'm sure Jim is expecting you back.' Her facial expression made him realise something was wrong. 'What's the matter?'

Jackie looked away for a moment, the colour in her cheeks rising. 'I wasn't going to mention this. You have enough to think about.'

'Jackie?'

'OK, I was interviewed by the two detectives again this afternoon.' She hesitated, as the waitress brought over a basket of bread and another beer for Charlie. 'They asked again about the night Angela was attacked, about Jim, about when he got home.'

'Surely, they can't think he had anything to do with it.' Charlie was trying not to raise his voice, but all the time he was thinking that the two detectives were pulling at straws. 'Angie always talked about Jim, what a good friend, surely?'

'Sometimes appearances can be deceiving.'

'What are you saying Jackie? Tell me, I need to know.' There was a hint of irritation in his voice now.

'I'm sorry Charlie, you're right, they were good friends and Jim is very fond of Angela. I wasn't trying to imply the two of them had a problem.'

'Then what are you saying?' But before Jackie could answer, the waitress was back with their meals. It took a few minutes to unload her tray and see that they had everything they needed.

'You're starving, let's eat and then I will tell you more over coffee. Meanwhile, tell me about this fishing trip you were having when you got the phone call.'

Charlie wanted to know what was going on, but

178

when he saw the food, he suddenly realised how little he had eaten over the past few days and how tired he was. He needed the food so that he could cope with what was to come, back at the hospital and also, for what else Jackie might have to say. He didn't know the woman all that well really, just through Angela and he had never spent any time alone with her. But he knew how close she and Angie were, so that counted for a lot with him. He also remembered the question Annie had asked him about Jim, Jackie and his sister. What exactly was happening here?

38

He was pacing up and down the kitchen, holding the photograph of Angela Goodman she'd given him that night. He'd described the one he wanted and she knew it immediately. He knew at the time she was only trying to pacify him. Telling him lies. Saying how sorry she was; saying those things so he wouldn't hurt her.

Now, all these days later, he got it out of the drawer and took it over to the table, placing it down carefully so he could study it. Under the kitchen light, she almost seemed to have a halo around her. Twisting his whisky glass in his hand, he knew that he could never accept what she did to him, that whatever revenge he was taking would never be enough. It would never make up for the consequences of her actions.

Suddenly he picked up the photograph again, talking to her, wanting her to hear his words.

'Angela ... you bitch. You know how long I'd been planning this? Yes, since the day of your lies. How could you? I loved you – you knew that. How could you turn it into something so dirty? All those gifts I gave you. All my time, all my attention. I wanted you to have all those things. I wanted you to have me. You deserved me.'

'And you know bitch that she didn't deserve it. You knew she relied on me. Even when you had become my world. I was prepared to give everything up for you. She noticed how I had changed. How my affections were elsewhere and I think she was jealous of you, of how you were stealing my soul. How could you not know the effect you had on me? How could you stand there and tell all those lies? Make me sound like a madman. You twisted everything.'

'How could I fail? When it came to it, you wouldn't even admit it was your fault. You said some awful things, still twisting the truth. You said it was because of me, not because of you. How could you say that? That was worse than all those lies you told in that courtroom. The way you made everyone believe you. They were taken in by you, just like I was.'

'But I won't fail again. I owe it to her.'

He stared at the photograph for a long time in complete silence, finally picking up the whisky glass again and swigging the remainder. Then he took the photograph over to the sink and held his lighter to one corner. He smiled as he saw the last burning fragment fall into the sink.

39

It was unusual for Jackie not to answer her phone and Jim was getting very irritated. When he thought about it, it seemed that she'd been getting more secretive of late. There had been more trips to the mall, with precious little shopping to show for it. Maybe she was having an affair. Once or twice when her cell phone rang, she disappeared into the kitchen. She never left it lying about so he might chance on answering it. Whenever he questioned her, it was always a wrong number or her service provider wanting to offer her free minutes or something. There had to be more to it.

'God damn you, Jackie, pick the phone up.' The cell phone went on to her voicemail before he slammed the phone down on the kitchen counter, got his coat on and grabbed his car keys for the second time that evening.

*****

Dave Ellison poured them each a glass of wine. Annie had had just enough time to tidy up the apartment and have a quick shower before he arrived. After the day she'd had, she needed to relax. The message from Paul had really spooked her. She didn't know what she would have done or how she would have felt if she'd been home to answer it. But there was that selfishness again: thinking of herself and her reactions, rather than the content of the message. Andrew was going to pull through. She swore he had nine lives, just like the kitten her parents had bought them when they were little. Andrew didn't really know how to treat a kitten and Annie was jealous because no matter how overly enthusiastic Andrew was with the kitten, it followed him everywhere. Annie could never entice the kitten to play. The memory made her smile.

'Is this a Scottish custom, eating pizza on a plate with a knife and fork.' Ellison's comment brought her out of her reverie.

Annie looked at the neatly set table and smiled. 'Sorry, I forgot how informal you Americans are. I'm used to eating pizza at the dinner table with a knife and fork, but I am happy to bow to my host country's customs.' She started to remove the cutlery, but Ellison reached over and took her hand to stop her. His touch made her blush and she had to look away, hoping he didn't notice.

Ellison smiled, 'I couldn't make you change who you are: the table it is'. As he brought the two glasses of wine over and sat down, Annie apologised again for her wet hair. Ellison didn't seem to mind.

'Haven't seen much of you the last day or two. Are you getting some breaks with the case or is Bronski just wanting to keep you to himself?'

Annie laughed. 'I think it's 'No' to both of those. We're keeping a close eye on Jim Moorcroft, the guy with the previous you found, although somehow I'm not convinced. His ex-wife seems pretty frightened of him, even though she hasn't seen him for years. From what she told us, he did more to her than came out in the records.'

Ellison was already on his second piece of pizza, when he noticed Annie looking at him quizzically. 'Sorry, I'll slow down. I didn't realise how starving I was. You were saying?'

'Maybe I better eat and not talk if I'm going to have any of this pizza.'

'OK, I hear you. I'm stopping now till you catch up.'

Annie took a few bites and had some wine while Ellison leaned back in the chair, completely relaxed. Annie could tell that he enjoyed being right where he was, but now she was feeling self-conscious. He really was quite attractive and she was feeling more like abandoning the pizza altogether and curling up on the couch next to him. But her personal rule about relationships at work nagged at the back of her mind. 'Now you are embarrassing me. Eat will you?'

Ellison laughed and then picked up another piece of pizza. 'So you were saying about the ex-wife.'

'She was really nervous talking to us, almost as if we might bring her into contact with him again. Obviously, the last thing she wanted.'

'So, there was more to it than just the loss of temper he claimed it was?'

'Aye, including marital rape which she never reported.'

'Um.'

'Then, of course, once we finished interviewing her, we were interested in whether or not he was still abusing women. He had been so adamant when we interviewed him that what had happened with his ex-wife was a single event, that he was provoked. Well, you know the story and you've probably heard stories like it a hundred times.'

Ellison nodded. 'I was called out to a lot of domestic violence cases when I was a rookie. The thing I never understood was how the women always went back. We'd go to the same houses over and over.'

'I know, depressing, isn't it? I don't know how some cops specialise in domestic violence. Anyway, so you see where we were coming from. I was convinced he'd still be at it, so we also interviewed Jackie Winters, the woman he lives with now.' Annie paused to sip some wine and have more pizza.

'Isn't she the good friend of Angela's who's been keeping a vigil at the hospital? The cops stationed outside the room have mentioned her.'

'Aye, she seems very close to Angela, although she met her through Jim Moorcroft who has known Angela for years. Jackie Winters came on the scene a year or two ago and moved in with Moorcroft soon after. All three of them work together. Angela is the section manager, so in effect, they both work for her.'

'Interesting that she was Moorcroft's boss.'

'Interesting how?'

'I was just wondering how things were at work. Was Moorcroft frustrated that he was in a junior position to Angela? Were they really friends or did he harbour some resentment towards her? Did she get a promotion that he went for too, that kind of thing? Just a thought.'

'Thanks, I'll try and get some more details, find out if they ever competed for the job, but what I was leading on to was our talk with Jackie Winters. I was surprised that she really took umbrage at our questions, especially when we asked if she'd experienced his temper. Suffice it to say, she stormed out.'

'Your interpretation of that being?' Ellison was cradling his wine glass, having had his fill of the pizza.

'I think she has been his victim too, but maybe she's too frightened to say anything to us.'

'Wouldn't be the first time, would it?'

*****

Charlie knew that there was still something on Jackie's mind. They hadn't finished the conversation about the interview with the two detectives. The plates had been cleared away and they were both having coffee. No chance of being interrupted by the waitress for a little while. The time was right to bring it up again.

'There's something else, isn't there? You've listened to me all night, now is there something more about the interview with the two detectives?'

'A perceptive male and still a bachelor. How does that happen?' Jackie had a twinkle in her eye.

Charlie knew he was blushing. Even though he was a captain in the army and had just finished a tour of active duty in Afghanistan, part of him was still that scared little boy: wanting his big sister to take care of him; wanting his mother's love that he'd never had. 'Come on, this is about you now, not me. There's something the matter, isn't there?'

Jackie had been drawing imaginary circles with her coffee spoon on the table. Now she looked up at him, her eyes immensely sad. 'You have enough on your mind, this isn't really your problem,' she said hesitantly.

'Jackie, you've been at the hospital day and night since Angie was admitted. I owe you. So tell me, what was said in the interview that's bothered you?' Charlie had put his coffee cup to one side and was focusing all his attention on her.

It was a good feeling for her, but not something that could go anywhere.

'I guess it's probably the third time I have seen those two detectives. I find Detective Bronski all right, but that Scottish woman is too abrupt for my liking.'

Charlie kept his own counsel on that one. 'Was it her manner or something she said or asked that's bothering you?'

'A bit of both, really. She said that Jim had been married before, but I knew that; he's told me. Something happened in the past. Detective Macpherson said he'd been arrested for assaulting her while they were still married.'

'What do you mean? Has he been in prison? Did you know about that?'

'Charlie, are you accusing me of something?' Jackie was getting visibly upset.

'No, of course not. It's just that he was the last one to see Angie, drove her home. What if something happened, what if he ...?'

'Stop it! I would know.' Then Jackie started to fill up with tears. 'Excuse me a minute, I'm going to ...' She was up before she could finish the sentence. The waitress saw the sudden departure and Charlie asked for the check somewhat abruptly. He was standing with Jackie's sweater by the entrance to the diner as she came out.

Franconi was in his room expecting them. Annie remembered not to bring in her Starbuck's coffee. She'd been warned that Franconi never drank the stuff and brewed his own. After he got up and poured himself a second cup, he looked at the two of them. 'Want one?'

Both detectives politely refused, so Franconi sat back down at his desk, ready for business.

'So how goes it?' He took a sip of his coffee and then picked up a paper clip and started cleaning under his fingernails. Annie hoped that her face didn't show that she would have preferred him just to toy with it.

The two detectives didn't hesitate. They'd already decided that Bronski would take the lead. 'We've just been in touch with the hospital. Angela Goodman was operated on again in the early hours of this morning. She survived the second bout of brain surgery but has still not regained consciousness. The doctors have said that the next forty-eight hours will be critical.'

Franconi's face, for once, seemed to be expressing genuine concern. 'Well at least we're not into a murder inquiry.'

'No, let's hope it doesn't come to that.' Bronski looked over at Annie momentarily and she was also nodding. He continued. 'We're still following up a few leads. We interviewed Linda Moorcroft, Jim Moorcroft's ex-wife. There was more to the arrest than what's on file. There were charges she never pressed, including marital rape, because she couldn't bear to testify to that in court. She also dropped the assault charge, probably out of fear and because she didn't want to admit to adultery. But from the account she gave us, she was certainly the victim of domestic violence.'

'So, it sounds like he was capable of the assault on Angela Goodman?' Franconi looked away from his nails momentarily.

'We think so Sir, but we have no firm evidence yet.' Annie butted in even though Bronski was leading. He didn't seem to mind, nodded and then continued.

'We spoke to Jackie Winters as well. She wasn't going to admit that there are any problems between them but we obviously touched a raw nerve because she stormed out when we asked if he had a temper.'

'Too close to home, we think.'

'What do you make of this Jackie Winters? Strike you as the type who would suffer in silence?' Franconi threw the paperclip in the bin and stared at his nails even as he spoke.

Bronski turned to Annie for her opinion. 'No, not really, unless he has some kind of hold over her. Some men seem to intimidate even the strongest of women. We gave her an opportunity to talk to us. She wouldn't or couldn't but I don't think we should leave it at that. I think we should speak to her again. She could be protecting him.'

'You've got a point, Detective. We need to know more about those two. At first they seemed like the Good Samaritans and then we find he has an arrest record. How goes the search into her background?'

'Dave Ellison has been helping with that but we seem to have drawn some blanks with her background check. Can't find anything about her before the last five years,' replied Bronski.

Franconi just murmured. 'Strange. Tell him to keep at it. What about the soon to be divorced Mr Goodman, is he out of the picture?'

Bronski came in again. 'Can't really see a motive. It's not like she was stalling on the divorce, so he was free to carry on with Genevieve Montgomery. The affair was common knowledge by the time of the assault, so there'd be no point in beating her up. It might have been different if she was being awkward about it. None of our searches has brought up anything about him. A womaniser maybe but no previous for anything.'

'Has the brother, what's his name, got any ideas?' Franconi put a second paperclip down and glanced over at Annie.

'Aye, Captain Hegarty. He can't believe anyone would do this to his sister. He admits he doesn't know a lot of things about her past as there is an age gap but they appear close. He showed me an email from her though, that said she had things she wanted to tell him, things he didn't know. She was looking forward to him coming home so they could talk.' Annie paused.

'And he has no idea what that could be about?'

'Not when I spoke to him, although he's had more time to reflect. I'll ask him again today. I need to ring him anyway, as he wants to know if he can access his sister's house. He wants to try and clear up some of the mess. I have some details of specialist cleaning companies to give him. They'll need to do some of it. We're just waiting for clearance that Glen Heaviley's team are finished with it.'

Franconi pushed his chair back and the two detectives knew that it was a signal that the interview was coming to an end.

'You need more on this woman's past: maybe there's something there. From the state of the crime scene, this wasn't random. Someone wanted to kill Angela Goodman but they just stopped short, probably by accident. Did you say before that she had another husband, before Goodman?'

Annie came in this time. 'Captain Hegarty gave us his name and we're trying to locate an address for him: then we'll have a word with him.'

'And we still have someone at the door to her room, don't we?'

'Yes, Sir.'

'OK let me know any developments.' With that Franconi picked up his pen and dragged some paperwork over.

When they got back to their desks, Bronski picked up a pink slip. 'It's a message from Hegarty. He's at the hospital; wants to speak to one of us. Left his cell phone number and says he'll have it on in half an hour.'

'Want me to ring him?' Annie asked.

'Let's just go down there. We need to ask him some more questions anyway.'

Annie grabbed a last sip of coffee and put her jacket on but then stopped a moment. 'Can I just ring Glen Heaviley and find out if they are finished with the house? Might be useful to give him some news.'

The traffic was awful and it took them the best part

of an hour to get through it, find a space in the parking lot and get up to the ward. As they approached the nurses' station, one of the nurses finished making a phone call and switched over to using the computer. It took her a couple of minutes to acknowledge the two detectives at the desk. Annie held her badge out.

'Detective Macpherson and Detective Bronski. We're here to see Angela Goodman. How is she?'

Annie assumed that nurses in the US would be more business like, with the payments required for hospital care. This nurse was a bit too officious for Annie's liking. 'About the same; still hasn't come around from the operation.' With that, she picked up a file and came around the side of the desk, making it obvious that further questions would have to wait. Bronski and Annie walked the length of the ward and nodded to the cop on duty.

'How's it going?' Bronski knew the cop and introduced Annie.

'Not too well. The brother is still in there; has been most of the night. Only popped out this morning to get a change of clothes and came right back. He looks awful, poor guy.'

As they entered the room, Annie felt a bit sick, as a memory came flooding back. It was the last days of her dad's terminal illness and the shock at seeing him wasting away. Her hero, her mentor and the man who was the reason she became a cop, lying in the hospital bed had become reduced to skin and bone. She still shuddered thinking about it. Now here was a woman, lying there motionless, just as he had.

The morning sun was shining into the room, even though the curtains were still drawn. Charlie was in a chair facing his sister's bed. He was asleep. Bronski motioned to Annie to touch him on the shoulder. As soon as Annie did so, he reacted instantly, like the trained soldier he was. His quick response made Annie jump.

'I'm sorry I didn't mean to startle you,' she said.

Charlie quickly regained his composure. 'Sorry, I drifted off; haven't had much sleep lately.'

Then he noticed Bronski on the other side of the bed. Bronski's gaze was intent on Angela Goodman, his voice barely a whisper. 'How's she doing?'

Charlie got up from the chair, stretching and rubbing his neck. Annie noticed for herself how exhausted he looked. Touching his sister's hand, he replied to Bronski, again speaking in a very low voice. 'It doesn't appear there's been much change. I was hoping this latest surgery ...'

'But it's still early, isn't it?' Annie touched his arm again and this time he didn't flinch.

'At least she survived the surgery. I'm told that is the trickiest part. Should we go outside to talk? I could do with a coffee. What time is it anyway?'

The three of them decided to go to the diner across the road, avoiding the crowded hospital canteen. They ordered as soon as they sat down and when the coffee was poured, Annie broke the awkwardness.

'You left a message for one of us to telephone you. We thought we would come by and see how Angela was, knowing you were here.'

Charlie took a long drink of coffee before responding. 'I expect you thought you might see a change in her. God knows, every time I come in I pray for that but she's still the same. I worry that I have put her through needless surgery and that I'm going to be faced with having to make a decision about switching off the life support.' For a moment, he put his face in his hands.

Annie and Bronski waited for him to recover.

'The surgeon said it could still be forty-eight hours before we know if there will be any change, so I keep trying to remind myself of that. Anyway, why I telephoned you. There were two things: I wanted to know where you were up to with releasing the house and then ...'

As Charlie hesitated, Annie came in on his first thought. 'We've been in touch with the forensics team and they can release the house this week. I also have some details for you of those specialist cleaning companies I think I mentioned to you already.' Annie reached into her handbag to retrieve a slip of paper with several names and telephone numbers. 'I can make the arrangements if that would help.'

'Thanks, but I'll take care of it. More than anything right now, I just want to fix the place up for her. She can't see it like that.'

'Will you have the time? What about your service commitments? When do you have to get back to your base?' Annie realised that time was passing and Charlie was a serving soldier.

'I've been granted a six month leave of absence. It starts next week when my leave would have finished. I need to be here for Angela. I'm all she has.'

41

It had been nearly two days since he'd staged the accident and all he could find on the Internet was an item from the local newspaper. It seemed as if there was nothing suspicious being reported.

He smiled to himself. When are you going to realise that there are two cars but only one body? But hey, he was many miles away, in a different State, with nothing to connect him to Carol Wojinski.

There was no need to discuss what he'd been up to either. This wasn't part of the plan they'd shared. He took one of those long very hot showers, the ones that cleansed him, made him feel whole again. Then after his usual nightcap, he crawled into bed.

Two hours later he woke suddenly, with a choking sensation. Rushing into the bathroom he barely had time to switch the light on before he vomited into the toilet. As he sat on the bathroom floor, with an arm still propped up on the toilet seat, the dream came flooding back. It was a variation on the recurring one he'd had for months now. Sometimes there were only disjointed snippets of the dream but tonight there was more of a sequence.

In the dream, he was in a prison cell but he didn't recognise anything about it. The walls were a strange colour and it was eerily quiet. Then the silence was broken by the sound of someone unlocking the door. He'd heard their footsteps but somehow couldn't get his eyes to open so that he could see who it was. He'd felt the hands around his neck and no matter how hard he tried he couldn't release the grip, nor could he get his eyes to open.

As that part of the dream came flooding back, he found himself being sick again. His ribs ached from the force of the heaving. A part of him wanted to remember the rest of the dream while another part of him wanted to curl up, right there on the bathroom floor. Despite that urge, he forced himself to remember, the sour taste of the vomit still in his mouth.

The next sound in the dream was that of water dripping and finally his eyes opened. A woman was there, her face covered but she was trying to help him, frantically pulling on the man's arm until he released his grip. But when he reached for her, water came flooding out of her mouth and all he could feel was dampness, the dampness of his own sweat.

As he got up from the floor, he reached for the glass and swilled his mouth out. With his heart still drumming and the sweat pouring off him, he went back to the bedroom. He looked at the clock – 2 am. No chance of sleeping now. He walked into the study, turned on the desk lamp and switched on the laptop.

42

'So what did you make of the other thing he had on his mind?' Bronski was seeking Annie's view about Hegarty's questioning of them with regard to Jim Moorcroft.

Annie thought about the encounter. Charlie's anger had been palpable. Was there something going on between him and Jackie Winters? It certainly seemed as if Jackie was using his shoulder to cry on. There was something about the woman Annie didn't trust. She replied with her own question. 'Are all American men so protective of women or is that characteristic of a military man?'

'Come on, stop the stereotyping. Besides, I thought chivalry started in your country: something about knights, wasn't it?' Bronski laughed, as he pulled out of the hospital parking lot.

Annie smiled. 'OK, my view is that Charlie is genuinely worried about Jim Moorcroft. I think he's feeling that Jackie Winters could be in danger from him and wonders why we're not doing anything about it.'

'Hmm ... you don't think he'll do anything himself, do you?'

'Well, I wouldn't want to have another assault victim on our hands. I think we need to talk to Jackie Winters and Jim Moorcroft again. They're both holding back; I'm just not sure what.'

Bronski glanced over at Annie. 'So, let's see if they're both at work.'

By the time the two detectives reached the office building and confirmed that Jim Moorcroft and Jackie Winters were in, they'd decided to interview Jackie Winters first. They'd been shown to an empty office and one of the personnel staff had gone to get Jackie. Bronski had made it clear that she should be brought straight to them and that Jim Moorcroft was not to be contacted until they said so. Annie thought that word would still get around, despite their precautions.

The knock on the door was expected. The personnel woman popped her head around the door. 'Jackie Winters for you. Is there anything else you require, coffee perhaps?'

'No thank you,' Annie replied, as she closed the door.

Jackie took a seat opposite them without a word but her face could barely contain her feelings. 'I thought we covered everything you wanted yesterday. Why do you keep showing up here? I haven't done anything wrong and it's embarrassing. I have to work in this building and things are starting to be said.' Her arms were folded tightly across her chest and she was noticeably bristling.

'We appreciate that this isn't easy for you but we are investigating a very serious assault and we think you have been less than honest with us.' Annie was taking the lead and wasn't in the mood to play games. The sight of Angela Goodman had sickened her.

'I have no idea what you mean. I have told you everything I know. I am trying to carry on working while spending as much time as I can visiting my best friend and supporting her brother. Pardon me if that isn't good enough for you.'

'We need to know more about your relationship with Mr Moorcroft.'

'Oh please, this is too much. What do our personal lives have to do with anything? He's my partner. We've been together for nearly two years and that's it; nothing more to tell you.'

Jackie shifted in her seat and Annie thought for a moment that she might get up and leave. After all, she was speaking to them voluntarily, so Annie had to be careful. 'I will come straight to the point. Angela Goodman was brutally assaulted. Whoever did this, left her for dead. If you and Jim hadn't gone to her house when you did, she probably wouldn't have survived.' Annie paused for a minute, wanting to be sure she had Jackie's full attention. 'You two were the last ones to see her the evening before, apart from the perpetrator and were also the ones who discovered her. Your partner's finger marks were on a glass in the kitchen, so he went into the house that night. The question for me is whether there was something going on between them and whether Jim Moorcroft had a motive for assaulting Angela Goodman.'

Annie leaned back in her chair and noticed the intensity with which Bronski was staring at Jackie Winters. But Jackie's body language hadn't changed and she was clearly still angry at the intrusiveness of their questions.

'No, no, no. They're friends, that's all. It was Jim who introduced me to Angie. When her husband left, we were very much a threesome. He's been very supportive of her over the break up of her marriage; we both have. We're friends, that's all. He loves me and that's the whole story; nothing sordid as you seem to want to imply. Now if there isn't anything else.' Jackie started to get up from her chair.

This time Bronski came in before Annie could. 'Are we to take it that he has never been violent to you?'

Jackie turned back, her hand already on the door. 'Not that it's any business of yours but, no, he has never been violent to me.' With that she walked out of the room, without looking back.

The two detectives took the personnel woman up on her offer and sat with their coffees, leaving Jim Moorcroft more time to wait.

'So, do you want to lead on this one?' Annie asked as she finished her drink.

'Sure. You about ready?' When Annie nodded, Bronski made the internal phone call.

This time the woman from personnel just opened the door and shut it again without a word. Jim Moorcroft started talking even before he took a seat. 'What is with you? Why can't you leave me alone? I have done nothing, apart from saving Angela's life. What if we didn't go over that morning, then what? We wouldn't be suspects, that's what.'

It was obvious he had seen Jackie before he came in for the interview. He was gesturing now and barely sitting down. Bronski leaned forward.

'We appreciate you talking to us again. There are one or two things we just want to go over again.' Bronski directed the questions at his first marriage but Moorcroft remained circumspect, only reporting what would be in official records anyway. But then Bronski caught him off guard by asking what he knew about Angela's first marriage.

'Surely, you're not thinking Dennis had anything to do with this. You are way off base on that one.'

'How so?'

Perhaps relieved that the questioning wasn't about his previous marriage any more, Jim Moorcroft visibly relaxed. 'Dennis worshipped her, thought she was his soul mate but she was too wrapped up at the time with her mother's illness and trying to ensure her brother was taken care of. She didn't have much left over for him even though he didn't demand much. He desperately wanted to start a family but she wouldn't even consider it. She rejected him before he ever got close to rejecting her.'

'Were the two of you friends?'

'I wouldn't describe us as friends exactly. Sure, the occasional beer, card games now and then. He didn't know a lot of people, only knew me through Angie. He was from Rhode Island originally and went back quite a bit to see his parents. She was a bitch to him, to be honest but I never said anything to her about it.' Jim started to shift in his seat now and glanced at his watch. 'It's getting close to the lunch break, are we finished?'

'Just a couple more questions.'

By the time Jim Moorcroft left the room, the two detectives were feeling less sure of his guilt. The interview confirmed that they needed to locate Dennis Cullen and get more on that marriage. It certainly seemed that Angela Goodman had problems in her relationships.

43

When Annie and Bronski got back to the station after lunch, Dave Ellison was waiting to see them.

'Two messages: Glen Heaviley is sending the keys over this afternoon. He assumed you would let the brother know.'

'I will. That's great, even sooner than I thought. And the second?'

'I've managed to track down the first husband, Dennis Cullen. He lives in Rhode Island now. I thought I'd save you some time by making a few phone calls. I spoke to his personal assistant. He's in New York on business for the next week. I have the telephone number of his motel but he may not even go back there tonight, as he is expecting to be in negotiations all night over some deal. Anyway, she insisted that he can't be disturbed but she will give him a message that you want to speak to him. She has the numbers here and also both your cell phones.'

By now, Annie was sitting at her desk making notes and Bronski was listening, while sorting through other messages on his desk. It was Annie who acknowledged the information first. 'Thanks, Dave, that's very helpful. I guess we'll have to wait for Dennis Cullen to ring us but I might just leave a message at the motel, make sure he knows we really want to speak to him.'

Annie looked over at Dave and he winked at her after assuring himself that Bronski wasn't looking their way. Then he got up and put the message with the telephone numbers for Dennis Cullen on her desk, brushing her hand in the process.

As he sat back down, Annie glanced over at Bronski who still had his head down skimming other messages. Turning to Ellison again, she said 'Any more background on Jackie Winters?'

'You took the next part right out of my mouth. Still nothing beyond five years, which is a bit strange. Do you know if Winters is a married name?'

'She's never mentioned being married, nor has Jim Moorcroft but then again we never specifically asked. I'll make a note to follow that up.'

As Annie was finishing her sentence, Bronski's phone rang.

'Well I'll be damned. Thanks Sarge. Detective Macpherson and I will be down in a minute. Can you put her in an interview room? Give her a cup of coffee.'

'Don't tell me, Jackie Winters is downstairs.'

'No, Detective, guess again.' Bronski smiled. 'You aren't going to believe this. It's our old friend, Genevieve Montgomery, downstairs. Says she's here to report an assault; came straight from the ER.'

Bronski laughed at the look on Annie's face. 'You weren't expecting that one were you?'

Anne pushed her chair back and stood up, putting her jacket back on. 'No, she wasn't the female I was expecting. So has Mr Goodman been up to no good, I wonder?'

'Let's find out, shall we?'

When the two detectives came through the door of the interview room, it was clear from the look on her face that Genevieve Montgomery wasn't happy to see

Annie with Bronski.

'This doesn't need two of you. I asked to speak to Detective Bronski.'

'How about we decide that,' Bronski replied, as he and Annie sat down opposite Genevieve Montgomery, who picked up her drink and finished it. She was clearly ill at ease and Annie was taken aback by the look of her face. It was very swollen and her right eye was half closed. Her lower lip was split and it looked as if it would be painful to speak. But she still had that superior air about her that had been so noticeable the first time they'd met her.

'So Ms Montgomery, would you like to tell us what happened?' enquired Bronski.

At first she hesitated as if she were about to change her mind and then blurted out, 'George did this; had a few too many last night when I was with him and carried on drinking today. Came into the boutique and demanded that I come into his car with him. It was clear that he was too drunk to drive, so I took the keys from him and drove him back to his apartment.'

Before continuing, she asked for a glass of water, which Annie arranged. After a few sips, she seemed to compose herself once again. Annie felt herself warming to the woman at last. This was clearly difficult for her.

'He turned nasty as soon as I got him into his apartment. Started calling me names, swearing at me, saying it was my fault that Angela was in hospital fighting for her life. I was so shocked I didn't know what to say.'

'What did he mean that it was your fault?'

'I don't know really; he never explained. He became incoherent, started mumbling about how much he loved her but that she frustrated him. He said she was never good in bed, that he wanted to love her but she wouldn't let him.'

Genevieve Montgomery was clearly becoming distressed and her voice was breaking. Annie knew that a strong woman like her would be humiliated at being assaulted by a man, especially one that she trusted.

'I loved him and I thought he loved me. Maybe it was all an act, maybe he just wanted the sex. I thought he wanted more. I did.' She began crying and Bronski and Annie gave her time to gain some control before they recorded more of the specifics about the time the attack happened, how she managed to get away from him and so on. She agreed that she wanted to press charges and Bronski left the room to organise the arrest of George Goodman.

When Annie and Genevieve Montgomery were alone, Annie focused on the question she knew the woman wouldn't want to answer. 'Did he say if he attacked Angela Goodman, if he was the one responsible for the condition she is in now?' Annie wasn't sure if the woman would answer, even though she clearly wanted him arrested for the assault on her.

'He didn't say he did but he didn't deny it either. He started hitting me when I asked him if he was responsible for it.'

Annie and Bronski took Genevieve Montgomery's statement and after it was signed, Annie arranged for one of the woman's staff to come to the station and accompany her back to her apartment house. When Annie got back up to the office, Bronski was on the phone. 'So he'll be here in about fifteen minutes; too drunk to interview? OK, I'll arrange it.'

44

When Annie finally opened her own front door, all she could think about was running a hot bath and having a long soak. It had been quite a day. The light was flashing on her answer machine. At first she was comforted to hear her mother's voice but the news wasn't good. Andrew wasn't being discharged from hospital as they'd hoped. More tests were required. The epilepsy was still not under control. More than anything, the emotional part of her wanted to get on a plane home and see her family. Her rational self knew differently. She was thousands of miles away and, realistically, there was nothing she could do.

After her bath, Annie telephoned her mum. Luckily, Mrs Macpherson was at home, getting a change of clothing for Andrew, so for once Annie managed to speak to her directly.

'Mum, I could arrange to come back.'

'No dear, I won't hear of it. You're having an opportunity that will probably never come again and besides, you know Andrew. He'll come round, he always does. It's just taking a while longer this time.'

Annie paced around the room, still listening to her mother. The guilt she was feeling wasn't helped by the fact that her mother continued the conversation by praising Annie's ex-fiancé for his support. Although Annie was grateful for his concern, part of her felt that it wasn't his business any more and his involvement with her family just made things more difficult for her. The next part of the conversation was predictable.

'Sweetheart, I think Paul still has feelings for you. He doesn't say it but I can tell and he's ...'

'Mum, please. This doesn't help. I can't go on justifying what I did. It's over, Mum.'

'I'm sorry, dear, it's just that ...' Annie had to listen to her mum's views yet again. The instant relief she felt when she put the phone down turned to anger.

'Over three-thousand miles and I still can't get away from you,' she shouted as she went into the kitchen. Opening the refrigerator, the contents offered little inspiration nor did she really have the energy to prepare anything. 'Thanks, Paul,' she yelled, slamming the refrigerator door shut. Weariness suddenly overwhelmed her. Wandering into the living room, she settled on to the couch and switched the TV on.

'Oh thanks, hundreds of channels and nothing decent to watch.' Drawing the throw around her and snuggling down, Annie found that she couldn't keep her eyes open.

The sound of her cell phone roused her and reaching into her bathrobe pocket, she checked her watch quickly. She realised she'd been asleep nearly an hour.

The caller ID read: 'Capt Hegarty'.

Annie answered, trying to compose herself. 'Detective Macpherson.'

'Hi Annie.'

'Hi Charlie. Is everything all right? Angela? Has something happened?' Pulling her robe around her, Annie wasn't sure she could face hearing the worst and knowing that their investigation would turn into a murder inquiry.

'It's not Angela: she's still holding her own. Your partner, Detective Bronski has just phoned me about arresting George. Listen, can we talk? I ...'

'Sure, do you want me to come down to the hospital? I can get a taxi pretty quickly.'

'No, but thanks for the offer. If I'm being honest, I need to get out of here for a while. The nurses have told me to go out and get something to eat.'

'They're right, you've been there non stop.' Her words echoed similar things she'd said to her mum a couple of hours earlier.

'Only, I'm sick of eating alone, so I was just wondering if you've eaten yet?'

They'd decided that rather than sit in a restaurant, Charlie would pick up some Chinese food and come over to Annie's. The half hour had afforded her time to change into a pair of black jeans and a fresh linen blouse. Her long blond curls had dried naturally while she was asleep on the couch.

Pausing in the kitchen, she looked around. The built in table was set with plates and knives and forks and she also put out some chopsticks that she found in a drawer. She wondered if it would be rude to have a glass of wine before he arrived. She needed something to settle herself. Pouring a glass out, for a split second she let herself imagine that this was a date, rather than business but then her professional self took charge.

'Will I ever find a man I can feel comfortable with?' she asked herself. Her reverie was broken by the sound of the apartment buzzer.

Charlie looked exhausted. Clearly the nurses were

right and although she and Bronski had only seen him the day before, he'd deteriorated further in that time.

'Come in. I'll take those. Have a seat. I've started some white wine but I have red or a beer.'

'Thanks, I'll just have a beer. I'll be driving soon. Besides, a glass of wine might put me to sleep.' Annie took a bottle of beer from the refrigerator and Charlie declined a glass.

'Maybe that wouldn't be such a bad thing. You look as if you could sleep for a week.'

Charlie took a swig of beer as Annie opened the boxes of food. 'This is all so bizarre, I can't get my head around it. I left Afghanistan less than a month ago. Then I was fly fishing in Montana, now I'm here, listening to machines keeping my sister alive, wondering every moment who could have done this to her, willing her to wake up and tell me.'

'She's our only witness and there isn't much evidence to go on. Apart from Jim Moorcroft's finger marks, the rest is circumstantial, certainly not enough to arrest anyone at this stage. We seem to have more questions than answers.' By now Annie had given up on the chopsticks and resorted to her fork. Charlie was much more adept.

'So what's all this about George? Your detective colleague didn't say much.'

'He's sleeping in a cell right now. We can't interview him until the morning, when he's cleared by the doctor. It will be about an alleged assault on Genevieve Montgomery.'

'She's the woman he was having the affair with?'

'Aye, but while we are at it, we will press him again

about Angela, of course.'

'It's not him, I know it.' Charlie picked his beer up and took another swig.

'What do you mean? Are you saying that he didn't assault Genevieve Montgomery or that he didn't attack your sister?'

'I don't know about the Montgomery woman but I know George Goodman. I don't think he is capable of causing the injuries that Angela has. She would have told me if he was violent. You get a feel for people being in the forces, as you must do in your job.'

Annie didn't want to admit how wrong she'd been about his sister. 'I have to say, I didn't like George much when we interviewed him but he didn't strike me as the perpetrator and there was no real evidence linking him and ...'

'What, is there something else?' Charlie stopped eating, waiting for Annie to reply.

'Just something, that is still in the back of my mind. Remember the night I talked to you in the hospital and you showed me the email from Angela?'

'I remember, I still have it on my phone. It's in my jacket.'

'We'll find it again in a minute but as I recall, she said something about wanting to talk to you, that there were things she needed to tell you.'

Charlie put his chopsticks down and retrieved his jacket. Taking his phone out of the pocket, he scanned his emails again. 'Here it is,' and he read it out loud for them both. 'So what are you thinking?' he said as he finished.

'Could she have wanted to tell you that George was a problem, that maybe she was being subjected to domestic violence?'

Charlie placed the phone back in his jacket pocket and then finished his beer. It was clear to Annie that he was taking his time to reply.

'No, I can't say why but I just don't buy it. I am sure she would have told me that. There must have been something else that she wanted to tell me. There was never any hint that there were problems with George.' Charlie pushed his plate away, no longer interested in the food.

'Without stating the obvious, then why the affair? Why Genevieve Montgomery?' Annie too had finished her food. This wasn't really a conversation to have over a meal and Annie regretted that she hadn't said as much at the beginning.

Charlie put his head in his hands and began to knead his forehead. 'I don't know, I just don't know. Look, I'm sorry, maybe I need a coffee.'

'Sure, why don't you go into the living room. I'll clear these up and then bring the coffee through.' While Charlie was in the living room, Annie heard him speaking to the nurse on duty, catching up on Angela's condition. Annie busied herself making the coffee, trying not to eavesdrop but the apartment was so small she could overhear everything he said. She hesitated going in until he had finished the call.

'There's no change,' he said to Annie as she put the two cups down on the coffee table and sat next to him.

'So, you interview George in the morning? I guess

it's a matter of seeing what he says.'

'We should know more soon enough. Tell me about the first husband, Dennis Cullen.'

'Not much to tell really. He seemed OK to me but I was a lot younger at the time so I wouldn't have picked up if there were any problems. He didn't come to our house very often and Angie was with us most days. He must have got sick of that. I think she left him though, not the other way around.'

'He lives in Rhode Island now.'

'Oh, so you managed to trace him?'

'At the moment, he's in New York on business. We're waiting for him to return our calls.'

'I think you'll find that he hasn't been in contact with Angie for years. I don't even know if he's remarried or not.'

'We may be able to fill you in when we've been in touch.'

Annie didn't know if they should continue talking about the case. She really wanted to know more about him. Something about him fascinated her. Maybe it was the military manner or the fact that he was really good looking but she couldn't help thinking whether he would be in her apartment now if they'd met under other circumstances.

Charlie had gone quiet for a few minutes and then put his coffee cup on the table. 'I know you probably want to change the subject but there is something worrying me a bit. Jackie hasn't been to the hospital today at all.'

'Is she visiting every day?' Annie looked at him but

hoped he wouldn't detect any sign of jealousy.

'Yes, and if not, she usually texts me to let me know.'

'Maybe she's busy at work.' Annie recalled their last conversation and her manner. There wasn't much to like about the woman, in Annie's view. What was Charlie seeing in her – a vulnerable female?

'Maybe, but she's not returning my calls. I might go over to her workplace in the morning. Speaking of morning, I really ought to think about going.'

'Are you going back to the hospital or to the motel?' Annie asked as the two of them got up and took the cups through to the kitchen.

'I'm not sure I can go back tonight and sleep on the chair again. The nurse told me off as I was leaving to come here and said that I need to sleep in a proper bed tonight. Perhaps she's right but I feel like I have to be there, like she needs me.'

'Charlie, you need to be selfish, just this once. When Angela regains consciousness they'll let you know. She'll need you then.'

'You're right.' Charlie leaned across and kissed her on the cheek. 'Thanks for listening to me.'

Annie could still smell his aftershave when he'd gone.

Later, Annie was just switching off her bedside lamp when she got a text message. It was Charlie saying that he was back at the motel and thanking her for the company. Annie smiled as she read the text a second time. She was definitely warming to Captain Charles Hegarty.

45

Jim Moorcroft was pacing up and down the living room, periodically looking through the curtains. Three cars, then four passed the house. One slowed down to park in front of his neighbour's house. Finally, he heard Jackie pull her car into the drive, the headlights illuminating the living room window. Glancing at his watch, he confirmed that it was past 11 pm and she'd been out for hours. His fists clenched, he drew back from the window and walked into the hall.

Jackie put her key in the lock and as she opened the door, he was only inches away from her.

'Jim, what's going on? You gave me a fright.' Jackie turned her back on him as she shut the door behind her.

'Where have you been?'

There was a tone in his voice that scared her, but she dared not show it. Remain calm, she told herself. 'I texted you; said I was going to stop at the mall on the way home and then I decided to have something to eat while I was out.' Jackie Winters moved past him in the hallway, unbuttoning her jacket as she tried to judge his mood further. His silence was more ominous than the shouting. She had to break it.

'What's bothering you?'

'You haven't got any shopping bags.' Jim Moorcroft followed her into the kitchen. Abandoning the idea of taking her jacket off, she filled the kettle with water and turned on the stove instead.

'There was nothing left in the sales. Everything was picked over and what there was, still wasn't reduced enough to make me want to buy it. It's not a crime coming home empty handed, is it?' After placing the two cups on the counter, she slowly walked over to the refrigerator for the milk. Her movements belied how she felt.

'It is, if you never went to the mall in the first place.' This time his voice was definitely raised.

'What?' Jackie looked at him quizzically.

'Where were you really? I know you're lying to me.'

With her back to him, Jackie paused for a moment, no longer interested in preparing a late night drink. Slowly turning around, she tried to judge where the conversation was going. Her stomach was churning.

'What's this about Jim? What are you implying?' Her voice held steady, just.

'Jennie and Sarah know what you're up to. I overheard them by the water cooler, giggling about your affair.' By now he was pacing in the kitchen, never a good sign.

'I'm not having an affair. They must have been talking about someone else. Besides, we're not married, so strictly speaking I can't have an affair.'

'Don't play the smart bitch with me, Jackie.'

'I can do what I want, when I want and I'm not being subjected to accusations in my own home, nor am I going to justify myself to you.' Jackie tried to muster some bravado, which she didn't actually feel, while all the time she considered the best way of getting out of the situation, before he did anything to her.

'That's where you're wrong Jackie. This isn't your home, it's mine and you're only here because I want you to be, but that can change.'

Jackie felt herself shiver, hoping that it didn't show.

'You know that I hate liars and you're lying to me. I followed you tonight. I know you went right past the mall and into New Britain. I followed you all the way to an apartment house and you've been gone hours.'

Jackie had heard enough. Backing out of the kitchen, she snatched up her handbag in the hall. Jim Moorcroft followed her, grabbing her arm.

'Let go of me,' she screamed, pushing him so hard he fell back against the hallway table.

'You bitch, where do you think you're going now? I haven't finished with you, I want answers.'

Managing to get to the door, Jackie slammed it behind her. She scrambled into her car and started the engine just as Jim Moorcroft ran down the drive after her. Revving the engine fiercely, she reversed on to the road before he could reach her.

'Don't come back,' was the last thing she heard him shout, as her heart thumped in her chest and tears ran down her cheeks. A neighbour three doors down opened his curtains at hearing the sound of her wheels screeching and she noticed him shaking his head as she looked in her rear view mirror. No one behaved like that on their street normally and she was surprised that no one else came out. There were so many windows open in the warm summer night.

When she turned the next corner, Jackie Winters pulled her car over, checking to make sure that he wasn't following her. She waited a few minutes, wondering what to do. Picking up her cell phone, she checked for messages, still keeping an eye on the rear view mirror. There were no missed calls from Jim, which made sense if he really had been following her. From Charlie, there were three text messages. As her hands stopped shaking, she scrolled down to read them. Each one asked if she was all right and to call him. Her fingers hovered over the phone momentarily before she shut it and dropped it back in her bag. She smiled as she pulled away from the kerb.

46

Gus's in-laws were clearing away the supper dishes. Watching them, he began thinking how different this all was from when Carol was there. She didn't like anyone else in her kitchen and the two of them always did the tidying up, while she would insist that her parents relax. Now he was letting them do it all.

Gus kept picturing the jewellery that Detective Malin had shown him the previous day. Until then he had harboured hopes that Carol was still alive, maybe had lost her memory or something, anything and that she would be coming back. The sight of the necklace, the rings and the watch had crushed all hope. Trying desperately to motivate himself, he stood up and walked over to the sink.

'Here, let me do that. You two take a break. I know where everything goes: it's easier for me.'

'Gus, we're nearly done,' replied Gillian Tyler, but then sensing that her son-in-law needed to do this simple mundane task, she passed him the plate still in her hands.

Her husband took the signal as well and moved away from the sink where he had been putting the scraps down the waste disposal. Gus took over and they retreated into the den. As her husband put the TV on, Gillian heard the doorbell ring. At first she assumed that it was Gus's mom, who had left the three of them an hour or so before to do some shopping in the mall. She realised that she hadn't packed enough things when she'd flown up from Florida after Gus's call.

Gillian automatically started to get up but then sat back down. After all, this wasn't her house. When they heard Gus address the caller as Detective Malin, they were unsure whether they should join them in the kitchen.

A few seconds later, Gus popped his head around the door of the den.

'Come in the kitchen. Detective Malin wants to update us on what's been happening with the investigation.'

Without a word, Gillian and Fred Tyler joined their son-in-law and he introduced them to Detective Malin.

'I am sorry for your loss, Mr and Mrs Tyler. I know this must have come as a great shock to you. I thought it best if you all hear what I have to say. The three of them sat down on the stools at the breakfast bar while Gus stood by the sink.

'Our forensics team has done some preliminary analyses of the road markings and the damage to both cars. At this stage, it looks as if the two cars didn't go over the ravine together which is what we thought at first.'

'I don't understand. I thought we were assuming that the other car hit Carol's and they both went though the barrier.' Fred Tyler appeared quite confused.

'Yes, Sir, that is exactly what we thought at first, but now we think that Carol's car went over but the second car stopped. The second set of skid marks would indicate that. We are speculating that the car was then pushed over the edge, through the barrier, which had already been damaged by Carol's car. There is paint from two cars on what is left of the barriers, but the amounts, thickness and so on would suggest that only one of them went through at speed.'

Malin glanced at the three people, all in a state of shock. He knew that they would probably forget some of the detail, but he felt obliged to provide it. Questions would come later, in his experience. So he continued. 'The trajectories would also indicate that this is a more likely scenario. Then there is the damage to each car, relative to the other and the points of impact.' Malin hesitated for a few moments giving this last piece of information time to sink in, before he revealed the most distressing aspect of the investigation so far.

'The other thing is that a second body hasn't been found.'

'You mean, not yet? Surely there has to be a second body.' Gus was rubbing his forehead as if he couldn't quite get what was being said. Over the last few days, he had wondered if another family was missing a loved one and not knowing where they were.

'No. What I'm saying is that we don't think there is a second body. We've done thermal imaging of the whole area. If there was a body in that vicinity we would have found it by now, or else the ground searches would have turned up something, but there is no trace of a second body.'

Gillian and Fred looked at Detective Malin in disbelief and then at their son-in-law, who could barely get his words out.

'It's rough ground out there, lots of tree cover and animals ...' Gus looked at Detective Malin before he even finished his sentence, realising that his arguments were pointless. The next words nearly choked him to get out. 'So what are you saying exactly?'

'Look, I know that this is hard to hear, but I want to be straight with you.' Detective Malin glanced at the Tylers and then turned to face Gus directly. 'We think that what happened to your wife wasn't an accident. We believe that her car was deliberately rammed so that it went over the edge and that the driver of the second car then pushed his car over the edge to make it look like an accident.' Malin hesitated for a second, before adding: 'We are now treating the case as a murder inquiry.'

Gillian Tyler's hand went to her mouth to stifle a scream and her husband put his arm around her. Gus just stared at the Detective in disbelief.

'But who, why? We're just ordinary people. She was a bookshop manager, for God's sake. What possible motive would anyone have to kill her? This can't be right, it just can't be.' Gus's distress filled the room.

'Look, I will need to come back and talk to you again. In the meantime I want you to think about whether there is anything, anything at all that we should be looking at. We are going to need to know as much about Carol as we can, explore all the possibilities.' Malin was seasoned enough to know that tonight wasn't the time for this. The family needed to think through what he'd said.

'I'll come back in the morning and we'll go through things again. I will also need a list of her close friends, now or in the past.'

Gus showed the detective to the door, just as Mrs

Wojinski pulled into the drive. Malin hesitated for a moment.

'Thanks, Detective. I'll explain to my mother what you've told us.'

Detective Malin just nodded to Mrs Wojinski as she got out of the car.

47

Charlie had just drifted off to sleep when the phone in his motel room rang. Reaching across, he answered groggily.

'Yes?'

'Captain Hegarty?'

His heart started pounding in his chest, sensing this was the call he had been dreading. 'What is it?' He felt himself almost shouting, anxiety mounting, as he threw the sheet off and started to get out of bed.

'There's a woman at reception asking to speak to you urgently. Her name is Jackie Winters.' The desk clerk hesitated for a moment and then continued. 'Do you want to speak to her on the phone or will you come down? The bar's still open. I could ask her to wait for you in there.'

Charlie reached for his watch, the dial illuminated in the darkened room. It was nearly midnight. 'OK, tell her to get a drink and put it on my room tab. I'll be down in ten minutes.' Switching on the bedside lamp, he half debated whether to have a quick shower, but then decided that Jackie must want something urgently to come all the way down to the motel at this time of night. So he got dressed, grabbed his room key and headed for the bar.

The bartender nodded to him as he entered the room and then motioned towards the corner table, where Jackie was sitting with her back to the bar. That immediately seemed strange. Why wasn't she keeping an eye out for him? But then he noticed that her shoulders were moving very slightly. When he took the leather corner seat opposite, he saw that she was crying. Not sobbing, more like a whimper.

Reaching across, he took her hands in his. 'What is it Jackie, what's happened?' As she looked at him through her teary eyes, he had a flashback of his mother: finding her downstairs, late at night, whimpering for her husband in the months after he died. The vision had the power to reduce him to that scared child again, wanting so much to comfort, but not really being able to help. He saw himself squeezing Jackie's hands, just like he had his mother's all those years ago, repeating the same motions.

'Tell me,' he coaxed, but it was a few minutes before she regained her composure. By then a fairly drunk couple had come into the bar and were giggling as they tried to order their drinks. The bartender was standing with his hands splayed on the bar as if he had all night for them to make up their minds. Charlie tried not to get distracted. Right now, he wanted some privacy for Jackie's sake. 'Listen, I guess you're not going back home tonight.'

Jackie nodded.

'Why don't I see if there is another room free in the motel? We'll go up there and talk.'

*****

Over breakfast, Annie jotted down a few reminders. First on the list was to mention to Bronski that Jackie hadn't been to see Angela, which had struck Charlie as odd when he'd mentioned it to her. As Annie made a note of that, she wondered if Jackie was trying to distance herself because of Jim Moorcroft. Her background was still bothering Annie as well. Charlie also thought it strange that there was nothing on file about her prior to five years ago. He had only known of her for a couple of years and until his last furlough, had never met her. It was Jim that Angela had been friendly with initially and then the two of them as a couple. But in recent months, Angela and Jackie had become much closer. Maybe Jim Moorcroft had become jealous.

Annie tapped her pen on the pad while she put a few question marks down on the page. Then she made a note to give Charlie the details of the specialist cleaning company, which Glen Heaviley had recommended. The firm had a reputation for doing a good job of decontamination and at a reasonable price. There was a lot of blood and other contaminants to clean up. The police still had a set of keys at the station and she had checked that these could be returned to Charlie. Annie knew how keen he was to get in there and redecorate for his sister. Last night he was so convinced that she was going to pull through, that Annie had started to believe it too. As she rinsed her cereal bowl, her cell phone rang.

The caller ID was Bronski.

'Morning Detective, I'm circling by to pick you up. I've had a message from dispatch. Guess who's turned up at the hospital, demanding to see Angela Goodman?'

Annie felt the adrenaline. 'Jim Moorcroft?'

'No, Dennis Cullen, the very man who couldn't be disturbed yesterday because he was in New York on some big business trip.'

'Interesting and surprising. Wonder what his secretary said to him.'

'Who knows? But it saves us a trip to New York. I'll be with you in ten minutes.'

Annie nearly said, 'But I wanted to see the Empire State Building,' but then thought better of it.

As Annie waited in front of her apartment house, she decided to text Charlie to see if he was at the hospital. Bronski hadn't provided much detail. As soon as she closed her phone, Bronski pulled up in his car and leaned over to open the passenger door.

'Good morning.'

'Let's hope so. What do we know?'

Bronski signalled to get back into the lane. 'Just that he turned up about a half hour ago. The cop on guard wouldn't let him in to see her and called dispatch to alert us. Then he asked him to wait in the visitors' room. He wasn't too pleased. Said he'd been driving since the early hours to get there and why wasn't he allowed in. He started ranting. Seems one of the nurses calmed him down.'

'Hmm and to our knowledge he hasn't seen her since the divorce, throughout her second marriage?'

'Who knows? Nothing would surprise me.' The traffic was building up and the hospital route was busier than the usual one to the station. Bronski was impatient and resorted to his horn.

Annie wondered if he would put his flashing lights on, but he resisted. She waited until there was more of a break in the traffic. 'So how is our other friend? Did he have a comfortable night? I bet he has a sore head this morning.'

Bronski laughed. 'I spoke to Dave Ellison right after I called you. Says that George Goodman is waiting to see the doctor to clear that he's OK to be interviewed. He'll also have some breakfast so we've got some time. If we get delayed, I'll get Ellison to start the process.'

'Funny how all the exes are turning up at once, just like buses.'

'I don't get that.'

'Sorry, it's a saying back home. You wait ages for a bus and then two come at once.'

Bronski nodded. 'Let's just hope this is the last of them – husbands I mean.'

'The other thing is that I saw Charlie again last night.'

'What do you mean, did you go down to the hospital?' Bronski sounded curious.

'No, he rang me and asked if he could pop round with a Chinese, said he was fed up eating on his own.'

'He's a real charmer.'

'I hardly think that was his intention Sir,' Annie quipped back. 'He's exhausted spending so much time at the hospital. He was really looking forward to seeing his sister. The whole thing has been a shock to him.'

'Hmm ...' Bronski signalled to turn into the underground parking lot. Annie decided to finish the conversation about last night later on. Now they had to concentrate on Dennis Cullen.

The officer at Angela's door was passing the time of

day with one of the hospital staff, but stopped abruptly when he saw the two detectives. After he greeted them, he showed them to the visitors' room. As soon as the door opened, a short man with prematurely grey hair closed his cell phone and got up from his seat.

'Dennis Cullen?'

'And you are?'

*****

Charlie drew up to Jackie Winter's place, having followed her in his car. He'd insisted in case there was any more trouble with Jim. He parked and got out as she was locking her car door. 'Want me to go in first?'

Jackie placed her hand on his arm. 'Thanks Charlie, but you've done enough. And thanks again for rescuing me last night. Jim's car isn't here so I expect he's at work. I'll check with one of my friends before I leave.'

'I could come in, just to be on the safe side.'

'No honestly, I'll be fine. Shall I come down to the hospital after work?'

'That would be a help. But won't that cause more of a problem with Jim?'

'I'll sort it. He's OK with me going to the hospital.'

'Good. Sometimes I think I'll go crazy in there on my own. I'm hoping to get over to Angie's house today. I want to get a specialist cleaning firm in to clean it up, so I can assess what I need to do, but I should be back by the time you get there.'

Jackie leaned across and gave him a kiss on the cheek. 'Thanks again,' she said, turning to go up the front steps.

Charlie waited for a few minutes and then got back in his car. He would stop for breakfast before going up to the ward. Prior to driving off, he checked his cell phone for messages.

48

'The waiting room is fairly crowded and I expect you'll want some privacy,' said the nurse. 'I'll show you to an interview room and make sure you aren't disturbed.'

Bronski nodded. 'Much appreciated.'

Dennis Cullen took the seat by the window, leaving the two detectives to take the chairs with their backs to the door.

'So when do I get to see Angie? I'm tired and I need to get some sleep before I head back to NY first thing in the morning. I need to get a motel room and have a shower, freshen up.'

Annie started the interview. 'What have you been told about Mrs Goodman?'

'What do you mean? I only know that some bastard attacked her and that she's not doing too well.' The man was clearly agitated.

'And that's all you know?'

'I don't know what you think you're implying, but yes, that's all I know. I haven't seen her for ...' Cullen hesitated, trying to remember, 'five years. I saw her for the last time just before she married Goodman.'

Neither detective said anything at the mention of George Goodman and Cullen picked up on their silence.

'That bastard, it was him, wasn't it? He did this to her!' Cullen rose from his seat, fists clenched.

'Mr Cullen, sit down. No one has been charged with her assault as yet. We have interviewed Mr Goodman and will do so again, if need be. Right now, we are interested in anything you can tell us.' Bronski wasn't about to give away the fact that George Goodman was in the cells, awaiting their return.

The man suddenly appeared wearier than he had when they first entered the interview room. He rubbed his eyes and looked quite distressed. 'I loved that woman. We were so happy at first, but I had to share her with her mother and Charlie. That's her brother, Charlie Hegarty.'

Annie nodded. 'We know Captain Hegarty.'

'Captain, eh? It has been a long time.'

But then Cullen realised that the two detectives were waiting for him to continue. 'I was about to say, Angie was more of a mother to Charlie than their mother ever was. After their dad died, their mother went to pieces. Charlie was still a kid, needed support. Angie was there for him, more than she was for me, to be honest.'

'Is that what broke up the marriage?' Annie was still trying to establish the background.

'I wanted a family of our own, but she said she wasn't ready. She said she needed to support Charlie first, that our time would come. I got sick of waiting, I guess you could say.' Again he rubbed his eyes. 'The worst decision I ever made in my life was leaving that woman. I still love her. No one else has ever come close.' Cullen hesitated for a minute and then added, 'Look, I'll answer any questions you have, but right now, all I want to do is see her.'

Annie glanced over at Bronski and he took the cue. 'All right, we'll take you down to see her now and we'll stay with you. Once you've seen her, we have more questions to ask.'

'Fine by me.'

As they walked down the corridor, Officer Whelan stood up. Bronski and Annie showed their badges.

'Officer, you can take a break, grab a coffee and come back in twenty minutes.'

Officer Whelan nodded. 'I just need the names for the log.'

Bronski filled in the three names, while Annie opened the door. She entered the room first, followed by Angela Goodman's ex-husband. He pulled a chair up next to the bed and a moment or two later, took her hand in his and kissed it gently. Annie thought she detected a flicker of movement from Angela Goodman. Bronski came into the room and stood solemnly beside Cullen, ready to intervene if anything was required.

Annie positioned herself on the other side of the bed, remembering her own shock the first time she'd seen Angela Goodman in the bed, with tubes, drips and the ventilator. It had taken her a minute to process the whole scene and Angela Goodman didn't look any better now. Annie couldn't help wondering how Charlie coped with being there over the past several days. It seemed clear that Angela Goodman was not going to recover.

As Charlie passed the nurses' station, one of the nurses stopped him.

'Captain Hegarty, your sister has three people in with her.'

Charlie looked a bit surprised. 'I wasn't expecting anyone.'

The nurse looked down at her sheet. 'Two detectives, Bronski and Macpherson and a Dennis Cullen.'

'Dennis?' Charlie didn't wait any longer and hurried down the corridor. As he approached his sister's room, he noticed that the cop usually on duty outside the room was gone.

*****

Jackie Winters looked in the parking lot on her way into her office building and couldn't spot Jim's car. Climbing the stairs to the office, her mind ran through excuses in case anyone asked about him.

'Good morning Jackie, Jim not with you?' It was Helen, one of the section leads.

'I thought he was already here. I had to stay at a sick friend's last night.'

There was a bit of laughter from one of the girls who overheard the conversation. 'Lover's spat, was it?' Jackie wasn't about to countenance the remark with a reply and simply went to her cubicle.

Settled at her desk, Jackie wondered what to do to save face. But more importantly, where was Jim? Last night talking things through with Charlie, it was obvious she would have to leave Jim. She told Charlie that she was frightened of Jim and what he might do to her. She hadn't said outright that it might have been Jim who assaulted Angela, but her uncertainty had been enough to throw suspicion his way. For once, she didn't feel safe at work. He could come in any minute and make a scene. When would all of this be over?

The nurse had ushered them out of the room while the doctors did their rounds. Charlie stayed behind to speak to the doctor. The two detectives and Dennis Cullen arranged to meet him in the canteen, which was surprisingly empty considering the number of staff who worked in the hospital and the daily number of visitors. Bronski went off to find a table out of earshot, just in case the place did start to fill up. Annie scanned the list of food being served, but didn't have much of an appetite. Hospitals did that to her.

Cullen picked up a tray and passed in front of her, ordering the all day breakfast. Seeing his plate being piled up with food made the decision for her. She asked for a muffin for herself and a pastry for Bronski and two large coffees. She got another coffee for Charlie and a second pastry.

Back at the table, they let Dennis Cullen eat in silence. Just as he was finishing his last mouthful, Annie noticed Charlie coming through the door. She motioned him to join them.

He was surprised when the bell rang. At first he was going to ignore it, but then considered it might be the delivery he was expecting. It wasn't, but he recognised the guy on the intercom camera. He hadn't expected it to happen this way, although there had always been a scenario for an eventuality like this. It was important to remain calm, remain focused. The guy was no match for him.

'What do you want?'

'I think we both know that.'

'You don't know anything,' he said out loud as he buzzed the intercom.

The rest was easy and it was surprising what he could get people to do. The story was convincing enough to get them both into the guy's house. None of the neighbours seemed to take any notice and once inside the garage, they were invisible to the road. When he had completed the first part of the task, he retrieved his sports bag from the car. An hour later, he checked the car one final time, meticulous as ever. After all, he'd had years to perfect his plans and was also very good at improvising.

Back at his apartment, he went through his cleaning ritual before carefully typing out a second note and sealing it in a special delivery envelope. Putting on his motorcycle helmet, there was one final task for the day. The receptionist didn't question the delivery.

Annie never ceased to be amazed at people who could eat heartily when they were stressed. Her problem was the opposite. The sight of food at that time made her feel sick. She'd lost nearly twenty pounds when she called off her engagement to Paul. Watching Dennis Cullen putting down his knife and fork and taking the last swig of his coffee, she wondered if the rest of the interview would play havoc with his digestion.

'I wasn't prepared to see Angie like that, Charlie. I'm so sorry.'

Charlie nodded. 'It's been a shock for all of us.'

Cullen then focused his gaze on Annie and Bronski. 'You two need to find the bastard who did this to her. God, I hope she pulls through.'

It was Charlie who responded to the last part, 'She will, Dennis, she has to.' The strain on his face was really starting to show. Annie noticed a difference even from the previous night. She'd been hoping that a night's sleep might have helped him and wanted to have a quiet word with him, ask him how he was doing, but now was not the time. Bronski was in charge and clearly wanting to finish this interview and get back to the station. George Goodman was still waiting there to be interviewed. By now the doctor should have cleared him as fit to be questioned.

'So, Mr Cullen.'

'Call me Dennis.'

'Thank you, but Mr Cullen will do for now. Is there anything from Mrs Goodman's past that might help us to look at the motive for this assault?'

'I've been thinking about that a lot, all the way here from New York. Angie was always a mystery to me.'

'What do you mean by that, Dennis?' Charlie asked.

Bronski, unhappy about his questioning being interrupted, cut back in. 'Captain Hegarty, if you would let me ask the questions.'

Charlie leaned back in his chair and didn't reply. Annie looked at him, trying to ascertain his thoughts, but his face was blank.

'Mr Cullen, you were talking about Mrs Goodman being a mystery.'

Cullen shifted in his chair now and pushed his plate to one side, placing his elbows on the table and folding his arms. It was a few seconds before he continued. 'I think something happened before I met her. It must have been when she was in the army, at least that's all I can work out. There was always a distance, like there were places she wouldn't allow me into, if you know what I mean.'

Bronski nodded for him to continue.

'She kept diaries. I'm sure they went back years. Each year she would get a new one. Always took herself off to a private space to write in them, but I knew what she was doing. I asked her a few times about them, about what she was writing. She told me not to worry, that they were personal to her and that she needed to keep them. It was obvious it was something she didn't want to share with me.'

'I remember the diaries too.' Charlie added. 'She always told me that she wanted to be a writer and that it was a good discipline writing every day. She said she'd read that in a magazine. I never took much notice.'

'That wasn't the impression I got, Charlie. I always saw them as her secret world, her innermost thoughts and I must admit I sometimes thought of them as a wall between us. It got so she resented me asking her about them, so I gave up, but it was just another thing that remained a problem between us.'

'Where did she keep these diaries? Were they locked away? It sounds as if she never wanted anyone to see them.' It was Annie's turn to become part of the interview and somehow she felt the diaries might be significant.

Both men responded almost in unison. 'The blue trunk.'

Then Charlie continued. 'It's up in her attic. I remember putting it up there for her when she moved into her house, just before she married George. It was too heavy for her. Do you think there may be something in those diaries that might help?'

'Charlie, that email from Angela ...'

'What email is that?' Bronski interrupted. He had a vague memory of Annie mentioning an email before.

Charlie took out his phone and scrolled through his emails, as he had the previous night when he was with Annie. 'This was it, written two days before the assault, while I was still in Livingston fishing. Let me see. This is the relevant part.' Charlie read the passage to them.

'You know there are things you never knew about me, reasons why I get nervy and stuff I've never told you. May-

be when you're here we can have a good heart to heart. It just seemed such an age gap when you were younger, but now you're a serving officer, fighting for our country. There are things you need to know about my past so you understand me better, little brother. But all that can wait until you have your dream vacation. I don't mind taking a back seat to the Yellowstone.'

Annie was relieved that he hadn't read out the part about Angela's visit to the police station and their interview. That would probably have incited Cullen. Annie would have to remember to thank Charlie for that when they were on their own.

Charlie turned to his former brother-in-law. 'The crucial part is the reference to there being things about her I never knew. She was going to tell me something and my bet is that whatever it was, it's probably in the diaries. If you're right, maybe it was something from her time in the army. I'm trying to think of what those years would be.'

By the time the four people left the canteen, they knew which years to prioritise, although Annie suspected that diaries either side of those years might also be important. There was another task at the head of the schedule now though, the interview with George Goodman. Cullen gave them further contact numbers for him, before the two detectives made their way to the parking lot.

Before Charlie and Cullen left the hospital, the former brothers-in-law went back to Angela's room. Charlie watched while Dennis Cullen gently touched his ex-wife's arm and leaned over and kissed her cheek. Memories came flooding back, especially the times Dennis had taken him to Red Sox games, while Angela spent time with their mother. Charlie had been too young to really understand that his mother was suffering from depression. Looking at Angie now in the bed, with her ex-husband holding her hand, he realised again how much she'd sheltered him and how much she'd sacrificed her own marriage to ensure that his childhood was full of happier memories than his mother could give him. Now he asked himself, what could he do for her?

The text alert sounded on Charlie's cell phone, just as the two men left the hospital. The decontamination cleaning team were waiting to be let in and Charlie had to get back with the keys. He was also anxious to assess the work he needed to do in the house once they finished the clean up. Now he had a further task, to get into the attic and search for the trunk storing his sister's memories. He was haunted by the thought that, soon, those diaries might be all he would have left of her.

The two men hugged before going their separate ways.

51

When the alarm went off, Connie pressed the snooze button. It was now over a week since she'd heard from Jason. As she reached across and touched the pillow on his side of the bed, she forced back the tears. 'Jason, where are you?' she kept repeating as she hugged the pillow to herself.

An hour later, as she walked into work, she stopped suddenly. It was a sensation – a feeling that he was there, behind her. Jason – it just felt like him. Turning quickly, she faced a complete stranger. Clearly startled by her sudden movement, the man stopped abruptly.

'Sorry, I thought you were someone else.'

But the grey haired man just looked at her as if she'd lost her mind and moved swiftly past her into the next doorway.

'I have to find out,' she mumbled to herself as she entered her office building, oblivious to people saying good morning to her. Opening her handbag, she took out the small address book and looked up the telephone number of the police station and dialled it. This time she was determined not to take 'No' for an answer.

'Detective Kelsey, it's Connie Lombardi. You took a statement from me last week about my boyfriend, Jason Craven, when I reported him missing.'

The flat, uninterested voice said, 'I remember.'

Flustered, Connie started to feel foolish, picturing the detective twiddling with his pen and probably rolling his eyes at the others in the squad room. But now she had to continue, for herself if nothing else. 'I just wanted to let you know that I still haven't been able to contact him and I'm frightened that something has happened to him. Only I was thinking, what if I could give you something with his DNA on it?' She'd been working through this idea for a few days now. She couldn't quite remember how DNA was gathered but was sure she'd seen something on TV about it. Wasn't there something about a toothbrush, or the hairs from a comb?

'Miss Lombardi, I can't request a forensic examination of something for DNA traces when no crime has been committed. You seem to forget that Mr Craven is a grown man and so far, you haven't given us anything to investigate. People go missing all the time for all sorts of reasons. Now, if there's nothing else.'

As she hung the phone up, she noticed a couple of her colleagues were eavesdropping and she felt her face flush. Grabbing her handbag, she made her way to the restroom. As she closed the cubicle door, tears started welling up. Rubbing her eyes, she tried to force them back. The last thing she needed in the small office was to have red eyes and a blotchy face.

52

'Morning Detective Macpherson.' The desk sergeant smiled, always pleased to see Annie arrive at the station.

Annie smiled back, but Bronski was more abrupt. 'So how is Mr Goodman doing today? I'm presuming he's received medical attention and that we are clear to interview him Sergeant?'

'That's right Detective. He's even had a shower, specially for Detective Macpherson.' The desk sergeant winked this time.

'Great. Have him transferred to interview room one. We'll be there when we've caught up with messages.'

Dave Ellison was at his desk as the two detectives walked in. 'How did it go at the hospital; get a confession yet?'

Annie smiled, but Bronski ignored the question and busied himself reading the messages on his desk. Annie wandered over to the coffee machine and Ellison joined her. They were out of earshot of Annie's supervisor.

'So what's up with Bronski?' Ellison asked as Annie handed him a coffee.

'I think he's frustrated. We seem to be getting nowhere fast. Dennis Cullen appears to be in the clear. He couldn't tell us a lot and the only thing that might be useful is that Angela Goodman kept diaries, which she never shared with him. They might be illuminating, but who knows? I wish to God she would just wake up and we could talk to her.' Annie took a sip of her coffee and then glanced over Ellison's shoulder to see Bronski coming towards them.

'Ready to interview Mr Goodman, Detective?'

Annie emptied the rest of her coffee down the sink, hoping that Bronski hadn't heard her comments to Dave Ellison.

George Goodman didn't look much better for his shower but his lawyer seemed ready to get on with it, so Annie read him his rights for the tape and the allegations made by Genevieve Montgomery. She was just about to start questioning him when George Goodman put his hand up to signal her to stop.

'I have a statement to make.'

'Please proceed, Mr Goodman.'

'I deny all the allegations made by Ms Montgomery. Two days ago, I told her that our relationship was over. We were at her apartment at the time. She became extremely angry. In fact, I would describe her behaviour as irrational. She lunged at me with her fists flying, screaming that I couldn't do this to her, that she would see to it that I would pay for treating her like this. The scratches on my face were caused by her.' George Goodman hesitated for a moment, touching his face where the scratches appeared to be healing.

His lawyer nodded for him to continue.

'I tried to push her away, but she's a strong woman. I fell over on to her couch while she was still attacking me. I managed to push her off, but she hit her eye on the wooden arm of the couch. That stopped her momentarily, but then she carried on screaming at me. It was as if she was possessed.' Again he paused.

'Please continue.' Annie noticed that his voice wasn't as loud as when he'd first started.

245

'She kept shouting that she hadn't waited all this time for me to leave *that bitch*, that was how she always referred to Angela, just for me to drop her. I kept trying to free myself from her, but it was really difficult. I have never seen her like that. Like I've said, it was as if she was possessed or something. I finally managed to get out of the living room and I pulled the door shut and just held on to it. She started kicking the door and I knew I just had to get out. I grabbed my coat from the hallway and ran out. That was the last time I saw Genevieve Montgomery. I swear that I never touched her except to defend myself.'

The rest of the questioning was perfunctory and in the end they had to let George Goodman go. However, they cautioned him that they would be continuing their inquiries and would be in touch with him again.

*****

Charlie pulled up in front of his sister's house. A white truck was backed up in the driveway, with two guys in the front seat. Their doors opened as soon as he got out.

'Captain Hegarty?' Charlie nodded and extended his hand. 'I'm Dave Carlson and this is my partner Wayne Davos. We're sorry for what's happened to your sister.'

'Thanks, let me show you around the house and please, call me Charlie.' He opened the door with his keys. Natural light flooded into the hallway.

The three men stood there for a few minutes and Charlie watched their reaction to the damage. Then he led them into the living room and the kitchen.

'So far, this looks like vandalism,' Dave remarked. 'As you know, Charlie, we specialise in cleaning up contamination: blood spills, that kind of stuff but we know people who could help you out with this kind of damage.'

'That's OK. I was hoping to do most of this myself, once you've taken care of the rest of it. Come and have a look upstairs.'

The two men surveyed the bedroom, noting the patches of blood on the wooden floor and the bed.

It was Wayne who commented. 'We'll get the lights on all of this so we can see the extent better. We'll be able to clean up these floorboards. I'm guessing there will also be blood on some of the walls, but it's hard to see in this light.' Then he focused on the bed. 'We usually take away anything that can't be cleaned. This mattress ...'

'Just get rid of it, I'll arrange to get her a new one.'

'OK, we'll get started. Then we'll have more of an idea what we're dealing with.'

Dave and Wayne were very businesslike. Charlie opened the garage door for them and they backed the truck inside. Within minutes they had protective clothing on and were setting up equipment. Charlie wandered into the kitchen on his own, leaving them to it. He surveyed the damage again wondering where he would make a start. Just as he was figuring out how much paint he would need, his cell phone went off. The display read 'Jackie.'

'R U free about 6. No sign of J. Don't want to go

home alone. Can I meet u at hosp.'

Charlie texted 'yes' back, wondering what games Jim Moorcroft was playing. Although he was happy to follow Jackie home, he didn't want to end up spending the evening with her. There was too much to do. He looked at his watch. There was just enough time to get some supplies, drop them back at the house and get over to the hospital.

An hour later, as Charlie entered the hospital, he felt weary physically, but his thoughts were racing. How many hours of his leave had he spent here already? Was his sister ever going to come out of the coma? What if he had to plan a funeral, rather than a homecoming? But he knew he had to take one day at a time. Suddenly, he remembered that he hadn't looked for the trunk with the diaries; maybe later tonight. It was awkward with the decontamination crew at the house. He didn't want them witnessing him searching through his sister's private things. He owed her that at least. Before he went upstairs to the ward, he grabbed a bite to eat. The last food he'd had was hours ago when he'd been with the two detectives and his former brother-in-law. Despite everything, when he thought of Annie, it made him smile.

Two hours passed quickly and as Charlie glanced at his watch, he realised he must have dozed off for at least some of the time. He now turned as the door of the room opened and Jackie walked in. She looked more apprehensive than when they'd parted that morning. He got up and gave her a hug.

'Thanks for coming, you've been a huge support for

Angela.'

'How's she doing?' Like everyone else who came into the room as visitors, she whispered. Charlie himself had only just started to speak at normal volume, realising this would be the best way to stimulate his sister.

'About the same. The doctor was here just as I arrived and he is still hopeful and so am I.' But he heard his own voice break with the last few words. Jackie touched his arm to comfort him.

A half hour later they got into their cars and Charlie followed her to the house she shared with Jim Moorcroft. On the way, he couldn't help but wonder what Jackie might face when they got back. This time he would insist on going in with her. If Jim Moorcroft was still angry, he didn't want Jackie taking the full brunt of it.

Annie finished the notes of the interview with George Goodman and updated the rest of the file. Not really much to show she thought, as she put it in the drawer. If only Angela Goodman would come out of the coma. But even if she did, would she remember who her attacker was?

Just as she reached for her jacket, Dave Ellison came by her desk. 'Want to get a bite to eat?'

'Thanks Dave, that's really kind of you, but tonight I just want to get home.'

'Turning me down, eh?' Ellison put on his really hurt look.

Annie smiled, but she didn't want to be persuaded. 'Sorry Dave, but I'll take a rain check.'

As Annie turned the key in her door, she had second thoughts about being alone and regretted turning down her only prospect of company. 'Pull yourself together, woman, you have been on your own a while now, enjoy it.' But the words, even said aloud, didn't help. The light on the answer machine was flashing. Once again, she'd missed a call from her mother. She listened to the message: this time the news of Andrew was good. The crisis was over and he'd soon be home.

Thankfully, her mother never mentioned Paul, but Annie couldn't help wondering if he'd stayed in touch with her mother after he returned to Stockport from his visit to Huntly. His continued involvement with her family bothered Annie. She knew he wanted her back and that her mother would be thinking that this time away would give Annie the space to realise that breaking off the engagement was a mistake. If anything, it was making her realise just how right her decision had been. Strangely enough, at this moment, she was feeling closer to Charlie than she ever had to Paul.

Using the remote, she half-heartedly searched the TV channels, just confirming to herself that there wasn't much to watch. Placing the remote back on the coffee table, she went back into the kitchen and took some meatballs and sauce from the freezer, putting them on the counter to start defrosting. Then she opened a bottle of red wine.

*****

Charlie parked in the drive next to Jackie. As he got out of his car, she was already peering through the side garage window. 'His car's in the garage.'

'I think I should go in first, talk to him, see what kind of mood he's in,' Charlie said, locking his car.

'I don't think he'd let you see how he's feeling, Charlie. After all you're someone who could stand up to him. He saves his feelings for me and who knows how many other women like me, knowing I won't retaliate.' Jackie's hands were shaking as she searched for her house keys.

'Look, why don't you wait in the car? Let me handle this. I'll tell him that I know he can be abusive and that I want to know that you'll be safe.'

'Don't get me wrong, Charlie, I appreciate what you're saying, but he's my partner and I got myself into this relationship. I can't keep hiding from it. You could come in with me for a few minutes, though, if you want. You could tell him about Angie. I know he respects you.'

Charlie nodded and they walked up the path. There were a couple of lights on, even though it wasn't dark out yet. Jim was definitely in the house, but what kind of state would he be in? In some ways, Charlie wanted to assess if Jim Moorcroft could have been the one who assaulted his sister. Once he knew that Jackie was OK in the house, he might ask Jim to come out with him for a drink, try and get a measure of the man. He let Jackie go ahead, just keeping a few steps behind her.

54

As insistent as they'd been, Gus Wojinski finally managed to persuade Carol's parents and his mother to go out for a meal without him. They had to be convinced first that he would eat, so he got out a frozen meal Carol had prepared last month and put it in the microwave to defrost. Seeing her writing on the label brought it all back home.

'Are you sure? We could all stay and I'll prepare something.' Mrs Wojinski clearly appeared ill at ease at the thought of leaving her son alone in the house.

'No Mom, you three get something decent to eat, take your mind off things.' Gus knew she still hadn't forgiven herself for not being there when Detective Malin had visited with the news that they were treating Carol's death as a homicide.

'Well, if you're sure?'

As soon as the door was shut behind them, Gus went back into the kitchen, opened the door of the microwave and spooned the contents of the container down the garbage disposal, before putting the container and a plate in the dishwasher and starting it up. That would make it look like he had eaten. He had no appetite and knew that he had already lost weight. That morning he'd had to tighten another notch on his belt, but the thought of eating only made him feel sick.

Walking into the den, he poured himself a whisky. Then he looked at the lists the four of them had been compiling all day. It was the funeral arrangements, although they couldn't finalise the details, as his wife's body was yet to be released. The identification had been made through her dental records, because her body had been so badly burned. At least he had been assured that she'd died from the impact, not the fire and he was spared having to have a devastating last image of his beautiful wife. No, he would picture her, as she was that last night, when she'd excitedly told him that she was going to buy the pregnancy testing kit the next morning. Then the plan was that she would do the test the next night and they would have their special meal, either as a celebration or commiseration with a determination to try again. Instead, that was the last night he ever saw her.

Sitting in his recliner, he pressed the control, trying to relax as the back of the chair eased and the weight was taken off his legs. Placing his glass on the side table, he shut his eyes. Carol's face came into clear view. The smile that had always enchanted him and what attracted him to her the first time they met, when friends had fixed them up on a date. It hadn't been the most auspicious start as he'd been wary, having broken off an engagement only weeks before. But she'd won him over and six months later they were married.

Now he was planning her funeral. As he felt the tears well up again, he put the chair back into an upright position and looked again at the list of the people he had to tell about the funeral. He could see that an old friend of Carol's was missing from the list. Rising from the chair, he went off in search of her address book, the one she used for Christmas cards. Now, what was the woman's second name?

55

Although a few steps behind Jackie as she opened the front door, Charlie noticed the smell first, a smell that conjured up for him his time in Afghanistan. But before he could grab Jackie and spare her, she let out an anguished cry.

'Oh my God, no ... no!'

He pulled Jackie towards him and shielded her from the view of the body hanging from the top landing, in clear view of the hallway. Then very gently, he eased her out of the house. She leaned over the porch steps and vomited. Charlie gave her his handkerchief and got out his cell phone. Instinctively he knew there was no point going back into the house and trying to revive Jim Moorcroft.

*****

Annie had finished her glass of wine and was getting a pan out to heat up the meatballs when her cell phone rang. Tempted at first to let it go on to voicemail, she then thought better of it. As she lifted it out of her handbag, Bronski's ID came up.

'I'm on my way over to your apartment house. Dispatch has just let me know that Captain Hegarty has dialled 911. He's with Jackie Winters at the house she shares, I mean 'shared' with Jim Moorcroft. They've just found his body. I thought you'd want to come with me.'

Annie couldn't believe what she was hearing and her mind started racing, but this wasn't the time to be asking questions. 'I'll be waiting out front.'

Annie shut her phone and leaned against the kitchen counter. 'What is going on?' she found herself saying out loud. She debated whether she should ring Charlie or not. No, he was a potential witness. Instead she put the container of meatballs back in the freezer and went into the bathroom to brush her teeth. The last thing she wanted was for Bronski to smell the wine on her, although officially she was off duty and she'd only had one glass.

In the car, Bronski filled her in with what he knew. As they approached the house, they could see the police cruiser and an ambulance. Jackie was being examined by a paramedic in the back of the ambulance. Bronski approached to speak to her while Annie moved towards the house.

Charlie was on the front porch, his back to her, on his cell phone. 'So there's no change ... the doctor will be round tomorrow? What time? OK, I'll be there ... no, not tonight ... see you in the morning.' As he put his cell phone away, he noticed Annie for the first time.

'It's not a pretty sight in there.'

'I'm sure not, but I have seen bodies before, including a teenager who hanged herself.' Annie didn't mean to sound so off hand with him and she surprised herself the way it came out.

'Sorry, I didn't mean to imply ...' Charlie realised that he had momentarily forgotten that she was a cop and this was her business.

'I know you didn't,' Annie interrupted, 'and I apologise for sounding so abrupt. We'll need to speak to you, get the details, but I need to go inside first. Where will you be?' Her tone had softened.

'I'll check on Jackie and then wait in the kitchen.'

Annie nodded, hoping her face didn't give away the tinge of jealousy she was feeling as he mentioned Jackie's name. 'I think Detective Bronski might be having a word with her.'

An hour later, as the body was being removed from the house, Annie walked into the kitchen to find Charlie sitting at the table drinking a cup of coffee, which one of the crime officers had given him. The thermos had been left in case anyone else needed one.

'Want one?'

'Thanks, I could do with one.' Annie sat down at the table.

As he poured the coffee, he commented, 'Jackie shouldn't be by herself tonight.'

'Bronski has taken care of it. The paramedics are taking her to the ER to get checked out for shock and one of her friends from work is meeting them there and has offered Jackie her spare room for as long as she needs it.'

'Thanks, I couldn't exactly offer to take her to Angie's.'

Annie noticed how concerned he was about Jackie and hoped that there wasn't anything developing between them. 'So, have you left the motel?'

'I'm staying at Angie's from tonight. It's easier and the decontamination crew have nearly finished. Then I want to get started on the redecoration.'

Annie felt that twinge of guilt again, thinking Charlie was only in this position because she hadn't taken his sister's story seriously. But even if she had, would that have prevented what happened? She would never know that for sure, especially if it was Jim Moorcroft who was responsible and not George Goodman, whom Angela had suspected.

But now, Annie had to go back to being a detective. Getting out her notebook, she started the interview. 'So tell me why you happened to be with Jackie tonight?' That was a question she wanted the answer to both personally and professionally.

'She sent me a text message earlier today asking if I would go back to the house with her. Then later when she came to the hospital, she explained that Jim hadn't been into work today. He'd phoned in this morning apparently, to say he was taking the day off. Jackie was frightened to go home alone in case he started on her again.'

'OK, we obviously need to check that out with his workplace, find out who spoke to him, how he sounded. Might also help us establish a time line. But what did you mean about him 'starting on her again'?'

Just as Charlie was about to answer, Bronski motioned to Annie.

'I'll be back in a minute, Charlie.'

Annie walked into the hallway where Bronski was waiting. He had been liaising with Glen Heaviley who was in charge of the crime scene investigation. Bronski passed her a piece of paper in a sealed plastic bag. Annie read it through the plastic. It was clearly a suicide note and a confession to the assault on Angela Goodman and it asked for Hegarty's forgiveness.

'Strange that Jackie Winters isn't even mentioned, don't you think?' Bronski offered.

'Strikes me as strange too, considering that they were living together. Should we show this to Charlie?'

'Don't see any reason why not,' Bronski said, 'but then again we can't be sure if it was typed by Moorcroft. Someone else could have typed it and left it for us to find. Until the post mortem is done, we don't know for sure whether he did kill himself or not. This could all have been staged.'

'So nothing firm yet. Still it would be interesting to see what Charlie's view on the note is.'

'It's sealed and labelled, so there's no problem you showing it to him. Still, you better ask him not to share it with Jackie Winters just yet. We'll have to interview her further when she's not in shock. She won't know about the note.'

Charlie wondered what Annie was carrying as she came back in the kitchen. The hall, landing and staircase were crowded with investigators and Bronski was basing himself in the master bedroom, where the note was found.

'What's up?' he asked as Annie placed the plastic envelope on the table in front of him.

'What do you make of this?'

He read the note word by word:

I can't live with my actions any longer. I am a danger to women. My temper is uncontrollable. I was in love with Angie, but it wasn't reciprocated. When she refused my advances that night, I lost it. I just lost it completely. It was like I went into an altered state. I couldn't believe what I'd done. I was so scared I just ran out. I thought she was dead. Charlie, I'm sorry. Your sister loves you. This is all my fault. One of these days she'll come out of that coma and tell you it was me. I can't live with that dread any longer or with what I have done. I want to ask your forgiveness, but I can't. It wouldn't be fair. Jim

Charlie slid it across the table to Annie, who looked at him expectantly.

'I'm confused – I just can't believe he did that to Angie. She never mentioned anything about the two of them, other than them just being friends.'

'Would you have been in a position to know?'

'Seems there is a lot about my sister that I didn't know. I can't believe this is happening. My gut instinct tells me that something is wrong here.'

'What do you mean?'

'I don't know what I mean.' Charlie got up and started to pace around the kitchen. Then he turned and faced Annie. 'I'm still trying to come to terms with what Jackie has been going through with him. That caught me unawares. I thought they made a really good couple. Just goes to show, eh? And now to think that he had feelings for Angie. Frankly, I just can't make sense of it. So what now?'

'I think there are more questions than answers. We'll have to show the note to Jackie when we interview her. But for now, Charlie, we need you to keep this to yourself.'

'Sure, but is that the end of the investigation of Angie's assault? I mean, do you really think Jim did it?' His eyes were firmly fixed on Annie and she tried to stop herself blushing.

'I'm not sure what I think just yet. Somehow this just seems too convenient.'

56

A half hour later, Annie joined Bronski while he had a final run through the events with Glen Heaviley. The forensics team would be in the house for a while yet. There was nothing else that either Annie or Bronski could do that night.

'So, shall I drop you back home, Detective?'

'Thanks Sir, but I'm going to go back to Angela's house with Charlie. I still want to look through those diaries of Angela's.'

'OK, but take some evidence bags, just in case they enlighten us about anything.'

'Of course.'

As Annie came back into the kitchen, Charlie looked like he was deep in thought. Annie wasn't sure if she wanted to ask him what was on his mind. For a man who had only recently come home on leave from Afghanistan, expecting a vacation in Montana and then time with his sister, instead to be faced with what he had been over the last several days, how does someone cope with that? Annie had to stay focused for both their sakes. Maybe the diaries would be important. He broke the silence.

'Want to get a bite to eat on the way to the house?'

'I never did get to eat before I was called out.'

It was getting late as they entered the diner. 'I think I'll have a sandwich. I'm sort of past eating, really,' Charlie said as he folded the menu.

'Tuna on toast sounds good to me.'

'So one tuna on toast and a BLT.' Charlie ordered the food and they both decided on another coffee. The one they'd had in the kitchen seemed like ages ago. As he put both menus back behind the paper napkin holder, he said, 'It would be nice just to take you out for a meal, not to be rushing from the hospital, or worse still, a crime scene.'

Annie smiled, 'Story of my life, I'm afraid.'

'Does that mean all your life you've been dating cops and you discuss cases over a meal?' he said, smiling.

'Something like that.' Annie could see that she hadn't satisfied his curiosity. Somehow she felt in the mood to tell him more. 'My ex-fiancé was a cop; I mean, is a cop, back home. We're in the same force but based at different stations.'

'Is that awkward if he's an ex?' Charlie took a drink of his coffee while he waited for her to reply.

'Sometimes. But we're more likely to come across each other outside work, rather than at work.' Annie sipped her coffee, unsure how much to say.

'Is that because he hasn't given up on being an ex?' He smiled. 'I can see why he wouldn't want to.'

Now Annie smiled. 'Unfortunately we come from the same place in Scotland as well. When I got the job in Stockport, we'd only just got engaged. It took him a few months longer to get a transfer. At the same time I was thinking about whether I should relocate my mum and brother to Manchester, so they could be near us. My brother has Down's Syndrome and severe epilepsy. He worships Paul and so does my mum.'

'And that made the break up more difficult?'

'Still does. My mother harbours an unshakeable belief that we'll get back together. While I've been away, Andrew, my brother has been in hospital. It was touch and go. Paul made the trip back home and was there for them. He even telephoned me to let me know how things were going.'

'Was that awkward, talking to him, I mean?'

'Thankfully, it was on the answer machine. I was at work when he phoned.'

'And Andrew, is he doing better now?' The waitress came with their orders just as Charlie asked the question. It took a minute or two for the waitress to establish they had everything they needed.

Annie resumed when the waitress had retreated. 'Aye, he's much better, for now at least. He's being discharged, but really I guess it's a matter of time. Each time he's admitted he seems to deteriorate a bit more, does less for himself when he comes out, doesn't bounce back as quickly. And each time we think that the new medication or the new dose of the old medication will lessen the attacks and it usually does for a short while and then the cycle repeats itself. Mum won't accept that they can't cure the epilepsy.' Annie paused to cut her sandwich into smaller pieces and to put ketchup on her French fries. 'Still, enough doom and gloom for one night; let's talk about something more pleasant.'

'Seems doom and gloom is all there is at the moment,' said Hegarty reflectively.

'Aye, but enough is enough for one day. Just while we eat, talk to me about something else. Tell me about Montana and the Yellowstone. I'm still jealous.'

Nearly an hour later, they were back in Charlie's car. 'It's getting late, are you sure you want to come back to Angie's and look for the diaries, or should I pick you up after work tomorrow and you can get them then?'

'How difficult will they be to find?'

'I'm not really sure. I'll have to go into the attic. I know the trunk is up there. I'm not sure how many of them there are and I guess it depends how far back you want to go. I don't know what else is in the attic. I might have to shift things around to get to the trunk.'

Annie hesitated, not sure how to answer. It didn't seem very practical to try and get them now, she had to admit.

Charlie broke in again. 'So, is tomorrow evening better? We could have something to eat first and then go into the attic. The guys from the decontamination company should be finished late morning. Then I'll be able to spend the afternoon with Angie.'

'Well, I guess the diaries can wait a bit longer. Tomorrow morning we'll be tied up interviewing Jackie Winters and sifting through evidence from the house.'

'OK, so why don't you call me when you're finished and I'll pick you up from the station.'

'Sure.'

When Annie got into the apartment, she checked her answer machine. At least there were no messages, so she knew all was well with Andrew and her mum.

57

Approaching the office of the South Mass News, Connie Lombardi needed every ounce of courage that she could muster. She could feel her heart thumping and her hands felt damp. A handwritten sign on the door said: Back in ten minutes.

'Damn.' Looking at her watch, she knew that if she waited the ten minutes, that would only give her just over five minutes to tell her story before she had to rush back to the office. Her determination was beginning to dissolve but as she turned around, a young man strode up to the door. Deciding to save him the trouble, she blurted out. 'There's no one there, the sign says they'll be back in ten minutes.'

'I know, I put it there. I'm Patrick Meehan, staff reporter.' Putting his hand out to shake hers, she was momentarily taken aback. He looked more like a college student than a reporter.

'Connie Lombardi.'

Holding the coffee in one hand, Patrick pulled his keys out of his trouser pocket with the other and let them in. Connie heard the beeping of the burglar alarm.

'Take a seat over by that desk while I turn this off.'

Connie looked around the office. It was smaller than she expected, but then again this was a local free newspaper. I just need to get through this, she thought, as Patrick Meehan took his seat behind the desk.

'Now, is it Ms, Miss or Mrs Lombardi?'

Connie smiled. She was certainly old enough to be his big sister, if not quite his mother.

'Connie, will do and it's Miss.'

'OK, Connie, how can I help you?'

'My boyfriend has disappeared, I've been to the police but frankly, they don't want to know. I have been thinking of putting posters up, as I am frightened that something has happened to him. He's never been out of touch for this long since we started going out.'

'And what? You want us to carry the poster?'

'I haven't actually done one yet. I guess I wanted some advice as to whether that would be a good thing.'

'Well, I guess that depends on how you're going to get them circulated. Most of these towns have ordinances. That means you can't just put posters up where you want to or you might find yourself with a fine.'

Connie blushed, that had never occurred to her.

'Tell you what, the story of one missing person, especially an adult male isn't exactly news, but if I can get an angle.' Patrick Meehan smiled and turned towards his computer. 'So you'd better tell me all about him.'

Walking back to the office, Connie felt hopeful for the first time in the last few weeks. Someone believed her, believed that Jason had no reason to go missing. Patrick Meehan was going to find out how many more men like him were out there. How many people were suffering like she was? What was the toll of the human misery left behind? Maybe someone would recognise his photo.

That was the only part that disappointed Patrick; she only had a single photo of Jason from her phone. Jason had never liked being photographed. She'd caught him unawares and told him she'd deleted it, but she hadn't. That way she could look at him whenever she wanted. Of course, she hadn't told him that. And when Jason was back and, if he was angry about the photo, so what? At least he'd be back.

He sat down in front of the TV, flicking through the channels. The crime programmes fascinated him. He smiled to himself now as one came on the screen. Watching it, he spotted all kinds of mistakes that the perpetrator had made. Not like him, his actions had been exemplary ... except, of course, for the bitch. But there was still time to get that right, if he had to – if the surgeons had managed some kind of miracle.

He thought about his earlier visit to the hospital. As usual, the cop outside the door couldn't do enough for him: 'Father this and Father that.' He made a mental note to find out if the officer had been an altar boy. But it was getting more difficult to contain himself when he went into her room. The urge to finish what he'd started was almost overwhelming, but the timing had to be right for that one final act, if indeed it became necessary. Before then, there was the added enjoyment of seeing her suffering prolonged, whispering in her ear. Not prayers, no not prayers. Yes, this was all an unexpected bonus and he could go into her room with impunity whenever he wanted. But he had to be careful, not seem over solicitous and be convincing that he visited other patients as well.

Just as the adverts came on, he thought, maybe I should write an episode for the TV, show people what you have to do.

'I hear you had an interesting night. Finding a dead body beat the prospect of having dinner with me, eh?' Dave Ellison was smiling at Annie while she took her jacket off and put it on the back of her chair.

Annie noticed that Ellison always seemed amused at her habitual morning routine. 'Not your usual pick up line, Dave. Want a coffee while I fill you in?'

Annie walked over to the kitchen and Ellison got up to follow her. 'Want a decent coffee downstairs, instead?'

'I would, but I've got lots of notes to write up. I imagine Franconi will want to catch up with us. Bronski should be here soon. Thanks for the offer, Dave, but I'd better stay put.'

Ellison leaned back on the counter, folding his arms. 'So, the body was one for the books, was it? Must admit I've seen some bodies in my time, but never one suspended from a rope.'

'Well, be grateful for small mercies, Dave. Believe me, it was not a pretty sight, especially since he'd been there for hours. And the smell, there is nothing like it.' Annie put the milk in the cups and then poured the coffee from the coffee maker.

'So Hegarty found him, eh? Why was he there?'

'Good question, Dave, but it was legitimate. Jackie Winters asked him to go back to the house with her after the problems she'd had with Moorcroft the previous night.'

'Convenient for her, then?'

Annie turned to Ellison while she passed him the coffee. 'Is that enough milk for you?'

'Great,' he said taking a sip.

'What do you mean by 'convenient for her'?'

Ellison paused for a moment. 'Well, it would have been different had she walked into that house alone, wouldn't it?' He took a sip of coffee.

'I guess so, but I'm still not getting your drift.'

Before they could finish the conversation, they heard Bronski walk in. Annie put her coffee down for a minute, as she poured another for her supervisor. Walking over to his desk, she put it down.

Ellison followed her out of the kitchen and sat back down at his desk to continue the computer search he had been doing before she arrived.

'Thanks Detective, I'm going to miss you when you go back to England. Could you teach Ellison to do that before you go?' quipped Bronski. But his focus on Annie was only momentary while he shifted stuff on his desk and checked the pink message slips. He never sat down until that task was completed.

Ellison leaned back in his chair. 'When you two have a minute, I've got a message for you both. Not sure it's what you want to hear, so don't 'shoot the messenger,' as they say.'

Annie glanced over at Ellison, trying to read the expression on his face and wondering why he hadn't said anything to her first, but she assumed he'd been waiting for Bronski to get in. He couldn't really show her any favouritism. He'd be working with Bronski long after her exchange ended.

Ellison's expression was neutral. What else can go wrong, thought Annie.

'Two minutes and we're all yours,' replied Bronski as he sorted his papers into two piles and pondered over one of the messages, while checking his watch.

Annie couldn't help wondering if she were the only impatient person in the place.

Finally, Bronski sat down facing his two colleagues. 'Right, what you got for us?'

'A message I took earlier this morning from George Goodman's lawyer.'

Annie visibly winced. 'What now, wrongful arrest?'

'No, he wants information from your interview with Genevieve Montgomery. Goodman is suing her for slander; says she wants to ruin him.'

Annie smiled. 'Now why doesn't that surprise me?'

'Well, he'll have to wait his turn. We've got a few more pressing things on our plate today. Is he putting it in writing, this lawyer?'

'Said he would.'

'Thanks, we'll wait and see. I'm glad you spoke to him. You're more diplomatic.' Now Bronski turned to Annie. 'We need to see Franconi this morning; update him on last night's events. He'll have heard from despatch and he'll want to know what we're doing about it.'

Right on cue, Franconi came through the door.

'Morning Detectives ... ten minutes ... my room.'

When he was out of earshot, Annie couldn't help mumbling a comment. 'Well at least he said good morning.'

'Must be your optimism, Detective,' Ellison retorted, 'I only heard him say 'morning', not 'good' morning.'

Even Bronski had to smile at that.

The intervening ten minutes gave Annie the chance to update the file on Angela Goodman, as Jim Moorcroft had been a part of that investigation. She also checked her notes from last night. A new file would need to be started on Moorcroft. The two events appeared to be related, but nevertheless a new investigation would be needed into his death.

'So Scotty, you're having an eventful exchange. Is this your first suicide?'

'No Sir, and to be fair, we're not sure yet if Mr Moorcroft's death is a suicide.'

Franconi picked up his pen and started to tap on his blotter. Annie was relieved that it wasn't the paper clip and the nail cleaning routine. 'And what do you think, Detective?' he asked, as his focus shifted to Bronski.

'Detective Macpherson is technically correct. It looks like a suicide. There is a note but it is typed and printed out from his computer. Anyone could have done that or could have forced him to do it. But unlike my partner, I'm tending to think he did commit suicide.'

Annie tried not to look at Bronski, knowing her face would betray how she felt. He could at least have backed me up at this early stage and not made me look a fool in front of Franconi, she thought. Also, she recalled he hadn't seemed so convinced last night. He was the one who said that it might have been staged to look like a suicide. But she tried to hold it together. She was here to learn, after all. Thankfully, Franconi needed a bit more to go on.

'Any sign of a struggle at the crime scene, any defence wounds on him?' Franconi's pen tapping was now getting rhythmical.

This question gave Annie the opening she needed. 'Not that we saw last night. The autopsy will give us more. I think, at this stage, we should be keeping an open mind.' Bronski might not like that comment, but it needed to be said.

'What did Jackie Winters have to say about it?'

Annie got out her notebook. 'The last time she saw him was the previous night. That's when she had an argument with him, went to see Captain Hegarty and stayed in the motel where he was staying. The next morning Captain Hegarty accompanied her back to the house but Moorcroft wasn't there.' Annie hesitated in case Franconi wanted to ask anything but he was too busy tapping his pen, so she continued. 'Then later in the day she sent a text to Hegarty and asked him if he would accompany her to the house. Hegarty showed me the text message and I've noted it verbatim and the time.'

'And?'

'She later met him at the hospital and told him more about her concerns about Moorcroft's mood the previous night. What was strange was that Moorcroft hadn't been at work yesterday.'

Franconi stood up and walked over to his coffee machine. He nodded to the two detectives but both declined a cup. He sat down again, this time focusing his attention on Annie.

'And does Hegarty back up the story?'

'Aye Sir, he does.'

'What's with the two of them?' Franconi was gazing at her intently. Annie was trying desperately to come over professionally, although she was taken aback. 'You mean Hegarty and Jackie Winters?'

'Of course, I mean them.'

Bronski shifted in his seat and Annie, sensing that he was about to take over, finished what she had to say. 'I understand that he knew Jackie Winters very little before the recent events with his sister. He had known Moorcroft much longer, as Moorcroft and his sister worked together and were friends for years. Jackie Winters only came into the picture a year or two ago and Hegarty only really knew of her from his sister's correspondence and telephone calls. He's been in Afghanistan for the past six months.'

Annie expected Franconi to make a comment. Instead, he changed the subject and addressed his next question to Bronski.

'What about the suicide note?'

Bronski passed the typed note to Franconi and waited in silence while he read it.

Passing the sealed evidence back to Bronski, Franconi carried on with his questioning. 'So, what does Jackie Winters make of the note? Does she believe what it says, this undying love for Angela Goodman, while he's living with her? Is she the jealous type?'

Here they were back to that woman again and her views. Annie couldn't really see the relevance. It was clear in her mind that they were seeking a male perpetrator and she was still convinced that they were missing something from Angela's past that was relevant. Somehow, Jim Moorcroft didn't fit into the puzzle for her, but he was obviously beginning to for Bronski and perhaps Franconi.

The next few minutes were spent tossing ideas around. Jackie Winters still had to be interviewed. That was part of the procedure and might be illuminating in some way. She'd been in no fit state to make a statement the previous evening but was due at the station later on in the morning. Annie and Bronski had already decided that they would interview her together.

'OK, I think we're through for now. Keep me informed. In the meantime, take the guard off the hospital room. It's costing too much and if Moorcroft did do it, then we're wasting money.' Franconi winked at Annie. 'After all, we need to keep track of our budgets or we may have to suspend the exchange.'

The wink made Annie uneasy, the budget comment felt like a veiled threat. Perhaps Franconi did feel that this all started with a misjudgement on her part and look at where they were now – a woman still fighting for her life and the man who found her was dead in suspicious circumstances. Consequently, as they walked out, Annie felt unnerved. Her intuition told her that the real perpetrator was as elusive as ever. What worried her more was her sense that Bronski and Franconi were settling on the suicide note being genuine. Her counterarguments were not being taken seriously. She could only hope that the autopsy would provide some evidence to the contrary. And she still needed to know more about Angela Goodman.

Dave Ellison tore up a pink message slip as Annie and Bronski got back to their desks. 'Good, you've just saved me writing out a message. Jackie Winters is waiting downstairs for you.'

60

Jackie Winters' appearance shocked Annie. For the first time, the pristine make-up wasn't in evidence and her hair looked as if it hadn't been washed. There were dark circles under her eyes and her lids were puffy. Bronski greeted her first. 'Thanks for coming down to the station. We're sorry for your loss. Although this is a difficult time, there are questions we need to ask you.'

Jackie Winters simply nodded to Bronski but made no eye contact with Annie. Once they were in the interview room, Bronski explained the procedure and then began his questions. 'Ms Winters, when was the last time you saw Mr Moorcroft alive?'

Jackie didn't hesitate, as if she'd already rehearsed her answer. 'Tuesday night. I went shopping at the mall and when I got back he just flew into a rage, asking me where I'd been, what I'd been doing. He was so angry I felt scared and ...'

'Go on, please.'

'I just grabbed my handbag and left the house.'

'He just let you go, didn't try to stop you?' Annie came in with her own question.

Jackie answered, but faced Bronski. 'I think he would have but I got away too quickly and jumped in the car. I pulled over a few minutes later to see if he was following me. Thankfully, he wasn't.'

'And what did you do next?'

'I drove to the motel where Charlie ... Captain Hegarty ... was staying. I went up to the reception desk and they telephoned his room for me. He had been asleep but he came down and met me in the bar.'

Annie knew that Charlie had not long since left her apartment and wondered whether he'd told Jackie that. If he had done, maybe that was the reason Jackie was avoiding eye contact with her. Bronski pursued what happened next, but Annie didn't really want to hear the next few answers or if there was anything going on between Charlie and Jackie. To her relief, the answers established only that they'd talked and then he'd arranged a room for her in the motel. They'd met again at breakfast. After that, he'd followed her back to the house in his car. As Moorcroft's car wasn't there, they had both assumed he was at work.

The questions then turned to Jim Moorcroft and his temper. Jackie admitted to them that sometimes she'd been frightened of him and that he had been abusive, but not severe enough for her to report it. The only time she'd been truly frightened was the last night she saw him.

Bronski opened the file and pulled out the suicide note. Jackie hadn't been shown it the night before. Bronski slid it across the table to her.

'We found this note in the main bedroom.'

Jackie hesitated, not knowing whether she should touch the plastic envelope or not, but then straightened it out in front of her and read it very slowly.

Her hand went to her mouth. 'Oh my God, no ... no, why?' And then she covered her face with her hands.

Bronski looked over at Annie, who took the cue. 'We know this is difficult but we have to ask you, do you believe that Jim Moorcroft wrote that note?'

Wiping away tears, she murmured. 'I don't want to believe it, all the lies, the deception. He never loved me, did he? He never spoke about Angie except as a friend. I had no idea he felt like that about her.' She picked up the note and read it again.

Annie poured Jackie Winters a glass of water and the two detectives waited while she composed herself. Once she appeared more settled, Bronski came in again. 'I am sure that part of the note is difficult for you, but do you believe what it says, that he really did commit suicide. Had he ever talked about suicide in the past?'

Jackie hesitated and when she finally spoke, her voice was barely above a whisper. 'Yes, right after we found Angela. He was really shook up at her house and while we were waiting for the ambulance to arrive, he started talking about death, how she deserved to live and other people didn't. At first I just thought he was in shock, you know, finding Angie like she was.' Jackie picked up the glass and drank from it. As she put it down, Annie gently prompted her to continue. 'Then he started to get morose, saying he didn't deserve to live. I just got angry at the time, told him to stop talking nonsense, that Angie needed him, that I needed him.'

'And?'

'I think the ambulance must have arrived because I don't remember him saying anything else about it and we never discussed it again. I never thought ...' It took a few minutes for Jackie Winters to compose herself again in order to continue. The two detectives remained silent as well.

Annie was thinking how painful the realisation

must be when someone commits suicide and you think you could have done something to help. But there was still that nagging feeling of whether this was suicide or not. Annie glanced briefly at Bronski. He's becoming more and more convinced of suicide, she thought.

Bronski asked a few more questions, mostly about the computer. Jackie confirmed that it was Moorcroft's and that she didn't use it. She said she had enough with computers at work. Finally they neared the end of their questions and Bronski asked her about Moorcroft's next of kin. She mentioned that he had a sister, Debbie, but that they weren't that close. She would need to find the address back at the house.

That final question prompted Jackie to ask whether she could return to the house, as she needed some clothes and things. 'Obviously I couldn't really pack anything last night and I'm going to run out of clothes.'

'Our forensic team is still there at the house, so we can't allow you in without police escort. Detective Macpherson will accompany you.'

This part hadn't been decided in advance and the last thing Annie wanted to do was to accompany Jackie Winters to her house. But maybe it would give her a chance to assess Jackie's mood once they were alone together. Just before they set off from the station, Annie sent a text message to Charlie, to confirm meeting up after work. The reply came back as she grabbed her jacket: 'Pick you up at 5:30 outside station. Text if changes. Charlie.'

Annie observed Jackie Winters as they approached the

front door of the house. Nervously, Jackie went in as the cop opened the door to them. There were still some technicians in the house. Jackie's eyes darted about as she tracked each person in what had been her home and what was now a crime scene. The senior technician introduced himself and expressed his sympathy for her loss. Annie was impressed, but like Jackie, wanted to get in and out as quickly as possible and let the technicians finish. In all, they were in there about twenty minutes.

61

Gus had been waiting for the phone call, ever since Detective Malin had left a message on the answer machine while he was in the shower. It was the first day for a week that he was going to be on his own. All the parents had gone home, awaiting news from him of the date of the funeral. It had been two days since he had last spoken to the detective and now he waited anxiously for the call. The glass of orange juice had burned as he swallowed it and he knew that the heartburn was from lack of proper food. Carol would be shouting at him if she were here.

If only ...

Just as he forced himself to take a bite of toast, the phone rang again. He recognised the detective's voice immediately.

'Sorry to phone you so early, Mr Wojinski, but I thought you would want to hear this from me, before we have to brief the local news reporters.'

Gus braced himself, leaning hard against the kitchen counter. He made himself reply. 'What?'

'I'm afraid that we are now officially treating your wife's death as a homicide, not an accident. As I told you the other night, there is no sign at all of a second body and now we have traced the other car. It was rented ten days ago in Springfield. We have the name of the customer – Jason Craven. Does that name mean anything to you?'

'I don't know anyone of that name and I can't recall Carol ever mentioning that name, but I can't be sure. He could have been a customer, an online buyer, a book dealer, perhaps. Do you know anything about him?'

The line went quiet for a few seconds. 'That's the thing, we've checked out the photocopy of the driving licence from the rental company. Jason Craven died three years ago in a plane crash, so we believe we are dealing with a case of identity fraud. The address doesn't check out either. It's a real street, just the house number doesn't exist, but as the guy paid in cash, they didn't bother with the usual checks. Some young kid was on duty at the time, just a summer job for him.' The detective finally paused.

'Were there any security cameras?'

'Yes, and we're checking out the tapes as we speak. The young kid who served him couldn't recall much about the customer, so we're just trying to identify people who were in line around the time on the docket. We're covering about an hour or so to be sure and we should finish later this morning. If we get any stills off the camera, I'll bring them around. You can see if you recognise anybody in them.'

'Maybe you should take them to the bookshop as well. Perhaps Sandra or Fiona will recognise a customer or a book distributor.' Gus was clutching at straws, but that was all he had. He felt so powerless.

'We'll do that. Can I get you later on this number?'

'I'll be here.'

Gus put the phone down. The terrible wrenching feeling in his stomach was back. He walked into their bedroom, took Carol's dressing gown from the hook behind the door and lay on the bed clutching it to his face as he sobbed.

62

When Annie got back to the station, Bronski was on the phone to the desk sergeant, letting him know that no one was needed to relieve the officer on duty outside the hospital room. 'Well that should cheer Franconi up, saving a few dollars. I don't know about you but it's about time to go home. How did the trip back to the house with Jackie Winters go?'

'It was fine. She didn't say a lot. Just got her things together. Kept trying not to glance at the spot where he killed himself.' What Annie left out was Jackie talking about Charlie and how good he had been to her. It was obvious that Jackie was developing feelings for him that Annie didn't want to hear about. After all, she was meeting him herself after work. Of course, she never mentioned that to Jackie. 'But she did say a bit more about Moorcroft. I think she was more afraid of him than she told us in the interview.'

'Her and the first wife, eh? By the way I guess we should let her know about his death. I'll do it now before I go home.'

As Bronski looked up the number, Annie read the messages on her desk. There was nothing that had to be dealt with immediately. Looking at her watch, she realised that she had about an hour to do some reports and update the time line in the file. The only distraction was overhearing Bronski on the phone to Linda Moorcroft. Annie glanced over at Bronski, as he put the phone down.

Turning towards her, he said: 'She believes the same

as you do.'

Annie looked at him quizzically, 'Meaning?'

'She said he is, sorry *was*, too arrogant to hang himself.'

'But you're still going with suicide for now?'

'We should have the autopsy results in the morning. Let's take it from there.' Bronski got up and grabbed his coat, shuffling in the pocket for his keys. 'See you in the morning Detective.'

'Aye.' Annie refocused on the last few tasks, relieved that Ellison was out. She hoped he wouldn't return in time to see her meeting Charlie, knowing it would annoy him.

Charlie was very punctual. As she got in the car, she debated whether or not to say anything about Jackie. Best not, she decided. 'How is your sister, any improvement?'

'It's hard to tell, although the doctors seem to think there is. Apparently the latest scan has shown that the swelling has gone down in the brain and she could come out of the coma in a day or two. They're going to call me if there is any change tonight.'

'Sounds more hopeful.'

'By the way, Officer Cunningham came in to say goodbye. Said that the detail is being taken off the door. What's that all about?' Charlie glanced at her and then concentrated on the traffic again.

'Franconi authorised it. Now that Moorcroft is being treated as the prime suspect in the assault on your sister, he didn't think it was required any more.' Annie hesitated a couple of seconds.

'Do I detect that you disagree?' he said, glancing at her again, while he signalled to turn right at the lights.

Annie wasn't sure how much to say. After all, her first loyalties were to her colleagues and she was a guest in their squad. 'I'm probably a bit more sceptical, should we say, than my colleagues, but the autopsy results shouldn't be too long now. They should confirm if Jim Moorcroft hanged himself or whether his death is suspicious.'

Charlie sighed. Annie noticed how tired he looked, how all of this was taking a toll on him. More than anything, she wanted to forget it all and just enjoy an evening together.

'But if it wasn't him, then someone could be out there who is still a danger to my sister.'

Annie had that fear as well. Even though she'd wanted to argue with Franconi about taking the cop off the door, she hadn't. There were times, she thought, when you had to let senior people make the decision, although it went against her gut instincts not to say anything. Maybe she should have had the courage to object. Charlie voicing his concern started to worry her, but she needed to reassure him. 'If it were someone else they would have made a move by now, probably in those early hours before the officer was assigned.'

'Unless they'd thought they'd accomplished what they set out to do on the night she was attacked. My sister was left for dead and it was a miracle she survived and is still hanging on to life.'

Annie didn't want to discuss the case any more.

There were too many unanswered questions in her own mind and the last thing she needed was for Charlie to start to doubt the investigation. 'I'll telephone the hospital when we get to the house and tell them to be vigilant for strangers.'

Twenty minutes later, they pulled into Angie's drive and Charlie let them into the house.

'Gosh, that decontamination company is good at their job, aren't they?' Annie was amazed at how different it looked compared to the last time she'd seen it.

Charlie shut the door. 'They were fantastic. Although it's not usually part of what they do, they also put a base coat of paint on all the walls. So all I have to do now is finish it off. The coverage is really good, except in the daylight when you can still see some of the streaks from the vandalism. A couple more coats should sort that out. Oh, and I ordered a carpet for her bedroom. Although they got the bloodstains out of the wooden floor, I just wanted the room to look different for her. I have to telephone the company tomorrow to confirm the colour. I'll show you some samples later and perhaps you can help me choose.'

He led Annie into the kitchen. Again this room looked so much better. 'The number for the hospital is in the memory, press '1' and you should get straight to the ward. When you're done, I'll talk to them as well.'

When Charlie hung the phone up, Annie said, 'Only Father Loftus has been in, said he'd check on her again tomorrow when he does his rounds. Said he would miss his talks with the officers outside the door.'

'I've never met him. I seem to miss him each time.

288

Perhaps I'll see him tomorrow. Now, some food, before we go in search of those diaries.'

An hour later, Annie helped Charlie make the decision about the bedroom carpet. Then it was time to look for the diaries in the attic. He took Annie into the spare room, which had a door opening on to a narrow staircase leading into the attic. He clicked the light switch.

'There's not much light in here, but from memory, the trunk is in the corner.'

Charlie led the way and soon found the trunk. Annie stepped carefully, avoiding an assortment of old furniture and boxes. The one light bulb hardly illuminated the space.

Charlie knelt down in front of the trunk. 'We're in luck, it isn't locked. That saves me searching for a key. Let's just take a handful each downstairs and then we can see what years we've got.'

He started to pass the diaries to Annie. There was an assortment of colours and sizes and only some were proper diaries with the year marked on the front. Others were notebooks of sorts. When they each had as many as they could manage, they started down the stairs.

Spreading them out in the living room, Hegarty topped up their wine glasses first. 'Not usually how I like to spend the evening after dinner.'

'No, but there has to be something we are missing, with the brutality of the attack, the damage to the house. I can't buy into it being Moorcroft, note or no note.'

'And you're convinced there is something from the past?'

'Something or someone and if it was Moorcroft, she must have had an inkling for years of how he felt.'

'OK, so what am I looking for?' Charlie asked as he picked up one of the diaries.

63

Detective Malin put the phone down. He really felt for Gus Wojinski. From the photos in the house, it was clear how attractive his wife had been. She had everything to live for. As he opened the file again, the phone started ringing.

'Detective Malin.'

'Hi, Detective, it's Penny Harrington, just wanting to catch up on the Carol Wojinski story.'

Penny Harrington was the local crime reporter. Not an unpleasant woman, he'd noted on many occasions. At least she wasn't as pushy as her predecessor, whom Malin couldn't stand. The papers were understandably eager for news. Carol Wojinski was known locally because of the bookshop and had lots of friends in the town. The first published story was just about the accident and reported that the police were assuming that both drivers had perished. However, as the days had passed and no second body was found, the local reporter was keen for a comment about the progress of the investigation. Malin had always believed that if you handled the press respectfully, they could be an asset in any investigation.

'OK, so ask away,' he said, doodling on his desk blotter.

'Great to have some co-operation Detective,' Penny Harrington laughed.

'Be fair, Penny, you know I will tell you what I can.' There was no tone of malice in his voice.

'True enough, but other times you've left me hanging.'

The two had known each other for several years and Malin knew that the little game of banter would soon be over. 'Alright, I'll try not to do it this time. Ask away.' He put his pen down and started to shuffle papers on his desk with his free hand. Now that he had spoken to Gus, he saw no reason not to release the name of the suspected driver of the other car and he knew that would be a key question.

'So, what do we know about the other car and the driver. Have you found the second body yet?'

'No, despite an extensive ground search with helicopter assistance using thermo-imaging. If there was one to be found we would have found it.' Malin paused and then added: 'We now believe that there isn't a second body.'

'No second body? How can that be?'

'We think that Carol Wojinski was forced off the road and that the second car was pushed over the edge. That seems to be consistent with what the accident investigators have found from the positions of the two cars, the tyre markings ...'

Before he could finish the sentence Harrington interrupted. 'Does that mean you are investigating a homicide?'

'You've got it.'

'Carol Wojinski was just an ordinary citizen. What possible motive could there be? I thought we were talking about a tragic accident, but deliberately forcing a woman, driving on her own, off the road ... well, it's another matter altogether.'

'Obviously we don't know who might have had a motive for this, but we do have the name of the man who rented the second car. We are issuing an alert for anyone who knows him to come forward with any details about him. I will be appearing on the lunch time local news with an appeal for information.'

'That's in an hour. I'll be there at the studio, but how about a scoop on this one?'

'Don't see why not. His name is Jason Craven. Have you ever heard the name before?'

'No.'

'Well let's hope some of the viewers, or your readers, have.'

'Does Gus Wojinski know this?'

'I spoke to him this morning.'

'I don't suppose you'll share his reaction?'

'I'm sure you can imagine. It's bad enough having to accept your wife's death is a tragic accident. It's another thing when you find out it's being investigated as a deliberate act.'

'I spoke to him briefly when he first heard: he was pretty devastated then.' Penny Harrington paused for a moment and then changed the subject. 'So, what do you know about this Jason Craven?'

'I can't say much at this point, but we are investigating him. At this stage all I am prepared to say is that he showed a Massachusetts licence when he rented the car.'

Penny Harrington knew Malin well enough to know that this was all she would get from him for now. She needed to do some searching herself. 'Thanks Detective, I'll make sure to print that anyone with information on this man should come forward.'

As he put the phone down, Malin wondered if he should have mentioned that Craven was probably a false identity. Even so, someone might recognise the name being used. Perhaps he would clear up the point in the news conference. After all, he had given Penny a heads up on the investigation.

As he was about to review his notes, one of his fellow detectives knocked on the door. Steiner had only joined them in the last month. 'What can I do for you Steiner?'

Steiner walked in the room shutting the door behind him. 'I heard one or two of the guys talking about the Wojinski case and they mentioned the name of the guy you're looking for ... Jason Craven.'

Malin looked at him intently. 'Go on.'

'Well, last week I took a call from a reporter in Boston. The guy works for the local free paper. Obviously, it's not in the same league as *The Globe*. Anyway, he was putting a story together about missing persons and was asking for information from one of our cold cases but, as we got talking, he said he was writing the story because a woman had come to see him about her partner who was missing. The partner's name was Jason Craven.'

Malin's face lit up. 'What details did he give you about this Jason Craven?'

'Not much really, just that this woman had been ignored by the police. You know the story: adults go missing all the time, maybe he had a reason, that sort of thing. But the woman wasn't convinced and obviously her story intrigued the reporter enough for him to decide to do a bigger article on missing persons.'

'Steiner, this is really good. I need the name of the reporter and the woman's name.'

'Thought you might. I've got my original notes here.

64

Breaking her usual habit of eating a quick sandwich in the office, Connie Lombardi decided instead to have lunch at the City Diner. As it was just around the corner, it was likely that there would be other people from work in there, but at least it was a change of scene. For probably the hundredth time that day, she checked her cell phone when she sat down. Still no message from Jason. As she looked at the menu, she knew she was just going through the motions of life: getting up every day, phoning her mother, forcing herself to go to work, always anxious to get home again in case he had written to her, put a note under her apartment door, left a message on her computer. Anything, anything at all that would let her know that he was still alive, that he was thinking about her. A month ago, her life had been so much more promising. Every day she'd woken up excited, knowing that she would see or at least talk to him but these last few weeks had really dragged.

Patrick Meehan, the reporter had been true to his word and written the article about people going missing. Disappointingly though, Jason's story didn't get the prominence she'd expected and assumed from their discussion. Instead, Meehan had managed to dig up an interesting tid bit about a local well known person whose brother had gone missing years before. That was the main story line, including a picture. No picture of Jason. In some ways, that was a relief. At least she didn't have to worry about him being angry with her if his photo had been in the paper. Would he be angry? She was beginning to doubt how well she even knew the man she'd been sleeping with for nearly six months.

The waitress approached to take her order. Connie didn't recognise her, but assumed she was a college kid earning a few bucks for the next semester. 'I'll have tuna on toast, white toast, no fries, extra coleslaw and a black coffee.' After she gave her order, she looked around, relieved that she didn't recognise anyone. A woman at the next table was in animated discussion with her husband and Connie engaged in her usual habit of eavesdropping.

'Such a shame about that woman in Springfield wasn't it?' The woman remarked as she bit into her burger.

'That woman whose car plunged down the ravine?'

'Yes, Carol something, managed a bookshop.'

'Blanche, don't you remember me talking about that route?'

'Can't say I do, Hank. What about it?'

'I used to take that road when I went to those district sales meetings. I know it very well, the drop must be a hundred feet.' Hank paused, concentrating on putting heaps of soured cream on his baked potato.

'Hank, I forgot about that. Gosh was that the same road?'

'Sure was. I hated that route, especially at night when I was tired.'

'I'm glad I didn't know about it at the time, I would have worried myself to death.'

The waitress brought Connie's coffee over as well as a glass of ice water. 'Your lunch won't be a minute.' Connie smiled, relieved that the waitress was quick, as she wanted to listen to the rest of the conversation without distraction. She remembered the news story the couple were discussing, although she hadn't heard any update on it. But instead, they began reminiscing about the years he travelled and the news story got lost. Just as well as her lunch arrived. She looked at her watch: only twenty minutes to eat and get back to her desk.

65

Annie walked into Angela's kitchen. Somehow it felt awkward being there the next morning. But why? After all, they were two single people. Last night it just seemed sensible that she should stay over in the guest room, rather than get a late taxi.

Charlie smiled as he put some toast on the table and poured coffee for the two of them. 'Sleep OK?'

'I did. That sofa bed is really comfortable.'

'I'm sorry I haven't got much food in; hope toast is enough to keep you going.'

Before Annie could answer, the phone rang.

Charlie looked at her. 'That could be the hospital.'

She watched him get up from the table, silently hoping that this wasn't the phone call he'd been fearing.

'I didn't catch your name ... Gus Wojinski.' Annie watched as Charlie noted the name down on the pad by the phone. 'No, Angela Goodman isn't here right now. I'm her brother, Charlie Hegarty. I'm staying at her house for a while.' Charlie hesitated while the man spoke and Annie was trying to get the gist of what was being said. 'I'm sorry for your loss. You must be devastated. No, I'm sorry, I don't recognise your wife's name. I was a kid when Angie was in the services. Of course, I'll let Angie know. Gus, give me your number.'

As Gus Wojinski was giving his number, he broke down on the phone. Charlie put his hand over the receiver and motioned to Annie. As he pressed the speaker button Annie could hear weeping. Charlie mouthed to her, 'I'm not very good at this.'

Annie stood there, debating whether to take the phone from Charlie but thought better of it. He hadn't said what the situation was with Angela, but something struck her as strange. She mouthed back to him, 'How did she die?' The cop in her wanted an explanation.

Charlie waited until the man at the other end of the phone had composed himself enough. 'Gus, I am really sorry for your loss. Was it sudden, unexpected?' He glanced at Annie, not feeling very comfortable talking to a stranger about his wife's death. All he really wanted to do was hang up the phone.

The voice through the speaker said: 'She died in a car crash, which we thought was an accident at first, but now the police are treating it as a homicide.'

Charlie and Annie looked at each other, the surprise showing in both their faces. Annie whispered to him to find out how Gus's wife knew Angela.

Gus was starting to explain that they'd been roommates in the army during basic training. Then Charlie heard voices in the background. It was obvious other people had arrived at the house. Minutes later, Gus said, 'I'll call again when I know the details. I know she would want Angela there.'

Again, Charlie couldn't bring himself to mention the situation with Angie. 'OK, we'll wait to hear from you. Gus, I'm sure Angie will be devastated over your loss. Thanks for letting us know.'

Putting the receiver down, Charlie repeated what they'd both heard. 'They were in the services together: hadn't met up in quite a few years, but Carol mentioned Angie from time to time. He knew Angie would want to know.'

Annie just nodded.

'I just couldn't tell him about Angie.'

'Charlie, he wasn't in a state to hear any more bad news. You did the right thing.'

Annie kept her own counsel for the time being, though in terms of the manner of Carol Wojinski's death, it would be bizarre if her death was linked somehow to the attack on Angela Goodman. Could there be a connection between what had happened to these two women? She needed to read the diaries covering the years Angela was in the army. There were several diaries in her bag already to take into work. Best to stay quiet until she'd learned more.

*****

That's strange, thought Annie as she came into the squad room an hour later. Unusually, Bronski had arrived before her, with his coffee already on the desk. Thanks, she thought, I usually do one for you. No return compliment, I see. The other unusual thing was that he hardly acknowledged her, so engrossed was he in what he was reading. He was also murmuring to himself. Annie decided to go off to the kitchen. She was planning how she would tell Bronski about the phone call Charlie had that morning without having to let on that she'd stayed the night with him. Bronski would probably read more into it than necessary. The diaries were in her bag, still to read. Maybe the information on the phone call could wait until she knew more.

She felt a bit hurt that Bronski hadn't acknowledged her yet this morning. Was it because she'd questioned, even subtly, both his and Franconi's judgement about Moorcroft's death? Even the interview with Jackie Winters, when she admitted that Moorcroft had spoken of suicide once before, hadn't convinced her. Bronski had been more persuaded, though. She could tell that much.

The coffee was fresh, at least. Hesitating in the kitchen for a few minutes, Annie looked across at the squad room. No one was there, except Bronski, still absorbed. No Dave Ellison this morning, but she expected he would be in later. He was working on a series of burglaries in Westford, the most expensive section of town, in which the Congressman for the State lived. That just wouldn't do. Annie smiled at the thought that money talked wherever you were in the world.

Finally, she spotted Bronski putting the file down. That was her signal to make her way back.

'So, Detective Macpherson, want a job with us?'

'I thought I already had one, Sir.'

'I mean we could do with a detective of your calibre on the force.' Bronski smiled at her before he continued. 'You were right all along. We're dealing with the homicide, not the suicide of Jim Moorcroft.'

'We are?' Annie was pleased, but didn't want to come over as too pleased.

'Let me explain.' Bronski got up from his desk.

For the first time since she'd met him, Bronski went over to the white board and started to draw pictures on it. 'So this was Moorcroft when we arrived at the scene.' The stick drawing portrayed the body hanging from the noose and the chair on the floor knocked over. 'Remember the signs we saw immediately, the signs of hypoxia?'

'The blue complexion, the chest extended because of the lungs.'

'... and the burst blood vessels in the eyes. All that is in the report.' Bronski listed the signs on the board. 'So the hanging itself isn't in doubt. The question is whether he was dead before his neck was placed in the noose or whether he died as a result of the hanging.' Bronski hesitated for a moment and then carried on. 'Now the report shows that the next bit isn't consistent with suicide. The rope marks on the neck don't have the inflamed edge of a 'vital reaction.' So this suggests homicide instead. So Moorcroft was dead before he was hanged.' Bronski drew another figure on the board.

'But there were no major signs of a struggle in the house. I imagine Moorcroft was pretty strong, so why didn't he fight his attacker?' Annie was leaning back in her chair.

Bronski put another arrow on the board. 'The autopsy found some bruising around the nose and mouth, not obvious at the scene because of the discolouration of the face from the hypoxia. They also found traces of an anaesthetic in the lungs.'

'So he was subdued and then what, strangled?'

'No, not strangled. The hypoid bone in the neck wasn't broken and it usually is in strangling, but not in hanging.' Bronski was standing in front of her with his arms crossed.

'So what then?'

'Jim Moorcroft was smothered. That's what the report is listing as cause of death – suffocation, but not as a result of hanging. So the hanging was intended to make it look like suicide. The note would have been a part of that.'

'But if he was smothered, then the perpetrator would have had to lift the body up.'

'Hmm, so the perpetrator is obviously strong and calculating. The noose would have had to be set up, the whole scene planned.'

'So I assume we are looking for a male, pretty fit?'

Bronski put a question mark on the board where he had been drawing the scenario. 'I agree, I think we are looking for a male. Jim Moorcroft was stocky and about five foot seven. Not sure many women would be able to lift that weight, certainly without help. Nothing to say that there weren't two people involved, of course, although we have nothing to show that as yet.'

'And are we thinking that his death has anything to do with the assault on Angela Goodman, apart from the obvious that the note mentions the assault?'

'Seems a coincidence, doesn't it? I think if we find out who killed Moorcroft, we will find Angela Goodman's attacker.'

'Are you going to tell Jackie Winters?'

'No need just yet, is there?'

66

Charlie was sitting with his sister. He noticed that the activity of hospital staff around her seemed less attentive than it had been just days ago. They're giving up on her, he thought, as he wiped some perspiration from her forehead. Staring again at the machine monitoring her every breath and heartbeat, he wondered when the staff would broach the idea of shutting it off. Her hand felt limp in his as he gently stroked it with his other hand, remembering all the times when he was little and she'd walked him hand in hand to the grocery store on the corner of their road. The list from their mother took priority, but she'd always managed to save a bit, searching for anything reduced in price so she could get him some candy. He was smiling now, but there were tears in his eyes.

An hour later, it was time for a coffee break. The hospital canteen felt like a second home as he got a cappuccino and an apple turnover. Placing the snack on the table, he glanced around, seeing if there was anyone else there he knew. Funny how he wasn't alone in keeping vigil over a relative, but today he didn't recognise anyone. Switching his phone on, there were three text messages in his inbox.

'Are u at hosp. Free for lunch? See u on ward at 12? Jackie x'

Before replying he opened the next one, 'Is house OK for u? Let us know if we missed anything. Dave & Wayne'. Good of the guys from the decontamination company to do a follow up, thought Charlie. In truth, he'd been amazed at how thorough they were.

The final text was from Annie, asking if she could see him that evening and to give her a call when he could. Deciding there was no time like the present he pressed return call.

'Macpherson.'

'Hi, it's me, Charlie. Got your text.'

'Hi, are you at the hospital?'

'Yeah, just taking a break in the canteen. What's up?'

'Just wanted to spend some time tonight going through the diaries. Is that OK with you?'

'Sure, should I pick you up when I leave the hospital?'

Next, he texted Jackie and confirmed a meet in the canteen for lunch. Taking a last swig of coffee and pushing the half eaten apple turnover to one side, he returned to the ward.

Waking up with a start, Charlie realised he must have dozed off. A glance at his watch told him that nearly an hour had passed since he'd come back to Angie's bedside. Hearing voices outside, he caught a glimpse of the Catholic priest talking to the ward sister: the priest's back was to him. Charlie retreated to his chair, secretly hoping the priest wouldn't want a word with him, as he had studiously avoided him so far. He hoped one of the nurses wouldn't insist on them meeting. Priests and he didn't mix, although he wouldn't deny his sister any prayers or blessings that were forthcoming.

The intrusive thought he'd spent years trying to push back into the recesses of his mind tumbled out. The evening service, being the privileged altar boy invited back into the sacristy to help the priest with his robes, remembering hearing the unzipping of the priest's fly and still not getting what he had in mind. Too embarrassed later to tell anyone, Angie included, that he had been held by one arm and had to watch the priest pleasuring himself. Remembering also how he'd recoiled when the priest wanted him to touch it too. Just thinking about it made him break out in a sweat. Charlie looked at his watch. It was only ten minutes now before he was due to meet Jackie, but he wasn't leaving the room until the voices died down and he was sure that the priest had left.

It was another twenty minutes before he ventured off the ward and headed for the canteen, spotting Jackie waving to him from a table in the corner. 'Sorry, I got a bit delayed on the ward. Have you been waiting long?'

Jackie Winters had been sipping a coffee, which was now half empty. 'No, just thought I'd have a coffee while I was waiting. Why don't you sit down and I'll get us a couple of sandwiches.'

'I can do that. What do you want?'

'Charlie, please, let me.'

'OK, I might just have one of those pizza slices they do and a bottle of water.' Charlie sat down watching Jackie moving gracefully to the ordering area. She was an attractive woman, tall and slim, much too attractive for Moorcroft, he mused. Although she looked subdued, he really didn't know to what extent Moorcroft's death was affecting her. Suicide was guilt provoking no matter what or who was to blame. But that note, professing love for his sister rather than for her, must have hurt her deeply. Would she resent Angie? This was her first visit since the death.

A few moments later Jackie Winters was back with their food, carefully placing everything on the table. She then returned the tray to the collection area before she took her seat again.

'So tell me, how is Angie today, any change?'

'Pretty much the same to be honest. Every time I go in I think things will be different. I'm dreading the doctors asking me to make a decision.'

'I'm so sorry Charlie. This is awful for you.' Jackie Winters reached across the table and placed her hand on his, just for a few seconds.

Charlie didn't look up at her. 'It's awful for Angie, but they keep assuring me that she isn't in any pain.' He picked up the slice of pizza, not really wanting it, but knowing that he had to eat. He'd already lost ten pounds. 'More to the point, how are you doing? Jim? I mean, it must be hard coming to terms with it.' He finally focused on Jackie and she put her fork down before answering.

'I guess I have mixed feelings. Sometimes I hate him for what he did – what he did to Angie I mean. I just don't understand why he never told me how he felt about her. I could have lived with that, let him go. They could have been together if that was what they wanted.' She hesitated, for a few minutes, taking a drink of her coffee before continuing. 'I would have moved on with my life, but now his suicide has made that so much harder. I feel this awful guilt.'

Charlie saw her eyes filling with tears and this time it was his turn to try and offer some comfort. Touching her hand, he smiled. 'What a pair, we make, eh?' Jackie smiled, wiping her eyes with her fingers.

'Will you go back to the house or find somewhere else?' he asked, taking another bite of the pizza.

'I'll have to go back and sort through all my things, when I'm allowed back in. Jim has a sister, Debbie and she's coming to sort through his things, decide what to do with the house. It was his. I never paid anything towards the mortgage and we just shared the bills. I guess he probably had a will and I imagine he left it all to her, as their parents are dead and there weren't any other brothers or sisters. He certainly never said that we should have a joint will or anything like that. But I expect if he had one, she'll find it.'

Charlie just nodded and Jackie continued. 'I couldn't live there anyway, even if she let me, not after finding him.' Her voice broke a bit, but then she composed herself. 'Besides I never really did get along with Debbie, although I only met her three or four times. I think she felt Jim could have done better than me. Maybe she was right.'

'She was wrong, Jackie, but I think you need to move out of there for your own sake. It will have too many memories. God knows, I'm trying to redecorate Angie's house, but that might not be enough to make her want to live there again. She may not get past the events of that night.' He paused, aware that what he was saying might just be wishful thinking on his part. Angie might not even survive, never mind move back into her house.

'What's happening with the police investigation? Have you heard anything?'

'I suspect they think it was Jim, following his confession in the note. At first I didn't want to believe it myself, but I guess it makes sense. I'm sorry, I know that's hard for you to hear. Selfishly, it stops me worrying that there is still someone out there who wants her dead.'

'Of course, that will be a huge relief for you. I didn't really think of that aspect.'

'Jackie, you've had enough to think about.' He smiled at her again and finished off his drink. Then he added, 'But I think Detective Macpherson is keeping more of an open mind, even though suicide seems the most likely scenario.'

'What makes you say that about Detective Macpherson keeping an open mind?'

'It's just that she's taken several of Angie's old diaries to look through. See if they have anything relevant in them.'

'Really?'

'I'm sure they won't add anything, but she seems determined to read through them anyway. I feel a bit uneasy as they are private to Angie.'

'Doesn't sound like she's convinced then, that it was Jim I mean.'

'I'm not really sure, but I think Detective Bronski is and he's the senior officer in the investigation.'

A few minutes later, Charlie made his way back to the ward. Jackie only had time to pop in on Angie for a few minutes. On her way out of the hospital, she stopped to switch her cell phone on. There was one missed message from Jim's sister, Debbie, saying they needed to talk about the house and offering to meet.

67

The afternoon had dragged and Connie Lombardi was relieved when it was time to go home, her lack of interest in her work starting to show. It would only be a matter of time before her boss asked to see her and she'd struggle to get another job so close to home. Berating herself, she stopped at the grocery store to pick up some cold cuts and salad, too despondent to make a proper meal. Besides, the temperature at this time in July was soaring and she couldn't be bothered cooking in the heat. Now if Jason were around she would have made the effort, even down to buying a bottle of his favourite wine. Damn you Jason, where are you?

Paying at the cash register, she picked up the Boston evening paper and the local Springfield one. Might just read the newspapers while I'm eating, she thought. A half hour later, opening her front door, she went straight into the kitchen dropping the groceries on the kitchen counter. Opening the refrigerator, she poured a glass of soda, topping the glass up with ice from the door. She switched on the portable air conditioning unit. Two minutes later, her plate was loaded with the prepared salad and the cold ham.

The front page of the Boston paper had the usual mix of national and local city news. Not interested in the politics of Washington DC, she flipped the paper open to the second page. The news headline caught her eye.

MAN SOUGHT IN HIT AND RUN DEATH

Always fascinated by accidents and crime, she read on:

By Penny Harrington

In a news conference this morning, Detective Thomas Malin announced that what the police originally thought was a tragic accident between two cars on Route 1 has turned into a murder inquiry. The accident, which happened around 7:30 last Wednesday morning, killed 39 year old bookshop manager Carol Wojinski.

'That's the woman that couple were talking about at the next table over lunch today,' Connie said out loud. It was a habit of hers to talk out loud when she was on her own in the house, a habit she'd had since childhood. But she'd always been careful not to do it in front of Jason, in case he thought that there was something wrong with her.

Turning her attention back to the page she read on:

Mrs Wojinski's death has devastated her many customers and flowers started arriving in front of the bookshop, as soon as the news reached the residents of Springfield. Fellow storekeepers expressed their sadness and many mentioned how dangerous Route 1 is and said that complaints about the safety of the road have gone unheeded. But no one was more devastated than her husband of 5 years, Gus Wojinski, a public accountant, also 39.

Connie was distracted for a moment by an advertisement, which had caught her eye, on the opposite page, for the Filenes' Basement sale. But then chastising herself for the easy distraction, she turned back to the story, deciding to at least skim read it.

Police are now looking for a man who had rented the other car involved, a brown Jeep. They have established that he rented the car two weeks ago from Value for U Rentals and supplied a Massachusetts driving licence in the name of Jason Craven. Police are unable to confirm if that is his true identity and are seeking the help of anyone who may know the man, described as 6 foot 1 inch with brown hair and eyes.

Connie's eyes widened and she dropped her fork on the table, when she read the last paragraph. 'Oh, my God … it can't be. Jason, it can't be you.' She felt the contents of her stomach rising up as she rushed off to the toilet.

Several minutes later, she poured a glass of water, but the queasiness was still there. Knowing she had to be sure, Connie read the article again, line by line. 'There must be another Jason Craven, surely. Besides he had a Connecticut driving licence, at least I think he did. God, I don't know anymore.' The article confirmed that no second body had been found, despite an extensive search and that police were now theorising that the crash of the second car had been staged and that Carol Wojinski's VW Beetle had been run off the road.

Sitting at the table, her head in her hands, she started to cry. Several times over the past couple of weeks she'd tried Jason's cell phone. At first, there was only the beep to leave a message. How many of those had she left? Earlier she'd tried again, but the tone was one she hadn't encountered before. Was this number disconnected, her only connection to him severed? But what if the police were mistaken? There had to be an explanation. The Jason she knew wasn't a murderer. But did she really know him?

Two hours later, the food having been consigned to the waste disposal, she was dozing on the couch, exhausted from her tears. The doorbell sounded, waking her suddenly. Disorientated by fear and exhaustion, she couldn't work out what was happening or even what time of day it was. The air conditioning had left the room chilled and she shuddered. The doorbell went again, this time more persistent. Before daring to answer it, she opened the living room curtains slightly and saw two men at the top of the stairs. One had his finger on the doorbell, about to ring it again. The other had seen the slight twitch of the curtain and pointed just as she let it go. There was no choice but to answer the door.

'Connie Lombardi?'

'Yes.'

'I'm Detective Malin and this is Detective Steiner, we would like to ask you some questions.'

Connie could feel the blush rising up from her neck, the way it always did when she was extremely embarrassed. Ushering them into the kitchen, they sat around the wooden table, the paper still opened at the story that had shocked her. There was no time to shut the paper and she realised that both men had spotted the opened page.

'I see you were reading the paper. Did that article mean anything to you?' Detective Malin pointed to the Harrington by line.

'I was just reading while I was eating. I wasn't really taking much notice. I just happened to leave the paper open.'

'Miss Lombardi, we are aware that you have been reporting a Jason Craven as missing to the Boston Police and that you also approached a newspaper reporter to help you find your boyfriend when the police didn't feel there was anything they could do.'

Connie blushed again, but didn't answer.

'Miss Lombardi, we believe that Jason Craven is an eyewitness to a fatal car accident and we need to interview him as a matter of urgency. Do you know Jason Craven?'

'My boyfriend's name is Jason Craven, but I am sure there must be several people with that name.'

'Does he meet this description?' Detective Malin read out the details from the driving licence.

Connie nearly smiled. She had loved his height, his strength, the brown eyes, his sandy hair that she had run her fingers through. God Jason, please don't let this be you. When Detective Malin finished, she nodded and then felt tears running down her face.

'We realise this is difficult for you, but we need to know all we can about Jason Craven.'

Connie nodded and answered the questions as best she could, although throughout she felt a sense of detachment. The man they were asking her about was not the man who was her lover. Then again, the more questions they asked her, the more she realised how little she really knew Jason Craven.

'No, I never met any friends of his.'

'What about family members?'

'I'm close to my mom. Well, she's close to me might be a better way of putting it. He never seemed to mind that we spoke on the telephone a lot but he never mentioned his own mother. I asked him once but he wasn't specific. Somehow, I got the feeling that she was dead, although he never actually said that. I guess I just assumed it. He never mentioned brothers or sisters.'

'What about work colleagues?'

'He had his own business, at least that's what he told me – imports or exports, I forget which. That's why he was away a lot of the time. Sometimes I didn't speak to him for a couple of days and his cell phone would be off, which is why I didn't worry at first when I hadn't heard from him, but then ...'

'How long was it before you reported him missing?'

'About a week or so. Three days was the longest time before, so when it got to be longer than that, I got really worried, especially as he hadn't said he'd be away. He always told me, always prepared me ...' The tears welled up again and she excused herself while she got a glass of water. At the sink she realised she'd never offered the two detectives a drink. 'Would either of you like a drink – a soda, ice tea?'

Malin shifted in his seat. 'Thank you, but we only have another couple of questions.'

As Connie sat back down, Malin asked, 'Do you have any photographs of Mr Craven?'

She could hardly lie, as she'd already mentioned one to the reporter. 'I only have one on my cell phone. I took it when he wasn't watching as he always said that he hated having his picture taken.' She passed the phone to Detective Steiner, who looked and then passed it to Malin.

'We need a copy of this and we need his cell phone number.'

Ten minutes later, they were on their way with both a print out of the photograph and an electronic copy sent to their email. Feeling a tremendous sense of betrayal, she shut the door behind them. The tears flowed freely as she reprimanded herself for going to the police in the first place and then the reporter. What had she set in motion? Where was it all going to end? Was Jason dead? Did he deliberately run that woman off the road?

The thought was shocking, as was the fact that he still had keys to her house. She resolved to get the locks changed in the morning. One thing she knew for sure, tonight she couldn't face the prospect of telling her mother what was going on.

68

Annie took advantage of a lull in activity in the squad room to take out one of Angela Goodman's diaries. She was plotting a timeline of what she was reading. This section of the diaries covered Angie's engagement and then her marriage to her first husband, Dennis Cullen. There was about an hour to go before she was due to meet Charlie downstairs for a quick meal and then more reading of the diaries.

'What'ya got there?' Ellison asked as he passed Annie's desk. He'd only just arrived back after being out all day.

'And hello to you too,' retorted Annie.

'Sorry, too abrupt for you? Hi Detective, is that better?'

Annie smiled. 'Definitely an improvement.'

The two laughed, as Ellison took his seat behind the desk.

'So what has you so engrossed and taking notes?'

'Angela Goodman's diaries. There are volumes of them. She was nothing if not meticulous. These are the five years from when she first left home after she married Dennis Cullen.'

'He was the first husband, right?'

'Aye, the one who turned up at the hospital.'

'So, are they helping to rule him out?'

'Well, the marriage wasn't the bed of roses he'd led us to believe. He wasn't averse to a little slapping when she annoyed him. It got more frequent towards the end, when she was telling him the marriage was going nowhere.'

'Hmm. We could do with more people keeping diaries.'

Annie returned to her reading.

'Hey, are you doing anything after work?' said Ellison.

'That was none too subtle a change of topic. I was beginning to think you were interested in my work.'

'Of course I am, Detective, but you're also very beautiful.'

'You know what they say about flattery, Dave. I'm sorry, but Captain Hegarty is picking me up after work to retrieve some more diaries. He's staying at Mrs Goodman's house now and they're all there.'

'I see.' Ellison said, turning to his computer, 'Not getting too close to the brother of the victim, are we?'

Annie shrugged.

'I'll take that as a 'No' then,' he replied, as he started to type.

A half hour later, Charlie picked her up in his car. 'Hi, how are you?'

'I'm good, you?'

'So, so. No change in Angie, but they haven't asked me the final question yet. Jackie visited for a bit. Honestly, she's been a rock through all of this.'

Annie inwardly cringed, but was determined not to show it. After all, she couldn't really say that she and Charlie had anything going between them, although she secretly hoped there could be. 'Did she say anything about Moorcroft?'

Charlie signalled as he turned down the main road, heading towards his sister's place. 'Not much really, she seems to still be in shock. She thinks Jim's sister will want her things out of his house, so I may help her to put them in storage. Oh, and she asked if you were convinced he was the one who attacked Angie.'

'She asked that?'

'Yeah. I told her you seemed sceptical still, that you were reading the diaries.' Charlie glanced at her briefly, while concentrating on the road.

'Oh,' Annie hesitated.

'What's the matter?'

'Nothing, but it probably would have been better not to mention that, as it is part of the investigation.'

'Come on, Annie, you can't be thinking that there's any problem mentioning the diaries to Jackie. I bet she already knew that Angie kept diaries. Besides, are you really convinced that my sister had some deep dark secret in her past that brought all this on?'

Annie didn't reply.

'I feel uncomfortable with it all, like we're invading her privacy.'

'Charlie, you need to let me do my job. Things don't add up for me. That's all I can say and her past could certainly be relevant. You told me yourself that the age gap makes it unlikely that you would know much from years ago. Already, Dennis Cullen hasn't been that truthful with us.'

'What?' Charlie glanced over again, just as they were approaching the house.

Annie regretted what she'd said but now that it was

out, she had to offer an explanation. 'Nothing too serious, only the marriage wasn't that great. Let's just say that Cullen had a temper and took it out on her at times.'

Charlie turned into the driveway and switched off the engine. He just sat there for a few seconds, staring at the house. 'I don't know what to believe any more. It's almost as if the Angie I am finding out about is a stranger. When I sit with her in the hospital, all I can think about is my childhood and how important she was to me. I love her, but can't help her.'

'Charlie, that's not true, you are doing everything you can. Please, let me handle my side of things. Just be there for her.'

69

A half hour later, as Charlie showered, Annie prepared a salad and coated two steaks with black pepper and olive oil, ready to barbecue on the patio. It was a beautiful summer evening and not for the first time, Annie wished she'd met Charlie under other circumstances. She was frustrated that she didn't have more answers for him. The thought still lingered that if only she'd believed Angela Goodman that day in the station, none of this might have happened. But, of course, she wouldn't have met Charlie either. 'You can't miss what you never had' her father would have said.

Charlie, walking into the kitchen, broke her train of thought. His hair was damp, but he looked more relaxed in his cargo shorts and cream T-shirt, which contrasted with his tanned skin. What Annie wanted to do was to give him a hug, but instead she passed him a glass of wine.

He handed over a few more diaries. 'I found these when I had a double check in the trunk. They were in a separate compartment that I didn't even realise it had. I also found this.' He passed her what looked like a scrapbook, with newspaper clippings, now yellowed with age. 'This was also in the same compartment. I haven't looked through it yet.'

As Annie opened up the scrapbook, Charlie picked up the steaks, took them outside and placed them on the barbecue.

'How do you like your steak?' he shouted a minute later. Annie decided she needed some time to relax, to stop being a detective, so she left the scrapbook and took her glass of wine outside.

'Medium rare, more rare than medium. Are we eating out here?'

'Sure. Grab the salad. Dressings are in the refrigerator. Pick what you want. I'll have any.'

Annie stepped back into the house and brought out everything they needed and set out the cutlery on the picnic table. A few minutes later, he passed her a plate with her steak on it.

'So, have the autopsy results come in yet?' Charlie queried, as he sat opposite her at the table.

'Charlie, could we eat first? Autopsies aren't exactly the topic of choice over dinner.'

He smiled. 'Sorry.'

Over dinner, Annie told him more about Scotland and growing up in Huntly, about the police training and about her dad. She hadn't talked so much about herself for years. Paul knew her background – she was never a stranger to him, since they virtually grew up together. Telling someone else was unusual for her. To her delight, Charlie seemed genuinely interested and asked lots of questions.

Later on, after they loaded the dishwasher and Annie poured them each another glass of wine, they went into the living room. She decided it was as good a time as ever to pick up on Charlie's earlier question.

'The results of the autopsy are back. Bronski and I reviewed them today.'

'So, did he commit suicide?'

'No.'

'No?' Charlie took another drink of wine, while he waited for Annie to continue.

'It was certainly made to look like suicide. But Moorcroft was suffocated, to be exact. I could give you the technical details, but that was the gist of the report.'

'So does that mean what I think it does?'

'We are definitely dealing with a homicide.'

Charlie took another drink of his wine. 'So, the note, the admission?'

'Someone typed it, presumably the person who suffocated him and then staged the hanging.'

'So, we are no further forward. I guess the next obvious question is, if Jim didn't attack Angie, then are her attacker and Jim's murderer the same person?'

Annie took a sip of wine herself, before responding. 'That would be my guess, but we have to keep an open mind. Bronski and I are going back to the house tomorrow to make sure we haven't missed anything. Forensics is still looking through his computer. So far, they haven't found much, apart from his penchant for porn.'

'Gee, what was Jackie putting up with?'

'She may not have known about the porn. When we asked her about the computer, she said she never used it.'

'How do you live with someone and not know these things?' Charlie put his glass down and leaned back on the couch, stifling a yawn. 'God I thought Afghanistan was complex. At least there I knew what I was doing. Here it's another story: nothing is as I expected it to be and no one is who I thought they were.'

'Charlie, we are going to solve this.' Annie got up

to use the bathroom, touching his arm as she passed him. When she came back a few minutes later, he had drifted off to sleep on the couch, his arms folded across his chest. For once there were no lines of worry on his face. As he slept, Annie went back into the kitchen and retrieved the scrapbook. At first it seemed to be in some chronological order, but then Annie realised that some items appeared to be years older in relation to other articles. She was fascinated by some of them:

CHEERLEADERS WIN CHAMPIONSHIP

The article discussed the recent win of the Westford High School squad at the Regional heats held in Boston. The now faded photograph showed a sixteen-year-old Angie, the Westford captain holding up the trophy while the other girls formed a semicircle on the floor behind her.

Juxtaposed on the opened out page was an engagement photo of Angie, with no date but describing her as a twenty-one year old. Dennis Cullen was named as the fiancé. The next several pages contained other engagement announcements and photos of marriages, all of which Annie assumed were friends of Angie's. The only name Annie knew from Angie's past was Carol Wojinski, but no one in any of the articles was called 'Carol' and there was no mention of a 'Gus'.

Annie felt herself nodding off reading the yellowed pages and Charlie was still sleeping. She realised that nothing had been said about whether Charlie was going to drop her home, or whether she was going to stay in the spare room again. As quietly as she could, she retreated to the kitchen and made herself a coffee. Looking around for a taxi number, her eyes scanned the cork message board that still reflected Angie's time in the house. There were numbers for pizza delivery and the local fitness club, as well as Jim and Jackie and a taxi company. When she unpinned it, she also noticed a Christmas card behind it.

Carefully, Annie unpinned the card, checking first that Charlie was still asleep. As she opened up the card, she noticed it was signed by Carol and Gus, but both names were in the same handwriting, presumably Carol's. There was also a note inside.

'Hoping you have a relaxing Christmas. Don't want to spook you, but I am sure I saw him two weeks ago – walked by the shop, looked in and stared. I just caught a glimpse, but you can imagine the effect. Maybe just my imagination, keep trying to forget it. It's been too long since we've met up. I'll get in touch in the New Year.'

Annie tapped the card in her hand. She would have to ask Charlie if she could take it. Bronski needed to see this and she also realised that Gus might have more information. Who was the 'him' that Carole was referring to? Why was she so spooked? And more importantly, why had forensics not had a look at the card?

Annie walked back into the living room and took her seat again, putting the card on the coffee table in front of her. Again she flicked through the scrapbook, scanning each item, even the seemingly irrelevant ones, just in case she'd missed anything. She smiled reading about Charlie's exploits on the football field at Westfield High School. Angie had saved various articles about him. She looked across at his relaxed face and decided not to wake him yet. His high school team got to some regional finals. Annie didn't have a clue about American football and Charlie looked really different with all the equipment on, including a big helmet. There was also an obituary notice for their mother. It just said that she had died at home but no cause of death was reported. There was nothing about their dad, at least nothing so far.

Annie sipped her coffee as she continued reading. Towards the end of the scrapbook, she found a double page spread from a newspaper, folded over several times. No particular article had been cut out of it, like the usual pattern in the scrapbook. It also struck her that, unlike the others, this one was not from a local newspaper, but was from the *Georgia Gazette*. Spreading it out on the coffee table, she began to scan the pages, wondering what was relevant. Just as she smoothed the paper out to get a better view, Charlie woke.

'Sorry, can't believe I dozed off. Have I been asleep long?' He stretched and then rubbed his face. 'Not very good manners falling asleep in front of a guest.'

'Don't worry, you obviously needed it.'

'What have you got there?'

'Just something I found in the scrapbook, only it wasn't pasted in like all the other stuff, like the photos of you and your football exploits.'

Charlie smiled. 'I didn't give you it for that, I can assure you.'

'Oh, aye. You just wanted me to know what a local hero you were, I know.'

Charlie smiled. 'I didn't even know she'd kept that stuff.'

'Angela was obviously a proud big sister, but I can't quite work out what this double page spread is about. There are lots of articles.' Annie smoothed the pages in front of her.

'Is that the Westford paper?' Charlie glanced across.

'No, the *Georgia Gazette.*'

Charlie got up and came and sat down beside Annie. 'Let's have a look. She was stationed in Georgia when she enlisted at eighteen.'

Charlie and Annie scanned the two-page spread together and in the bottom half of the second page, an article struck her first.

SECOND LIEUTENANT FACES CHARGES IN COURT MARTIAL

'Charlie, what about this?' Annie started to read the article out loud:

A court martial heard evidence today against Second Lieutenant John Hardman relating to the stalking of a Private in his company. The Private, a new recruit having completed basic training and pursuing her nurse training alleged that the Lieutenant had started to stalk her after she spurned his advances. He then subjected her to months of harassment, including leaving her scores of messages on her phone and accessing her quarters and leaving gifts for her. When she tried to complain, her Sergeant didn't believe her. If it hadn't been for her own persistence and that of a fellow colleague who was able to gather irrefutable evidence, the case might never have gone to court. That and the fact that his ultimate act of stalking was to rape her just prior to their deployment to Germany.

The Commanding Officer, who heard the case ruled that all charges were upheld and that the Second Lieutenant should be dishonourably discharged and should serve a minimum of ten years in a military prison for the torment he had subjected the Private to over a number of months. Her name has not been released nor that of her main witness.

Annie looked across at Charlie as she finished the article. His face was ashen.

'My God, I've never seen this before. Angie was a Private. She left before her two years were up, which is really unusual. She always said that it was because mum was ill and she needed to help her with me, but what if?'

'What if this is Angela in the article and what if the witness was Carol Wojinski? Charlie I need to show you this. I found it in the kitchen on the cork board.' Annie passed the Christmas card to Charlie.

He read the words and looked up at her. 'Gus said that they knew each other in the service. We need to know if he knows anything about this article, don't we?'

'Charlie, how far is it to Springfield? Would it be better if we went to see him tomorrow? The guy is still in a state of shock and he doesn't know about Angie. I might have to contact the detective in charge of his wife's case, if he can give us anything to go on.'

'I could call him back, what do you think?'

'Let me ring Bronski first and see what he advises. He could start getting a trace on the guy in this article. It may be nothing, but I just feel that this article is significant.'

He answered on the second ring.

'That wasn't what I wanted to hear.'

'I know.'

'I'll have to think this out.'

'Don't take too long, this needs to be finished.'

'And I don't know that?'

'I know, I'm sorry.'

'Have you sorted out the rest of it?'

'Of course, you told me to do that and I always do what I'm told.'

'I know, this time I'm sorry.'

He clicked the cell phone off and deleted the number from the call register.

They were up very early the next morning, neither of them having slept well. Annie had stayed up an hour after Charlie, still sifting through the rest of the scrapbook and some more of the diaries. But the diaries with the relevant years of Angela's army service appeared to be missing.

It was a lovely summer morning, the sun already shining and no hint of a breeze. The humidity was still a couple of hours away. 'So how long will it take to get to Gus's?'

'I guess about an hour or so, depending on the traffic. If I've timed this right, we'll miss the rush hour at this end at least. If we get there too early, then we'll stop somewhere for coffee.'

Annie would be ready for a coffee by then. Waiting for an opportune moment, Annie continued. 'Charlie, last night I finished off the scrapbook.'

'Anything else relevant?'

'No, but I also flicked through some diaries again. We seem to be missing the two years that she was in the army. Do you think those diaries could be somewhere else?'

Charlie was thoughtful for a moment. 'That's strange, but now that you mention it, when we went up to the attic the other night I had a feeling that the trunk had been opened not long ago. I thought it was my imagination, but now that I think about it.'

Signalling right, he turned on to the highway and increased his speed. Annie waited sensing that he wanted to say something else. 'Hey, do you think her attacker knew about the diaries? Only if it was that guy from the article ...'

'It's a possibility. He may have got her to hand them over, but let's be careful not to get ahead of ourselves here. We still have a long way to go on this ...'

Before Annie could finish her sentence, her cell phone rang.

'Where are you now?' Bronski asked.

Annie fed back Charlie's description of the route numbers. They made sense to Bronski, but Annie had never travelled in a car out of Westford before, so they meant nothing to her.

'I've got Ellison working with the Department of Defense, trying to get more information about the guy in the article. They're being really cagey, so if you can get anything more substantial from Gus Wojinski, especially if he can verify the story is relevant, then we can push a bit harder. Also I spoke to Detective Malin. He's going to meet you at the house. Said he'd let Mr Wojinski know he was coming.'

'Good, we need some luck. Let's just hope this leads us somewhere.'

'I'm here all day, keep in touch.'

An hour later, they found themselves on a tree-lined street. Nice neighbourhood, Annie thought, the sort of place where you'd feel safe. Gus Wojinski and his late wife lived in a red Cape Cod. At least that was the description Charlie gave her of the house type. The lawns outside had been carefully tended, but the summer sun and lack of rain had started to dry them out and some patches were turning brown. Annie imagined that the state of his lawns was probably the last thing on Gus Wojinski's mind right now.

Although they were about ten minutes early, as the car pulled up, Gus appeared at the screen door. He opened it as Charlie and Annie got out of the car and walked down the path to greet them. Annie was struck by his composure, but on the other hand suspected that he might only just be holding it together. Back in the house, he led them into the kitchen, where he had poured out glasses of fresh orange juice.

'So what can I help you folks with? I wasn't really sure after your phone call.'

Charlie looked at Annie, not sure who was taking the lead. Annie nodded for him to make a start.

'Gus, we know this is an awful time for you. I never met your wife. I was only a kid when my sister was in the army and met your wife there.'

'You'll have to excuse me, I can't seem to hold it together for very long'. Gus wiped a tear away. 'Carol enlisted straight from school; always said that a career in the army had been her dream. I think Angela joined around the same time, I know they met nearly right away.' He paused for a moment to drink some of his juice and Annie noticed that his hand was shaking as he lifted the glass. Neither she nor Charlie interrupted.

'They were inseparable, as much as you can be. Carol always used to say that Angie was the sister she never had.' His voice choked for a minute. 'But something happened. Carol told me parts over the years, never the whole story all at once.'

This was starting to confirm what Annie had suspected, but had never clearly formulated. 'Anything you can tell us would be a great help.'

'You have to remember that I am going on snippets told at different times and I never met Angela myself. I sensed that most of the time it seemed like a painful thing for Carol to discuss so I never pushed it. But what I understand is that Angela started a relationship with one of the officers, I don't know what his name was or even his rank.' Gus hesitated.

'That's OK, just tell us what you know,' said Charlie.

'I guess Carol tried to tell her it wasn't a good idea and I think at first it put some strain on their friendship, so Carol had to back off. As I said, as I understand it, Angela was really attracted to this guy, at least at first.'

'What do you mean?' Annie came in a bit more abruptly than she intended.

'Apparently quite quickly, Angela realised that it was only an infatuation and that there were things about him she didn't like. She tried to break it off but he wouldn't have it. Carol said that it started to get quite scary. That's when the two of them got close again. Angela needed her support. It seemed that everywhere they went, this guy would just turn up. Angela had gotten so she wouldn't leave the base on her own. So if Carol was on duty, Angela stayed in the barracks, but that didn't stop him.'

Gus shifted uncomfortably in his seat.

'Gus, I appreciate that this is difficult for you, but we really need to know,' said Annie.

After another drink of his juice, he continued. 'Carol said that he would get the master key and let himself into Angela's room while she was sleeping. Sometimes she would wake up and he would be there, just looking at her. The first time it frightened her to death, but he promised he wouldn't do it again. I guess just the thought of it affected Angela and her work started to slip, because she was too frightened to sleep. She never told anyone, apart from Carol, what was happening.'

'That must have been difficult for your wife, seeing her friend going through that and knowing that a fellow soldier was the cause of it.'

'That was the part that she found the hardest, but neither did she want to breach her friend's confidentiality, that and the fact that he never kept his promises and kept letting himself in. Sometimes Angela would wake in a fright to see her door just closing and then she knew he had been there again. Carol started to notice that Angela was becoming obsessive about showering and would scrub her skin until it was nearly raw. I remember her saying that this one time, her skin was really sore and then they were out on exercises and it was really hot and Angela got sunstroke. She was confined to the hospital wing for a couple of nights and the nurses asked her about the skin problems, but Angela wouldn't say anything.'

Gus hesitated and stared at Charlie. 'I'm sorry, this must be hard for you, hearing all this about your sister and especially being an officer yourself.'

Charlie nodded. 'At that stage she was my big sister, invincible, especially when she came home in her uniform. I wanted to join the army just like her. But now, I need to know what she went through, what she never told me all these years.' Suddenly, he remembered that email his sister had sent those few weeks ago, when she said there were things about her he didn't know. But this? It wasn't at all what he was expecting. 'Please Gus, finish the story.'

'I guess it must have been soon after she came out of the hospital, although I don't know that for sure. But I remember Carol saying that she was still too ill to re-join her colleagues, so it must have been around that time. Anyway, Carol described this one occasion where she helped Angela return to her room. When they opened the door, they were struck by the smell. The room was full of flowers, but they were all dead. Carol said that it was the last straw as far as she was concerned and she was ready to report the guy, but Angela begged her not to; said that it would only get worse if she did. So instead, Carol just got rid of all the flowers.'

Gus hesitated and then said, 'I remember that bit because she told me it one time when we'd left some flowers and came back after a weekend away. They were dead and she had to get them out of the house before she could even unpack. I couldn't understand why it was so important to her.'

'What a bastard.'

Annie hadn't heard Charlie swear before, but he said what she was thinking herself.

'I'm not sure how long it was after that, but he then started to leave her notes, saying that she'd ruined his life, that she was a bitch. Sometimes the notes would just say that one word. I suspect by now it was also affecting Carol, but Angela still refused to report him, convincing herself that he would stop, if she just ignored him.'

Gus stopped suddenly and looked at the two of them. 'Do you think there's a connection with this guy and what's happened to Carol?' His demeanour seemed to change, as if the story telling had completely drained him, but had also made him feel vulnerable and scared. 'You haven't told me anything about Angela, only that she's in the hospital. What's going on?'

Annie could hear the desperation in his voice and realised how unfair they'd been, not really being up front about their trip. 'I'm sorry Gus. We owe you a fuller explanation. We needed to hear what you had to say first, to consider whether there might be any relationship between your wife and Charlie's sister. I think I've heard enough. We told you Angela was in the hospital, but not why ...' Annie hesitated for a moment. Gus would find it hard to take in what she was about to say next. 'Angela was badly assaulted nearly three weeks ago and is still in a coma.'

'Three weeks ago.' Gus was repeating Angie's words as if allowing them to sink in.

'We have been exploring a number of angles, particularly with past relationships. We thought we had found the perpetrator. A close friend of hers, a Jim Moorcroft committed suicide last week and left a note saying that he was Angela's attacker.'

'So you got the guy? And is he the one from the army?'

'No, Jim Moorcroft was a friend of Angela's, a very close friend, definitely not the same man as the one you are describing to us. It's just that we now have reason to doubt what was left in the supposed suicide note.'

'Supposed suicide note; what does that mean?'

Annie realised how this all must be sounding to Gus, so tied up in his own grief. 'I'm sorry, Gus, let me explain. At first the note left by Mr Moorcroft seemed genuine enough, but then we got the autopsy result. Well, the autopsy showed that he was suffocated before he was hanged, so it wasn't suicide, after all.'

'Oh, my God, so he was murdered? And you think there is a connection with Angela's assault?' Gus looked at Charlie who could only shrug. Annie was about to explain further, but Gus came in again. 'But I still don't see what Carol has to do with all of this. They hadn't even seen each other for years. In fact I had forgotten Angela's name until I looked it up in Carol's address book, the one she kept for Christmas cards. I guess I hadn't even thought about the story I just told you, for a long time. It must be a few years since Carol even mentioned it. So, now I'm really confused. How does my wife fit in?'

The sound of the doorbell interrupted his words.

When Gus got up to answer the door, Annie and Charlie looked at one another and he squeezed her hand. A few seconds later, an older man followed Gus into the kitchen.

Introducing himself, he extended his hand to Annie.

'Detective Annie Macpherson, on an exchange with the Westford Police,' Annie replied, shaking his hand.

'I know, I've been speaking to Detective Bronski.' Malin then turned to Charlie and shook his hand. 'You must be Captain Hegarty, Mrs Goodman's brother. Detective Bronski filled me in on the case.'

'Yes, Sir,' Charlie responded as the older man sat down.

Malin continued. 'Sorry I'm late. Got caught up on my way out. I guess we all know why we are here. Perhaps we better go over what we know and what we're thinking.'

Over the next half hour, Gus repeated the connection between the two women and Annie provided details of what had happened to Angela Goodman and Jim Moorcroft. Then she took out the newspaper clipping from the scrapbook. Gus and Malin read it side by side on the table, while she and Charlie stayed silent.

When they finished, Annie continued with her explanation. 'So, that article got me wondering if there was a connection between Carol and Angela, as Gus had telephoned Charlie about his wife. I started to read Angela's old diaries but the two covering her army years are missing.'

'Carol never said anything about a rape. I never knew it went that far, but it has to be the same guy. The rest of the story is the same as Carol told me,' Gus added.

'It's still a bit tangential, don't you think?' Malin asked Annie.

'I wasn't sure of the significance myself, or the relationship with what happened to Carol, until I spotted this on the corkboard by Angela's telephone.' Annie handed over the Christmas card and again the two men read it.

'That was last year's card. We always send the same cards to everyone, but pick a new one each year,' said Gus. 'Carol never said anything about seeing someone and feeling frightened. She signed it for both of us, as she always did. I am hopeless with things like Christmas cards. I guess she didn't want to tell me about what she wrote in the card. Could it be this Hardman guy?'

Annie hesitated a moment, leaving time for Malin to come in. 'It sounds like there may be some connection. What we have so far is that the guy who rented the second car in the incident called himself Jason Craven. We've traced his girlfriend and she'd reported him missing a couple of weeks back. We now believe it's a case of stolen identity, as a Jason Craven died three years ago in a plane crash.'

Annie responded. 'We're trying to get more information on John Hardman. My colleagues are contacting the Department of Defense. We're hoping the information will include a photograph. The article says that he was convicted of rape and sentenced to ten years which means he could have got out two years ago.'

'Unless he was paroled earlier,' Charlie added.

'That's possible. What about the picture of Jason Craven?'

Malin opened his folder. 'We have two shots, neither very good.' He passed the photographs over to Annie. 'Gus has already confirmed that he doesn't recognise the guy.' Gus nodded as the detective spoke. Then Malin added. 'Too bad there isn't a photo in that news story you've got.'

'Maybe we'll get lucky with the Department of Defense.' Annie then turned her attention to the two photos. 'This first one from the security camera could be just about anyone. The face is quite obscured. The baseball cap doesn't help, of course. This second one?'

'Taken by the girlfriend. Again, only a side on shot. Apparently he told her never to take a picture of him but she sneaked this one. When he found out, he told her to delete it and she said she did, but then couldn't do it. She wanted to keep it, but said he'd go mad if he ever sees it in print.'

'Not a good shot but it's better than nothing. I guess if someone knew him or if we get a photo from the Department of Defense, we'll have some idea if it's the same guy or not. Detective Malin, can we have copies of these photos?'

'I'll get them to you.'

Annie glanced over at Charlie and they made their excuses to leave. Gus promised to let them know the details of his wife's funeral. Annie gave him a hug at the front door and apologised again for putting him through even more suffering. Malin stayed behind, promising again to send an email with the photos attached.

Then, just before Annie and Charlie got in the car, Gus shouted to them. They waited while he made his way down the drive. 'I've got to start sifting through Carol's things. I've been putting it off, but if I find out any more about this guy, I'll get in touch.' Charlie shook his hand again.

As they pulled away, another car arrived with an elderly couple in it. Annie turned to Charlie. 'What do you think, his parents or hers?'

'Who knows, but perhaps they can help him sort her things. Maybe they'll find something that will help.'

72

Annie's cell phone rang just as they got on the highway. Neither had felt much like sitting down to eat, so they'd grabbed a burger and had it in the car. That had saved them some time. Annie mouthed to Charlie that it was Bronski on the phone.

'Good and the photos from Detective Malin have come through. I know ... not that much use. So Dave's managed to speak to his commanding officer. I see. Oh ...' Annie started to rub her forehead as if she'd a nasty headache coming on and she just murmured for the next several minutes as Bronski spoke to her. 'I see. No, we're going to stop off at the hospital first, to see how Angela is doing. I can fill you in then ... talk later.'

'I got some of that, how about filling in the blanks?' Charlie said, as Annie ended the call.

'Charlie, you might not find this very easy.'

'Annie, just tell me. I've been through enough in the last few weeks.'

'I know. Dave Ellison spoke to John Hardman's commanding officer. He confirmed the details of the newspaper article, but apparently there were parts of the trial where the judge ordered reporting restrictions.'

'Which parts?'

'Charlie, maybe we should get off the highway and pull over for a bit.' Annie was feeling uncomfortable and wished Bronski hadn't gone into detail. Maybe she shouldn't have said anything to Charlie until they got back.

'Just tell me.'

'OK. You know about the rape, but he also held a gun to her head when he'd done it. Said he was going to kill her, but someone knocked on the door – her friend, Carol. Hardman held his hand over your sister's mouth and cocked the trigger. Eventually Carol went away when Angela didn't answer the door. Then he threatened to kill her if she told anyone and also threatened to kill Carol. Angela had a breakdown and the only person she eventually did tell was the army psychiatrist who acted on the information.'

Charlie went quiet for a little while. 'What I can't understand is why she's never told me any of this. She kept silent all these years. I could have helped her.'

*****

The hospital seemed quieter than usual as he took the stairs up to the fourth floor. The nurses had joked with him many times about being the fittest priest they knew: able to walk up four flights and not be out of breath. He'd made it a mission of his to keep fit and not for the purposes of the priesthood.

'Afternoon, Father.'

'Afternoon. How is Angela Goodman today?' His face held a look of real concern. It was all he could do to keep it like that.

'Can you perform miracles, Father?' The nurse joked, not for the first time.

'No. If I could you'd be putting me up for a sainthood, but I can pray for one.' Father Loftus replied. 'I'll sit with her for a bit, say a rosary. How is her brother?

Has he been in today?'

'Not yet, so it will be good for her to have some company.' The nurse smiled as she picked up a medical chart and headed down to the other end of the corridor. Then she turned back to the priest. 'And while you're at it Father, say a few prayers for me.'

Father Loftus smiled, thinking: if only you knew my dear, if only you knew.

He shut the door behind him, so familiar with the routine now that he knew he wouldn't be disturbed by any of the hospital staff for quite a while. And, Captain Hegarty, well, it sounded like he was out of the picture for the time being. The rosary beads went back in his pocket.

'Now bitch, it's time we had our final little talk. I'll do the talking. You just listen.'

*****

They pulled into the hospital parking lot.

'Charlie, I need to stop at the pharmacy on the way in and get something for this headache. Shall I meet you upstairs?'

Charlie locked the car door. 'I'll get some painkillers for you. There are one or two things I need anyway. Why don't you go up and I'll be there in a couple of minutes. It's too early for the doctors, so there's no rush for me.'

'Sure.'

The lift stopped at all the floors while an assortment of staff got in and out. It was still early for visitors. Annie thought she'd flash her badge if she were questioned. As it happened, when the door opened on Angela's floor, it was pretty quiet. Walking down the corridor she noticed that there weren't many staff about. Most of the rooms were singles, so staff could be in any of them. She felt a bit awkward going in to see Angela without Charlie, but he had asked her to and it was the least she could do.

Angela's room was the last down the corridor on the right. Somehow Annie had always felt better when the officer was stationed outside. She realised that she should have asked Bronski to reinstate the guard, taken off when Jim Moorcroft was found hanged. He was in the clear anyway, as far as she was concerned. The new worry was this John Hardman. There was no telling where he was. The picture of him flashed into her mind again.

Getting out her phone, she texted a quick message to Bronski about the guard and saying that she was at the hospital with Charlie. Closing the phone, she wondered whether to just wait outside the door until Charlie came, but then realised she was being silly. Besides there were no staff about and she didn't want Charlie to find her lingering in the corridor. She opened her phone again and switched it off. Couldn't do with it interfering with the machine.

73

Dave Ellison got up and went over to the printer. Attached to the email was a transcript summarising the trial and the conviction of John Hardman. The army couldn't confirm whether he was still in prison or not, although they thought it was likely he was out. Bronski was waiting for further confirmation from the prison authorities. They were even slower than the Department of Defense. The final page was the one Ellison wanted, a full face photograph of John Hardman, albeit well over a decade old.

Bronski looked up as Ellison approached his desk. 'One trial transcript summary and one full colour photograph.' He proffered them to Bronski, who put the transcript to one side and placed the photo flat on his desk, angling the desk light so that he got the best view.

'You can see the likeness from the side-on photo the girlfriend took. He's a bit greyer around the temples. The shot on the security camera at the car dealership could be anyone, frankly. Let's forward the photo to Malin and get him to run it past the girlfriend. That will get us definite confirmation that it's him, but tell him not to alert her to anything. Hardman might still show up at her house. Oh, and tell him to get it to the car rental place, get confirmation he's the man who identified himself as Jason Craven when he rented the car. Thanks, Detective, good work.'

'Sure.' Just as Ellison went back to his desk, one of the cops who'd been on duty at the hospital over the last few weeks came in.

'Detective Bronski, Sergeant said you wanted to see me.'

'Yeah, take a seat, Cunningham. Detective Macpherson thinks we need cover again outside Angela Goodman's room.'

'I thought someone was in the frame for that,' the young cop queried.

'Well we now know he was suffocated and it was made to look like suicide.'

'Oh, so whoever put Angela Goodman in hospital could still be out there?'

'That's right, but we think we may have a suspect.' Bronski picked up the printout and handed it to Cunningham. 'Don't suppose you saw this guy while you were sat outside her room?' Bronski wasn't expecting anything as the logged reports had been minimal, mainly the hospital staff.

There was an immediate reaction. 'I don't understand.'

'What do you mean?'

Ellison stopped what he was doing to listen to the conversation.

'But this looks like a much earlier photo of Father Loftus, the priest who covers Mrs Goodman's ward. He does his rounds most days; visited her a few times when I was on duty. I always logged him; very friendly guy.'

'Are you sure, absolutely sure?'

'Pretty sure. He's older than in this photo, greyer ...'

Bronski got out the other two photos, the one from the cell phone and the one from the security camera and passed them over.

Cunningham studied them again. 'I can't tell from this one, with the hat on, but I would swear this side-shot is Father Loftus.' Then the officer looked alarmed. 'The hospital said he was the new priest, I never thought to get him checked out and he was there so often, what's going on? Who is he?'

'Thanks Cunningham, I haven't got time to explain. I'll get back to you. That's all for now.'

As soon as the officer was out of the room, Bronski turned to Ellison.

'Get Macpherson on her cell phone. I'll call the hospital and then you and I need to get down there.'

74

Not wanting to disturb Angela, Annie eased the door open quietly. Of course, she knew the noise made no difference to a woman in a coma, but it was a sign of respect, nonetheless. For a heavy door, it opened easily.

Stepping silently into the room, it was the voice she processed first - a low, guttural chanting and the words, 'Bitch, bitch, bitch ...' A man was standing with his back to her. There was no white coat, no stethoscope. His broad shoulders were blocking any view of what his hands were doing, but his words were chilling enough.

'Stop, police.' Annie shouted.

Startled, the man turned towards her. The white of the clerical collar surprised Annie – a priest? Her eyes widened - something else was familiar about him.

John Hardman was standing a few feet away and he was smiling.

'Stay right where you are,' she demanded in a firm voice, heart pounding. She had no weapon, no police baton, only her training and experience. Annie desperately wanted to check Angela Goodman. What had Hardman been doing when she walked in? But she couldn't divert her attention from him, both for her sake and for Angela's. Hardman clenched his fists, smiling again.

His silence was eerie.

Then, as Hardman moved towards her, Annie countered, running towards him at full force, turning her shoulder at the last second, using this momentum to knock him backwards across the chair. While he was off balance, Annie tried desperately to check Angela.

Hardman scrambled back to his feet before she could finish.

Annie took a step back, trying to put some distance between them. The room seemed to be shrinking rapidly as Hardman loomed over her. Annie realised how frightening he must have been all those years ago. No wonder Angela had been unable to report his actions. She sensed his menace and her mind raced to come up with a plan, but it was too late for that. Hardman's fist smashed into her face and pain shot through her head. The room whirled around her as she fell sideways, sliding down and hitting her back against the end of the bed. Warm blood gushed from her split lip, dribbling down on to her neck and chest.

Hardman stepped forward again, grabbing her by the throat. Rage distorted his features and Annie could feel his hot stale breath on her, as he leaned forward applying more and more pressure. The stabbing pain in her back should have been excruciating but the iron fingers at her throat made it seem like a distant pinprick. Air rasped in her throat as she tried to take a breath. Her strength was starting to ebb as she scrabbled at his hands trying to prise his fingers from her neck.

Images of Hardman's attack on Angela and the damage he had done to her sharpened Annie's resolve to fight. He smiled again as he moved his elbows a matter of inches, just enough to block the use of her arms. Although his upper body was splayed across her, that slight movement created a gap between their bodies. Annie knew there was a chance here. She let both her feet slip, causing Hardman's weight to fall further forward on to her, but in that same second she raised her knee, thrusting it between his legs with as much force as she could muster.

The gripping hands loosened for a split second and Hardman's contorted face told Annie she'd made contact. That brief hiatus was just enough for her to push him off and break away from his sickening grip. Gasping for air, she slipped off the bed around to the other side. Still choking, she fumbled frantically for the emergency call button.

Hardman bent over in pain, rage in his eyes. 'Bitch, you'll regret this.' He started to skirt the bed for a further attack as Annie pressed the alarm button.

Hardman hesitated at the warning sound, spun round and headed for the door.

Annie stood up slowly, trying to steady her breathing. Her split lip was bleeding heavily, but she was more concerned about Angela Goodman. Checking the comatose woman again, she ensured that she hadn't dislodged anything when she'd fallen on the bed.

In the next second, the door swung open and two nurses and a doctor rushed in with the crash cart.

Shouting 'Police!' Annie struggled past them through the open door.

Hardman had a good lead and was half way down the corridor. Annie suddenly felt sick and couldn't stop herself doubling over until the sensation passed. Breathing deeply, she forced air into her lungs. As her quarry approached the lift, the door opened.

Charlie stepped out, a matter of feet away from

Hardman.

Annie could see another chance here but realised that Charlie hadn't spotted her or recognised the priest. Blood still dripping from her face, she screamed at him down the corridor. 'Charlie, it's Hardman.'

Hardman heard the shout and swerved. Charlie sidestepped and tackled him, bringing him down hard, as only an American footballer could. Winded, Hardman tried vainly to twist his way out of Charlie's grip but the soldier wouldn't let go and used his whole weight to hold the man down.

In the next second, Annie realised there was someone else a few steps away from the two men. Jackie Winters stood there stunned. She must have followed Charlie out of the lift.

'Jackie, get help,' Annie shouted. 'Call security!'

Jackie Winters glanced at Annie for a second and then ran up to Charlie and Hardman.

'No,' Annie shouted, 'get help!'

To Annie's amazement, Jackie Winters completely ignored her warning. Instead, she jumped on Charlie, hammering his head with her fists and screaming at him to let go. More surprised than hurt, he momentarily loosened his hold. Jackie heaved him off Hardman who then rolled away from his attacker. Jackie helped Hardman up, grabbing his arm and pulling him towards the stairway.

Annie reached them a few seconds later, just as the stairway door opened and a cleaning supervisor stood blocking the entrance with clipboard in hand. The woman was puzzled, unable to make out what was happening.

Annie barked at the woman. 'Police, call security.'

Hardman desperately tried to push past the woman but she was blocking the stairway door and seemed frozen to the spot. Charlie was now on his feet and tackled Hardman again, within inches of the woman, who started screaming. Just as it looked as if Jackie was going to wade in again, Annie approached from behind: encircling her neck with her right arm, using her knee to force Jackie to bend her legs. Avoiding Jackie's flailing arms and talon like nails, Annie gritted her teeth and with the last of her strength, forced the woman to the ground.

As Charlie wrestled Hardman to the floor, the supervisor finally had the presence of mind to sound her personal attack alarm, sending a signal to security. Annie was shouting further instructions to her as the lift doors opened again, disgorging Bronski and Ellison.

75

An hour had passed since the two were arrested. Annie was in the ER waiting for the all clear to leave. The staff had insisted that she lie down for a few minutes before being discharged. She'd had to have two stitches in her lip and bruises were appearing around her eye. The curtains parted and Charlie stood there.

'Sorry, I must look a sight.'

'You look beautiful.'

'Don't make me smile, these stitches are pulling.'

He walked over to the bed and gave her a hug, kissing her forehead. 'You saved Angie's life.'

'What have the doctors said? Has any further damage been done?'

'Thank God, no; all her vitals remain the same. He was trying to kill her.'

'I know.'

'It really makes me shudder. He's been visiting her most days, supposedly as Father Loftus. The nurses are really shocked. They never questioned him. Nor did any of the cops.'

'A real master of disguise, hey?'

'But Jackie? Do you know what's happening? I don't understand what's going on, why was she trying to set Hardman free?'

'We should know soon enough. Both have been arrested. Bronski should be interviewing him now and she's at the station too. I'm going down as soon as they discharge me.'

'I'll take you. I'll just see Angie first.'

'You should be home resting, Detective.' The desk sergeant had alerted Franconi that Annie was on her way up and he was waiting to greet her. The whole station knew that she'd saved Angela Goodman's life and her quick actions ensured that Hardman and Jackie Winters had been arrested.

'I know Sir, but I can't rest.'

Franconi grinned. 'No, I don't suppose you can. Just watch those painkillers wearing off.'

'I will, Sir. So where are things up to?' Annie took a seat at her desk. Suddenly, she felt incredibly tired.

'Bronski and Ellison are interviewing Hardman at the moment. We've got a search warrant for his property. Bronski kind of thought you might want to be in on that.'

'Thanks, Sir. What about Jackie Winters?'

'She's in a cell at the moment, a bit tight lipped. She can wait till Hardman is finished. We still don't know what she's got to do with all this. Listen, while you're waiting, I was just about to call Detective Malin. He left Bronski a message. Perhaps you want to give him a call?'

'Sure, Sir.' Annie took the proffered message, wondering if her voice would sound funny over the phone, given the state of her lip.

Malin answered on the first ring.

'How's it going Detective? What's with your voice?'

'I've got stitches in my lip after I was in a scuffle with John Hardman a few hours ago.'

'What? He's there; you've arrested him? Are you OK?'

Annie nearly smiled but caught herself. 'Thanks for

asking Sir. I have looked better; a cut lip and by morning a black eye, I suspect. I found him in Angela Goodman's hospital room trying to finish what he'd started.' She heard the audible groan from Malin and knew she had to continue to the better news. 'The doctors say she is stable again, still in a coma, but no worse for the attack. I'm just pleased I got in there when I did.' Now Annie had to hesitate. The painkillers were starting to wear off and her lip was throbbing.

'So, how did he get in there? No cop on the door?'

'We were just about to start the roster again. Apparently, he's been coming in to see her most days since the attack.' Again there was the audible groan. 'He's a master of disguise. Here, he's been Father Loftus, Catholic priest, giving her blessings, saying the rosary. The nurses and even the cops on duty were completely taken in. He fooled everyone.'

'Clever, guy. So that's at least three identities: John Hardman, Jason Craven and now Father Loftus. I wouldn't be surprised if there are more. That's what my call was about. We've had firm confirmation from the car rental place and from Connie Lombardi, the girlfriend, that Jason Craven is Hardman. They've seen the photo that Detective Ellison got through to me earlier on. Obviously he's aged. Connie Lombardi knew nothing of any military service. I think she's had a lucky escape from him. So, is he being interviewed?'

'Aye, by Detectives Bronski and Ellison. I missed out, being in the ER.'

As she said it, Annie realised how disappointed she was. After what she'd been through, not to have the chance to be in that interview room herself. She decided she would insist on being there to interview Jackie Winters.

'Must be frustrating for you. Any idea how they're getting along? I'll need to interview him myself about Carol Wojinski.'

'I'll get Bronski to liaise with you as soon as I see him. John Hardman is not going anywhere for a while. Initially, I suspect, he'll be charged with the attempted murder of Angela Goodman and for the assault on me, so there's plenty to hold him.'

As Annie put the phone down, she put her head in her hands, fighting off a wave of nausea. A few seconds later, Franconi reappeared.

'You OK?'

'Aye, Sir, feeling a bit sick; must be the pills. I'll be OK in a minute. I've just been talking to Detective Malin. He wants to interview Hardman about the death of Carol Wojinski.'

Franconi nodded. 'Bronski will sort that out with him. The search warrant has come through for Hardman's apartment.' He handed the document to her. Annie checked the listing of search items as Franconi stood by her desk. Annie nodded. 'We've got a lot of scope here. Let's just hope there's something there.'

A half hour later, Annie heard Bronski and Ellison before they appeared at the door. The looks on their faces gave it away.

'He's not saying anything, still sticking by the Father Loftus story, saying you completely misinterpreted what you saw. He says he was just trying to reposition her pillows to get her comfortable. You attacked him etc.'

'Oh, aye.'

'So, we need something from the search and something to tie him to the other identities.' By now, Dave Ellison was back at his computer. Bronski was staring intently at Annie.

'Are you OK? That lip looks pretty sore.'

'I'm fine, just frustrated to have missed out on the interview. Franconi asked me to return a call to Detective Malin while you were with Hardman.'

'Oh?' Bronski looked over at Dave Ellison, who nodded for Annie to continue.

Annie summarised her conversation with Malin. 'Oh and another piece of good news. Franconi gave me the search warrant. It gives us a lot of scope. Should we go there now?' Annie proffered the piece of paper.

'No time like the present, as they say. Let's go.' Bronski pulled his jacket off the back of his chair. 'You coming Detective Ellison?'

'Yeah, wouldn't miss it.'

76

'Take a look at this, Sir.' Annie had opened the desk drawer in the small study. There, in a metal box were two passports, one in the name of John Hardman and the other in the name of June Hardman. 'Who does this look like?'

Bronski took the two passports. The first was definitely the man claiming to be Father Loftus, whom they'd already identified from the army photograph as John Hardman. As Bronski opened the second one, his reaction was immediate. 'Jackie Winters. That explains a lot. But who is she, his wife?'

'Could be, but my guess is his sister. Look at the dates of birth. There's a good fifteen years between them.'

Just before they placed the two passports in evidence bags, Ellison came into the room. He was carrying a sports bag. Annie showed him the passports.

'Well, well, John Hardman and Jackie Winters, who is really June Hardman. So how is Father Loftus going to explain this away? Think maybe he had a conversion in prison and took his vows and changed his name?'

Bronski smiled at the sarcasm. 'Somehow, I don't think so. What have you got there in the sports bag?'

Ellison dropped the bag on the floor and opened it. Reaching in with his gloved hand, he retrieved two credit cards. He held one in each hand so his colleagues could read the name on the cards: 'James Moorcroft'.

Macpherson looked at them thoughtfully. 'I distinctly remember Jackie Winters saying nothing was missing, even when she looked in his wallet which was still in his trouser pocket. Was she lying to us?'

'Who knows, but you might also recognise this.' Next he opened the bag wider so they could both see a length of rope, which had clearly been cut at one end, together with a knife.

Annie and Bronski looked at one another, before Annie expressed what they were both thinking. 'Looks identical to the one used to stage the Moorcroft suicide, wouldn't you say?'

'Right we need a whole team in here. There's enough evidence already to tear this place apart.'

'One more thing,' Ellison said, 'wasn't her house vandalised with paint?'

'You've got a good memory. Now you're going to tell me you've found loads of paint cans,' said Bronski.

'No, but there's a chisel in here with lots of different paint colours on it, like it was used to lever cans open.'

'I knew he would have needed something.' Annie remembered how she'd questioned this the first time she'd seen the crime scene. 'We'll need to match the samples with the ones from the walls. This is getting interesting.' Then another thought came to her. 'Dave, there was a footprint found in her house in the paint, see if you can find any shoes with paint on them.'

While Bronski was phoning dispatch for a full search team, Ellison returned to the main bedroom where he'd found the sports bag. Annie moved on to the kitchen. She wondered how Charlie was going to react to the news that Jackie Winters wasn't Jackie Winters after all, but June Hardman. As yet they couldn't be sure of the relationship between her and Hardman and it still wasn't clear what role, if any, she'd had in this. Could she have been an accessory to Angela's assault and Moorcroft's murder? Annie thought back to her father's advice when she'd first started out in her career. 'Never be surprised. People do things you least expect, things you would never do yourself.' How many times had his advice been proven right?

The kitchen didn't appear to have anything of interest, although she spent some time opening cupboards. It appeared that John Hardman was excessively tidy. All the cupboards were neatly arranged, reminding her of Angela Goodman's. That thought made her shudder. A pretty ballerina figurine on the window ledge also intrigued Annie. It seemed an incongruous place for a statue and not something she would expect in John Hardman's apartment.

Annie finished searching the kitchen and walked into the back bedroom, which Hardman appeared to use as a second study. At least this was where he kept his computer. Ellison had only just started trying to get into the computer. 'No shoes with paint, at least not in his bedroom, but forensics might find something. Thought I'd have a quick look at this, while we're waiting for them.'

'Any joy?' Annie asked as she stood beside him.

'You give me joy, just looking at you,' he said, flashing that smile of his.

'Thanks, Dave. You're great for a girl's ego, especially one with a black eye and a swollen lip. What I meant was, how's the access going?'

Ellison turned back to the screen. 'I've only been at

it a couple of minutes, but I've tried all my usual tricks and no joy, as you would say. I think the forensics team will need to break this one. Let's hope there's still stuff on the hard drive and that he hasn't deleted everything. I've got a feeling this computer has a story to tell.'

Bronski reappeared. 'I've telephoned dispatch. A full team is on their way. I also found these.' He held out a set of boarding passes to Annie, who in turn read them out loud.

'Boston to Toronto, leaving tonight: two passengers, John Hardman and June Hardman.'

Bronski smiled. 'Let's hope he took out cancellation insurance.'

Annie had to force herself not to smile, as her swollen lip had started to throb. 'So they obviously had a plan. Angela must have been the last stop, taking care of unfinished business. Presumably Jackie, or should I now say, June, was meeting him at the hospital. Maybe running into Charlie was the only unplanned part and she was forced to come up in the elevator with him, not to ruin their cover.'

'Yeah, but instead, they literally run into you chasing John Hardman dressed as a priest and she has no choice but to try and free him from Hegarty and then herself from you.' Ellison added. 'Maybe, originally the plan was that she would be there when he suffocated Angela. When you entered the room, he was probably expecting her, not you. After all, both of them were regular visitors and wouldn't have aroused suspicion. We'd even withdrawn the police cover from the room, which was very convenient for them.'

Bronski looked at the two of them. 'I think we've got the gist of this. Now we need Jackie, I mean June, to confirm it. We could do with having some more to go on when we interview her. All we've got so far is the passport and boarding pass. How deeply was she involved in all this and what is her relationship to John Hardman? Any luck on the computer, Dave?'

Ellison shook his head. 'Afraid I will have to defer to the forensics team.'

Truck doors slammed outside. Before Bronski went out to the team, he said, 'I think we've done enough for now. We've got enough to hold them overnight. Let's take our time and interview them in the morning. Give each of them time to reflect, eh?'

'I'm fine with that, Sir.' Annie replied. She was exhausted and wanted to be fresh for the interviews.

'Macpherson, you need to get home and rest. Ellison could you drop her off at home, while I brief the team?'

Ellison smiled. 'My pleasure.'

77

The local newspaper hadn't updated the identity of Jason Craven as yet and Mrs Lombardi, who never read a newspaper until it was three days old, had only just came across the story. She claimed that a story three days old wasn't nearly as shocking as a breaking news story. But this one would have shocked her whenever she read it.

'Oh my God,' she repeated over and over to herself, as she telephoned her daughter's number.

Connie Lombardi decided to let the call go to the answer machine. She knew it was her mother and she'd been waiting for the call.

Detective Malin had only just left her house, having questioned her for over an hour, explaining that she could be considered an accessory if she held back any relevant information about Jason Craven. Connie recanted, handing over the T-shirt Jason had worn that last day with her and his comb, both carefully stored in plastic, in an attempt to preserve something of him. They were the only mementos of the lover she'd lost.

The story that Detective Malin had told her was so unbelievable. 'The man you knew as Jason Craven stole his identity from a man killed three years ago in an accident. His real name is John Hardman and he served ten years in a military prison for stalking, false imprisonment, rape and going AWOL. He was given a dishonourable discharge from the army.'

Connie had frozen when she'd heard those words, willing Detective Malin to stop talking about a man she'd started to realise she never really knew. This wasn't the Jason she'd fallen in love with.

'Now he is being questioned in Westford Connecticut for a vicious assault on the woman he stalked and raped all those years ago, who remains in a coma and is still fighting for her life. Have you ever heard him mention Angela Goodman?'

Her voice had been barely audible as she mouthed the word, 'No.'

'When the Westford Police finish interviewing him about that assault, I am going to interview him about the death of Carol Wojinski. Did he ever mention her by name to you?'

Again Connie felt like she was in some kind of bad dream. 'No, I only heard people talking about it in a restaurant and then I saw that article in the paper, the night you came to see me.' Connie felt as if she was being accused of something, but the only thing she'd done wrong was to be taken in by this man. 'He never talked about other women and although he never said anything, I always felt like he needed to be protected. Like maybe he had been hurt in the past, like a wounded animal. Do you know what I mean?'

Malin hadn't been able to square the man she wanted to describe to him with the one he was telling her about, the man now under arrest. It was as if they were two different people.

Had she been such a bad judge of character? That really frightened her. Finally, she knew she had to call her mother back. Mrs Lombardi would only get more frenzied if she didn't.

As Detective Malin started his car, dispatch radioed him. 'We've taken a call from a motel desk clerk at the Sleepy Glen Inn.'

'I know the motel.'

'She's only just seen the paper and recognised the man referred to as Jason Craven.'

'I'll go straight there. What's her name?'

78

Annie was afraid to look at herself in the mirror. Although she'd slept for eight hours, the swelling of her lip hadn't gone down and the bruising on her face was more pronounced. She thought a hot shower might help. After drying her hair, she made herself some toast. Her mouth moved more easily, despite the swelling and make-up hid some of the bruising. As she carefully sipped her coffee, her cell phone rang.

'Macpherson.'

'Hi Annie, I'm leaving for the hospital soon. Can I give you a ride to the station?'

'Thanks Charlie, I can be ready in ten minutes. I'll meet you downstairs.'

Charlie was waiting as she came down her front steps. The day was already warm and the sun felt good on her face. Before pulling away from the kerb, he leaned across and brushed her hair back to get a better view of her face. 'That looks a bit better than yesterday. How does it feel?'

The sensation of his hand on her hair was what Annie was feeling the most, but she couldn't give that away. 'I'll be fine in a few days. I was able to chew some toast, so that was a bonus. Anyway, I'm not the important one, how was Angela overnight?'

'I couldn't get much out of the nurse on duty when I called this morning, so I'll have to try and talk to one of the doctors when I'm there today. I'm still hoping for a miracle.'

Twenty minutes later, Annie walked into the squad room. Ellison was hanging up the phone, as she walked in. Bronski wasn't there yet.

'Hi beautiful,' he said and smiled.

'Thanks, Dave, only I can't smile back.'

'Pity, because I think you'll want to smile when I tell you what is about to be faxed to you and Bronski.'

'What's that?'

'The adoption record for June Hardman, also known as Jackie Winters, also known as Jane Lieberman.'

'Gosh, you have been busy.'

'Came back here last night after I dropped you off and you managed to resist the temptation to invite me in.' Ellison winked. 'So instead, I thought there might be another way to your heart. I got the paperwork together to release whatever files there were on June Hardman from the welfare department and the adoption agency. The permissions were signed last night and I have been making phone calls for the last half hour. I knew you'd have problems talking and besides I thought you would want to exercise those lips interviewing instead.'

'Dave, why haven't you been snapped up yet?'

'Because I've been waiting for you all my life.' Ellison winked at her again before going over to the fax machine. While Ellison was picking up pages cascading from the fax machine, Bronski appeared.

'Morning, how's the lip?'

'Fine, Sir, I should be OK for interviewing.'

'Just what I wanted to hear.'

Ellison popped back to his desk and explained what he was gathering up from the fax machine.

Bronski's face lit up. 'This is going to be a good day.' As Bronski poured coffee for the three of them, the desk sergeant phoned to ask about the interview schedule for Jackie Winters and Father Loftus. The two had steadfastly refused to provide any other names to the police.

'Give us an hour,' was Bronski's reply.

'OK Ellison, how about talking us through the record? What can we use this morning?'

Ellison skimmed and read out pieces that were pertinent. Annie took notes while Bronski listened intently.

'June Hardman, aged ten, was taken into care following the suicide, by prescription pills and drowning, of her mother Alison Hardman. The mother suffered from depression for years following the death of her husband. The suicide was on the 15th of April 1987.'

'Wait a minute.' Bronski got up and grabbed the notes from the military trial from his desk. It only took a minute for him to find the relevant part. 'I thought so; that's the date that Hardman was convicted and sent down for ten years.'

They all exchanged knowing looks.

'Let me see if anything of that is mentioned. It's too much of a coincidence.' Ellison scanned down the sheet of paper. 'Yeah, listen to this, the next of kin of June Hardman is her brother, John Hardman.'

'Well that clarifies the relationship,' interrupted Bronski. 'Macpherson, you were right again.'

Ellison continued reading '... who is fifteen years older than his sister. However, he is unable to participate in discussions about her future care as he has been sentenced to a ten-year prison sentence and therefore a judge will rule on the adoption. No other relatives have come forward.' Ellison paused for a moment and then turned the page. 'It has been reported that John Hardman telephoned his mother after his conviction and that it was only hours later that her body was found by her daughter.' Ellison took a breath.

'Obviously his conviction and sentencing pushed her over the edge,' responded Bronski.

'But to do it at home, knowing your ten year old daughter would find you, that's unforgivable for a mother,' Annie added.

'There's more. John Hardman was allowed home for the funeral of his mother and had a few minutes with his sister, who was very distressed when he was led away. That evening it was reported by the prison authorities that he badly assaulted one of the guards, who went in to check on him.'

'So we have a motive for both Angela Goodman and Carol Wojinski. Both testified against him. His mother commits suicide because of it and his sister ends up getting adopted. And it's all down to him.' Bronski was summing up.

'But a man like him will see himself as a victim and will want revenge on the two women he blames for all of this.'

Ellison turned to them both. 'Just remind me, Jackie Winters, or June Hardman, as we now know, had a key to Angela's house, didn't she? So motive and opportunity?'

'The lack of forced entry has always bothered us,' Annie said.

'Where did Moorcroft fit in? Was he part of it?' Ellison questioned.

The three were thoughtful for a few minutes. Then Annie offered her view. 'I think he was an innocent victim, a ploy to get access to Angela. I could never see Jackie and Moorcroft as equal partners in a relationship. My guess is that she was using him, but now we have to prove all these theories. It will be interesting how they each react when we present them with what we know. Should we decide how we're going to approach the interviews?'

'Yeah, but we need to brief Franconi first,' said Bronski. 'He should be in any minute. Ellison, keep skimming that document and let me know if there's anything else we can use.' Bronski grabbed his jacket from the back of his chair and walked back to his desk.

Annie knew he would need a few minutes to organise his thoughts. He always did before they saw Franconi.

Bronski's phone rang as he sat down at his desk. 'Morning, Glen ... I see, yeah, bring it in.'

'Well, well,' Bronski said, turning to his colleagues who were both at their desks now. 'Seems that Hardman tape-recorded his encounter with Angela Goodman and the forensics team found it hidden in the apartment. Glen Heaviley says the transcript will be dynamite. They talk about what happened and he makes her beg for mercy – not that he showed her any. Glen's bringing it up now.'

Annie took a deep breath. It was one thing imagining what had happened to Angela Goodman from seeing the extent of her injuries. It was going to be another listening to her terrified voice. All Annie could do was think of Charlie.

'And one more thing. They have found two diaries in the apartment with the name Angela Hegarty in them.'

An hour later, Bronski and Annie were back in the squad room having briefed Franconi. He was pleased with how things were going. They would need to brief him again after the interviews.

Bronski turned to Ellison. 'Anything else before we get started?'

Ellison sat back in his seat. 'Our girl didn't have an easy time of it. There is a catalogue of aborted placements for June Hardman, behaviour problems, foster parents not coping, even one adoption that ended because of her behaviour. She left the system when she was of a legal age and there the record stops. She obviously moved around after that and that's why she was so difficult to trace. I'm working on her adopted name now, seeing what else may come up, but all in all, I would say she had years and years to build up her resentment.'

'OK, keep on it.' Then turning to Annie, Bronski added, 'Are you ready, Detective?'

79

Annie couldn't believe that a week had passed since the arrest of John Hardman and his sister. She still thought of June Hardman as Jackie Winters. The forensic evidence from the apartment turned out to be overwhelming. The rope from the sports bag matched that used in the hanging of Jim Moorcroft and the credit cards, knife and rope contained John Hardman's finger marks. Then there was the tape recording, which still made Annie shudder when she thought about it. Charlie hadn't been told about the tape recording yet, although it would come out in the trial. So some time soon she would need to tell him. Records from Hardman's computer revealed the detailed planning that he'd engaged in over the previous three years. Their scheme had been meticulous and June Hardman had played her part with precision, duping both Jim Moorcroft and Angela Goodman. She'd inveigled her way into Jim's life so that she could befriend Angela and gain access to her for her brother.

Also found were the missing two years of Angela Goodman's diaries spelling out, in chilling detail, the stalking, rape and mind games that John Hardman had played to gain power over her. Carol Wojinski had clearly been through the whole ordeal with Angela and had been her main supporter throughout the trial. Carol had also taken the stand to corroborate Angela's story. In fact, the diaries revealed that Carol was instrumental in Angela reporting what had happened.

The evidence from some of the computer records

also helped Detective Malin to build up his case against Hardman, motive wise. The DNA evidence from the T-shirt and comb that Connie Lombardi handed over identified without a doubt, that the man known as Jason Craven was really John Hardman. The motel desk clerk was able to identify him in the vicinity on the day of the accident and the staff in the bookshop had also seen him passing by, as had other shop owners in the locality. The rental car employee picked him out as the man who had rented the second car in the accident. All that remained was for the prosecutors to be more definite about the final list of charges, which also included the assault on Annie in the hospital.

As Annie mulled all this over in her mind, waiting in front of her apartment, she spotted Charlie's car turning into the road. A minute later, he pulled up in front of her apartment house and opened the car door for her.

'Thanks for coming with me. We should be there in just over an hour or so.'

'It's going to be a very hard day for Gus and Carol's parents and his mother.'

'Yeah. I never knew Carol, but she was obviously a huge support for Angie and for that I will always be grateful to her. Perhaps one day soon, Angie will be able to talk to us all about this.'

'In good time.'

'You know, the part I still find hard to accept is Jackie, I mean June. I still can't believe how I was taken in by her. When I think that I trusted her with Angie. All that time she spent with me in the hospital. It really makes you start to doubt your judgement.'

'Charlie, you hardly knew her. You accepted her because she was Angela's friend and she appeared to be such a loyal friend, visiting as she did. None of us could have imagined the true extent of her involvement. She is one damaged lady, that's for sure. For all she did, I still can't get out of my mind, what it must have been like to be ten years old and come home to find your mom drowned in the bath.'

'The shock of that is hard to imagine,' Charlie commented.

They were both reflective for a few minutes. Then Annie added, 'The one I really feel sorry for is Jim Moorcroft. True he wasn't a nice man, if his ex-wife and her experience was anything to go by, but he was never a part of anything to do with Angela. He was a victim too.'

'I'm dreading Angie asking about him and about Jackie for that matter. She'll wonder why they aren't visiting. Still, all of that's a long way off. She's only just showing the early signs of recovery.'

*****

The church was nearly full by the time they arrived and minutes after they took their seats, the funeral procession began. Gus Wojinski followed his wife's coffin, flanked on either side by her parents with his mother behind. The women dabbed their eyes as they walked past the mourners. The funeral itself was a celebration of Carol Wojinski's life and numerous friends got up and talked about her and their times together. Both

Annie and Charlie were amazed that Gus was able to stand up and deliver the most moving account of what his wife had meant to him. Annie couldn't contain herself and the tears flowed freely. Charlie put a comforting arm around her.

On the way out of the church, Gus asked the two of them to come back to his house. Annie left Charlie speaking to Gus as she moved on ahead and joined Detective Malin, who was waiting by his car.

'The only consolation is that we got Hardman,' he said, as Annie approached.

'Aye. I hope it will be some solace for Gus.'

'Anything further on Captain Hegarty's sister?'

'Thankfully, some positive signs. The doctors say that she is emerging from the coma. It's some sleep and awake cycle. She's opening her eyes and has started tracking, but not yet when asked. She's still on the assisted breathing but it's the most hopeful it's been. Still early days, obviously. We hope that eventually she'll be able to identify Hardman as her attacker. She doesn't know about Carol yet.'

'No, I don't expect news like that would help her.' Glancing over at Charlie in his dress uniform, he added, 'She's lucky to have her brother. He looks like the sort of man who will stand by her.'

'The Department of Defense has been really accommodating. He's been given a leave of absence for six months to help her in her recovery. I think he's considering whether to resign his commission, but I guess he'll evaluate that as the next few months go by. Will we see you back at the house?'

'No, I already paid my respects. The best thing I can do for Mrs Wojinski now is to make sure our case is watertight. Thanks for all your help, Detective Macpherson and good luck with the rest of your exchange.'

Annie walked back to Charlie. They smiled at one another, joining hands as they headed for his car.